To my wife Marie, a woman
I would like to live with forever.

D1614523

JOHN 14:25,26—These things have I spoken unto you, being yet present with you. But the Comforter, which is the Holy ghost, whom the Father will send in my name, he shall teach you all things, and bring all things to your remembrance, whatsoever I have said unto you.

CHAPTER ONE

Only a small percentage of Multiple Myeloma victims beat their cancer, and it was obvious Lee's wife wouldn't be in that small percentage. There was a part of him that didn't want his wife to die, but it was only a small part. He was tired of seeing her in pain, tired of the fruitless appointments, chemotherapy, and prayers. He was just tired.

When the attending nurse quietly entered the room, Lee, with a smile of resignation, figuratively said goodbye to his wife by rendering his position. Like a wooden soldier, he stood respectfully at the end of her bed, guarding his wife's body; a friend, a little girl; a woman helplessly fighting for her life. When she failed to steal one more breath of hope, death slid into the room, filling every corner. Almost twenty-nine years of marriage gone in a breath. The silence was deafening.

Lee just stood and stared as if waiting for direction. He had no tears; they had already been shed. There was no remorse. How could anyone have remorse for a blessing? His gauntlet was finally over. The inevitable, having been with them for the past two years, had become inevitable. He felt sick, not for his wife, but himself. Only questions of procedure, and a tinge of guilt for feeling free, stood beside him.

However, as he looked at the nurse and saw her intense concentration, he felt something was wrong. He followed her stare and found what looked to be a pulsating bruise, one that was getting larger with each pulsation. Something didn't fit. Dead bodies don't move.

"What's on her neck?" he asked not really wanting to know.

As if not wanting to wake the woman whose hand she held, the nurse responded in a reverent whisper, "It's a vein."

Realizing he wanted more information, he asked, "Is my wife dead?"

"No, Mr. Richards. God hasn't taken her yet."

Anger smiled as Lee fought for control. Pastors, for the past two years, had paraded themselves in and out of their lives selling hope when everyone knew there was none. His wife had needed that charade, but he didn't, and as far as he was concerned, he didn't want anything to do with God, or anything resembling religion. He had given "God" his chance, and his wife's death confirmed what he had always known, that man created God, not the other way around.

With a pretentious smile, Lee softly asked, with emphases on each word, separated by a calculated pause, the only question he wanted answered. "Yes…or…no…is…my…wife…dead?"

Somewhat surprised and irritated by Lee's delivery, the nurse spoke in deliberate sentences as if teaching a disinterested child, the rules of a game he already knew.

"The answer to your question Mr. Richards is no. As you can see your wife's body is still alive. Her heart is unsuccessfully trying to supply oxygen to a body that can no longer accept it. That's the explanation for the size and frequency of the vein you are observing. In a very short time, the size and frequency of that pulsating vein will start to diminish. When it stops, I will point out the obvious. At that moment, your wife's body will be *medically* dead. I will then summon a doctor who will concur with my conclusion, and at that moment your wife's body will be *legally* dead. Have I answered your question?"

Lee didn't respond, and she didn't expect him to. His silence told her she had been rude and insensitive.

Both stared at Gayle's vein as if searching for a way out of an awkward moment, an awkward moment both had created.

Finally, too proud to apologize, but wanting to resume some type of dialog, Lee said, "Her pulsating vein reminds me of sand slipping through an hourglass."

"Yes, it does," the nurse said, happy for the opportunity to reconnect.

"And just as sand passing through an hourglass measures time, Gayle's blood passing through her vein is measuring her life, isn't it?" Lee said, not knowing where he was going with his analogy.

"I guess it is."

"It's also measuring my life."

The nurse looked at Lee. "What do you mean?"

"When Gayle dies, a part of me will die as well. The best part. I'm not afraid of my wife dying as much as I'm afraid of living without her. Her body might be giving up, but I gave up months ago." He paused as his eyes filled. "At least, I thought I had."

As if following a request, he began to relay little "nothings" of no importance. Some were sobering and thoughtful; some were funny. Only when he realized his wife's vein had stopped pulsating, did he stop in mid-sentence.

The nurse gently laid Gayle's hand on the bed, and with moist eyes studied Lee's face before speaking. "Mr. Richards, your wife has passed away."

When there was no response from Lee, she continued, "I will leave you now, and give you some time with your wife. When you're ready to leave, notify one of us, and we'll take care of her body."

"What happens now?" Lee said trying to find his voice.

"When you leave, we will contact the doctor on call, and he will legally verify that your wife is dead. Then we will take her body to the hospital morgue, where it will be picked up by the mortuary of your choosing."

"How long can I be with her?"

"As long as you want."

As the nurse started to leave, Lee gently pleaded, "Don't go. I need someone to talk to."

She stopped and waited for him to speak. After a long moment of silence, his words were barely audible. "I don't know what...." He stopped to search for a word, a sentence, anything. "I... I...."

Both stared at each other for a brief moment, before Lee smiled and said, "I'm sorry."

"May I tell you something you won't believe?" the nurse said with experience in her voice.

Lee's silence was all the permission she needed.

"Time heals. Time will make this loss more manageable. I'm not saying things will be as they were. I'm saying time is a healing balm that works if you let it work."

She waited a reasonable time for him to respond. When he didn't, she took both of his hands in hers and said, "Let it work, Mr. Richards."

Lee's smile was one of appreciation. "Thank you. I will always remember this moment. Would you tell me your name?"

Surprised but pleased, she let go of his hands and hesitated only for a second before responding. "Kerry. Kerry Howells."

His smile made the moment comfortable. She wanted to say more, but this was their time.

Lee became lost in the moment as he looked at his wife's body.

Realizing it was time for her to leave, Kerry quietly slipped out of the room.

Unaware of Kerry's departure, Lee stared at his wife. After several minutes he grabbed her wedding hand and said, "What am I supposed to do now?" He asked as if expecting a response. When none came, he seemed disappointed. It was the first time she hadn't been there for him.

Confused as to what he should do next, he went to his wife's body, and without concern for brittle bones or the pain they once housed, hugged her. After a few minutes, he laid her body down, and with a kiss, said goodbye to his wife and former life.

As he walked out of "their" room, he felt like he was trespassing; like he no longer belonged, like a guest checking out of a hotel. He tried to find stability as he searched the hospital waiting room for memories that would comfort him. When he failed to find one, he quickly headed for the elevators, knowing this would be the last time he would use them.

As he waited for the elevator, Lee mentally prepared himself for the labyrinth this hospital would present.

Wesley Medical Hospital, founded in 1912 by a religious organization of the Methodist Church, had become one of Wichita's largest hospitals, claiming a medical staff of nine hundred physicians, three thousand employees, and an annual visit from twenty-five thousand inpatients, as well as six thousand newborns. When funds became available, Wesley's physical structure grew, accumulating into one gigantic edifice of brick, interlaced with halls and elevators.

Thus, he was glad he had mentally marked every office, hall-way, and elevator on the first day of his wife's admittance. He knew his visits to this graveyard made of brick, would be tempo-rary. He knew the time would come when one hallway would be-come another, and his state of mind would need all the assistance it could get. He knew this day would come, and now it was here.

When the elevator reached the main floor, he exited without memory of the ride down, let alone getting on. His focus was the hallway before him, and the life he had to create.

Upon entering the hallway leading to the parking garage, he encountered an employee mirroring the movement of the electric buffer he was operating; lost in its echo, an echo which bounced off the walls of the abandoned hallway he was buffering. The fact he was obviously happy with his station in life, made Lee jealous.

The employee was surprised and pleased to see someone this early in the morning. He stopped his buffer and gave Lee a nod of acknowledgment. Lee, overcoming an urge to inform him of his wife's death, nodded back, and continued toward the parking garage.

As Lee approached the entrance to the parking garage, a pro-found thought fell into step, a thought that made him lengthen his stride. *Wesley Hospital might be a necessary evil to some, but it's no longer a necessity to me.*

As he entered the parking garage, Lee suddenly stopped and turned around, seeing the hospital from a view he normally saw going in. He then turned and looked at the parking garage as if for the first time. By juxtaposing the two views, Lee reached a deduction, which caused him to smile as he shook his head.

He suddenly realized that up until now the hospital had repre-sented death, the surrounding city indifference, and the parking garage a semi-permeable barrier separating the two. Although his deduction of the hospital and the city remained the same, his perception of the parking garage had changed dramatically. He now realized it had always been a refuge from his situational responsibilities, upcoming conversations with his wife, and her inevitable death. His recognition brought both guilt and comfort.

Putting the past behind him, he set out to find "his spot," a parking place offering a view of a cement wall, a wall that eliminated the distractions of incoming, guilt-ridden relatives, carrying flowers, burdens, and disinterest. It was his spot to hide from whatever he wanted to hide from, a sanctuary whose need was suddenly essential.

Upon arrival, he got in his car and waited for the solitude this spot always gave. This time it didn't come. Instead, hate slithered in beside him, a friend who didn't make promises of recovery like a cash cow, called cancer-treatment, nor gave elusive hope, like a manufactured crutch called religion. However, unlike times past, this friend, a friend who usually had to be driven away, didn't stay long.

Waiting for direction, something, anything, he sat looking at the cement wall for several minutes. Finally, mercy came and laid Lee's head on the steering wheel as he began to cry.

CHAPTER TWO

Kerry Howells didn't see Lee depart his wife's room. Instead, she was in her cubical trying to cope with being served divorce papers on Mother's Day. After reading the summons for the second time, she laid it down, and quietly asked the genesis of this embarrassment as if he was there, "Of all the days and places you could have served me divorce papers, why Mother's Day? And why at work in front of my co-workers? That's even low for you, you pig!"

She picked up her family portrait, found her husband, and stared at him for several minutes, trying to capture the moment she first met the man who was now leaving her and their twelve-year-old son, after thirteen years of marriage. There had been no arguments, no discussions, and no signs of trouble leading up to this moment. Simply put, she had been blind-sided. Yet, if she was honest with herself, the signs were there. Her denial was a realization more painful than the summons. The fact that her husband was leaving her for another woman, just made this moment more humiliating.

"Why shouldn't we have gotten married?" she defended herself to the portrait she held. "You were handsome, articulate, and a returned missionary, for heaven's sake." As she continued, her voice rose with each word. "Did I say a returned missionary? Who could have foreseen anything wrong with a union between "Peter Priesthood" and "Molly Mormon?""

The volume of her cathartic declaration drew silence from the floor nurses, as well as Kerry. She cringed as she waited for a comment, not turning to see if one was coming. Only when other conversations resumed, did she return to the portrait she was holding, and focus again on her soon-to-be ex-husband.

When she met Sam Howells, in a church institute class at Wichita State University, he was respectful and courteous. They became inseparable, and despite warnings from her parents and friends, she ignored common sense and married him within three months.

However, upon returning home from their honeymoon, he became a control freak. Nothing she could do was good enough, or too insignificant for his scrutiny. Disallowing any rebuttal, he barked out orders like a drill sergeant in boot camp.

On the other hand, at church, he treated his family with patience and compassion. He was always in a good mood, surrendering any control when the occasion demanded. He was the first to offer help and the last to offer advice. No wonder Church leaders were hard-pressed to hear her pleas. They only saw her husband as a righteous priesthood holder, and to be fair, at church, he was a righteous priesthood holder.

Tears filled her eyes when her gaze fell on her son's portrait. She knew he loved her, but she also knew he idolized his father. How would he handle the upcoming divorce, and his father's excommunication? Would he want to stay with her or go with his father?

"Kerry, stop it!" she said with uncertainty.

She kissed her son's portrait and said with compassion, "I'm sorry Jason. You don't deserve this. Please stay strong in the Church, even though your dad hasn't. Always remember your Heavenly Father loves you." Her last statement brought emotion.

"Kerry," a floor nurse cautiously said. "Mr. Richards has vacated his wife's room."

"Thanks, Christine," Kerry replied as she nodded her head in gratitude.

Once the nurse had closed the door, Kerry once again perused the portrait she held. Then she placed it in her handbag along with the divorce papers. She wanted to cry for her son, for her marriage, for herself, but it was time to go back to work. It was time to move on with her life.

CHAPTER THREE

Kerry watched the morning light gently distinguish the green glow coming from her alarm clock. Although she had purposely put off coming to bed, sleep was sporadic. Time and again, she would wake to find the passage of minutes instead of hours.

Eight years ago, this very day, she had been served divorce papers, and every Mother's Day, from that day to the present, brought with it the same sleepless night, followed by the same today-is-yesterday experience. She would go to church today, as she did every Mother's Day, and sit through talks given by biased mothers about the virtues of motherhood; talks from men, whose experiences of helping their wives, seemed to qualify them as experts on the subject; talks that would sear the hearts of those who would never become mothers or mothers who would eventually lose their son because of a divorce.

The divorce had been hard on Jason. At first, he had questions as to why his father was leaving instead of her. Those questions turned into accusations and faultfinding, which led to a Monday-to-Friday norm that found him virtually keeping to himself; longing for the freedom the weekend and his father provided him.

As he grew older his desire to live with his father became more intense. She didn't know if his intensity sprung from a desire to be with his father, or with a group of boys he met at his father's country club. Regardless, weekends always began with his excitement to leave, and always ended with complaints of coming home.

Over the years, this constant bickering between her and her son finally wore her down, and on his seventeenth birthday, she gave in and said he could live with his father. His excitement hurt her, but not for long.

When Jason told his father his mother was going to let him move in with him, his father wasn't excited at all. In fact, his father gave him several reasons why he should stay with his mother, all of them centering on his wellbeing. But Jason didn't buy what his father was selling, and for the first time in his young life, he saw his father for what he really was.

His father, having no clue as to the hurt he had caused, repeatedly invited his son for visits as if nothing had happened. Jason played his father's game, citing various reasons why he couldn't accept his father's invitations. That is, until the end of his senior year in high school, when suddenly and without explanation, he accepted his father's invitation to attend a dinner honoring the high school graduates of the members of his father's country club. Only later did Kerry find out the reason for her son's sudden change of heart, a reason that always brought a smile.

The glare of the rising sun snapped Kerry out of her "groundhog loop." She jumped out of bed, and into the shower. Her anticipation of meeting Jason kept her shower to a necessity. After toweling off, she donned a robe, entered a spare bedroom she used as a closet, and began the arduous task of selecting her wardrobe for this very important day.

Forty minutes later, she stood amongst a sea of discarded dresses, skirts, and blouses, staring into a full-length mirror with the eye of a detective searching a crime scene for clues. She found no clues, just a crime scene.

Looking in the mirror with brownish green eyes, eyes encircled with eight years of humiliation and anger, she saw a fifty-year-old looking back at a forty-year-old. Numbed by this reflecting evidence, she looked at her dress, a dress that hadn't stood the test of time; a dress that covered a five-ten, one hundred forty-pound frame; a frame topped with a bob hairstyle laced with grey strands of anxiety. She thought about makeup but decided against it, and then changed her mind. When tears blurred her reflection, she accepted a less than stellar product, turned, and headed for the kitchen without turning off the lights.

Upon entering the kitchen, Kerry retrieved a cup from the dishwasher, filled it with old coffee, and placed it in the microwave. She then went to her refrigerator and rescued a four-day-old doughnut.

When the microwave dinged, she retrieved her cup of coffee, and with the doughnut, sat down at her kitchen table. After a two-sentence prayer, a bite of a tough doughnut told her things had to change.

When she lifted the cup of coffee to her lips, instead of drinking it, she stared at the cup as if trying to discover a crack. After a long moment, she slowly placed the cup on the table, stood, and went to the hall closet to collect her coat and car keys.

Returning to the kitchen table, she again stared at the cup of coffee as she put her coat on. After failing at another attempt to take a drink, she placed the cup in the sink, turned off the kitchen light, and walked out of her house, forgetting to lock the door. Although she was apprehensive about what lay ahead, she walked to her car with conviction, metaphorically declaring, "Don't look back, you're not heading in that direction."

Once in the car, she looked into the rearview mirror and announced the parameters going forward. "This is the first time in almost a year you're going to be with your son, so be with him. If he wants to meet you in church, so be it! Church will only be an appetizer to a seven-course day of reconnection."

She buckled up, started the car, and backed down the driveway, failing to notice a gust of wind carrying tiny drops of rain.

CHAPTER FOUR

The rain was coming down with some force by the time Kerry drove into the church parking lot. Even though it was almost empty, anticipation, not rain, made it difficult for her to find a space. She wanted to be close enough to see Jason drive in, but not too close as to draw greetings from those entering the building.

She chose the outer edge of the parking lot and backed into a parking space so she could observe the entrance to the church. After backing in, she killed the engine and looked at the church as if seeing it for the first time.

As a child, church was more than a family requirement. It was a time in the week for camaraderie, gossip, and fun. Now, this excruciating habit was nothing more than three hours of internal conflict.

The monotonous rhythm of the rain tried to keep her in the past, but she would have nothing to do with it. Instead, she desperately tried to rehearse upcoming scenarios, but finally gave up.

She started the car and drove to a parking spot right in front of the main entrance of the church. Realizing the rain had let up, she got out of the car and headed for what she hoped would be a new future for her and her son.

As Kerry entered the chapel, she sat down in the first pew she came to. She certainly didn't want Jason to leave because he didn't see her, or she didn't see him. Her plan was to grab her son as he entered the chapel and whisk him to a location where salutations would be at a minimum.

"Good morning, Sister Howells," boomed a voice out of no-where, accompanied by a handshake.

"Good morning," she replied with a smile, frantically trying to remember the name of the man who had just greeted her. Fortunately for her, he was already grabbing the hand of someone else and seemed not to have noticed her awkwardness.

Kerry was glad his welcome had been short. There was only one person she wanted to talk to on this day.

Glancing at the chapel clock, Kerry started to panic. Church would begin in fifteen minutes, and her son was nowhere to be seen. She forced a smile as she looked at the floor seeing nothing but doubt.

"How's Kerry doing today?"

Expecting another meaningless greeting, she looked up to find Jean, her best friend, sporting a grin that would make a donkey eating a prickly pear, proud.

"Kerry is doing fine. How is Jean Atlee doing?" she responded in an octave higher than normal.

They both laughed as Jean sat down beside her.

Jean Atlee was a widow of seventy-six, who looked sixty-six, and acted like she was fifty-six. She was five feet at her best stretch and weighed a hundred pounds, that is if she was wearing a ten-pound coat at the time of her weighing. She wore a cap of white hair with dignity, and even though her voice sounded like a dry branch rubbing against a cold window, Kerry always found her comforting to talk to.

Jean, widowed several years before Kerry's divorce, had become a good friend, and a much-needed confidant during Kerry's rebound. Although she brought life, laughter, and spirituality to any subject, what Kerry appreciated most was her innate sense of personal space—she knew when to talk and when to be silent; when to visit, and when to leave.

"Jean Atlee is doing great, now that she has discovered her best friend in church on Mother's Day," Jean said, with a half-cocked head. "By the way what are you doing here on this day? I thought Mother's-Day-Sundays, as you call them, were not your favorite Sundays?"

"Nothing has changed on that score, and Mother's-Day talks are just *one* reason I hate this day."

"You have another reason?" Jean said with a smile and exaggerated eyes.

Kerry smiled. She loved the humor Jean always brought to a subject or situation. But she also wanted to express, for the millionth time, her views concerning Mother's Day. Unfortunately for Jean, she was the only person Kerry was close to.

"I'm serious, Jean."

"I know you are Kerry. I'm not belittling your feelings, sweetheart, but could I address the issue you have about Mother's-Day before you tell me what you tell me each year? I promise what I have to say concerning Mother's Day will be short."

Kerry admired Jean's honesty. Smiling as she patted Jean's hand, she nodded her consent.

"One, this Church didn't create Mother's Day. Two, Mother's Day is about motherhood, and motherhood is an attitude as much as it is an action. Almost any female can give birth. It's when a female decides to care for someone, whether she's given birth to that someone or not, does motherhood come into play.

Motherhood, the combination of action and attitude, is what is being celebrated today, and you don't have to have children to celebrate it."

"Thank you," Kerry said as she looked at her lap, humbled by the truth she had just heard. "Before the divorce, this day represented hope for my family. After the divorce, it became a three-hour block of embarrassment, and doubt. You, of all people, should know why. This is a family-orientated church. Its primary purpose is to help families return to our Heavenly Family. When you're not a "family" the Church doesn't know what to do with you."

"You're right to a point," said Jean in an understanding tone. "When my Fred died, everyone was kind and loving. However, shortly after the funeral, I felt, and I emphasis felt, like a third wheel, an invisible third wheel. Eventually, I realized I was the problem. Only when I began to take an interest in *their* lives, did things change in *my* life. Kerry, it's just as hard for them to adjust to us, as it is for us to adjust to them."

"At least you weren't divorced," Kerry reminded her. "You weren't blamed for your husband's death."

"No one blames you for your divorce."

"Oh, come on. If I heard the rumors, you must have heard them too."

Another greeting interrupted their conversation, giving Kerry an opportunity to sweep the congregation for any sign of Jason. Unsuccessful in her search, she returned to her friend with a weak smile.

"Remember," Jean said, "your ex-husband was the one who betrayed you, not the Church. Sam divorced you, the church didn't."

"Not exactly true," Kerry said in a calm tone of strength. "When Sam abandoned me and his son for another woman, I was the one who was put under the microscope, not Sam."

"People are people, and there are those who judge and those who don't," Jean answered.

"Jean, you were the only one that was concerned about Jason and me. Only when Sam dumped his mistress, married his secretary, and then dumped her within a year, did I get some credibility from this ward, and then it was at arm's length. Yes, I'm bitter, but I think I have a right to be."

Jean leaned back. "One, that's your perception, or should I say Satan's? Two, how's your bitterness working for you?"

Kerry knew she was right; however, this day wasn't going to be ruined with Sam-talk.

"Jean," Kerry said as she grabbed Jean's hands, and scooted as close as their knees would allow. "My son is joining me for church!"

Their squeals drew unwanted attention. "How long has it been? How's he doing? Is he still in college? Is he coming for Sunday School and Priesthood, or will you two go and eat after church? What is—"

"Wait a minute! Hold on." One, it's been four years since he's been to church. Two, he sounds okay. Three, I think he's still a student majoring in journalism at Wichita State University. Four, he only promised me a sacrament meeting, and yes, I hope he will go to lunch with me, and if he will, I'll take him to any restaurant he wants, even if we have to leave before the opening prayer! I just want to be with my son."

The bishop's approach to the pulpit didn't give Jean a chance to ask another question. Kerry, resembling a cook looking for a needed spice, frantically searched the chapel for her son. Seeing no sign of his presence, she put her phone on vibrate and held on to it with a grip of hope.

She tried to listen to the opening announcements but couldn't concentrate. She even tried to sing the opening hymn but found herself searching the chapel at the beginning of each stanza. During the invocation, she mentally checked out, and the two subsequent blessings only reminded her of what she didn't have in her life. The sacrament was robotic, and the first talk was just noise. By the time the second speaker began her talk, Kerry's hope of having her son by her side was gone.

The vibration of her cell phone almost caused her to drop it. She came off her pew like a racehorse leaving the starting gate. She didn't even look to see who was calling as she headed for an exit. Just before she stepped outside the chapel, in a voice much louder than she intended, she answered her phone.

"Hello. Hello, Jason is that you?"

"Hi mom, it's me."

"Where are you? Are you okay?" her interrogation was impersonal and direct.

"I'm fine mom. I—"

"Are you going to make it to church?" she interrupted, tears in her eyes, knowing the answer, wishing she hadn't asked."

"No mom. I'm sorry."

"Have I done something wrong?"

"No mom. I've been in a car accident."

CHAPTER FIVE

Jason looked in the rearview mirror of the car he had just parked in his driveway. He didn't see his brown hair and brown eyes, or his hundred and eighty-pound body advertising a lifetime of minimal movement shoved into a five-foot eight-inch body frame. Nor did he see a man who would be turning nineteen in a couple of weeks. He only saw a twelve-year-old boy, who one day woke up as a child of loving parents, only to retire that evening, the property of a contested divorce.

However, some good had come out of his parent's selfishness. Their game of one-upmanship, where he was their human ping-pong ball, had taught Jason tactical approaches to life's problems. For example, he soon discovered he could get a new video game from his father by letting him know of his mother's disapproval. Likewise, informing his mother of his desire to live with his father, brought all the attention and perks his mother could give.

But that was then, and this was now. Jason's leverage waned with the passage of time. No longer a parental pawn, it didn't take long for his father to become an infrequent visitor, and his mother an absent breadwinner.

With nobody to turn to, Jason turned to books. Books offered him worlds of adventure, love, and needed companionship.

However, as he grew older, his self-esteem demanded more than someone else's world, it demanded a world of his making; a world where he could create *what was, what wasn't,* and *what should be.* For that reason, he turned his attention to writing.

Writing honed the skills he had already acquired. It didn't take him long to become proficient in commingling truth with fiction, combining survival instincts with opportunity. The house he was parked in front of, was proof of that. It was also a reminder of how it came to be.

When his father sidestepped the opportunity to have Jason live with him, their relationship became frozen at best. However, when his father invited him to a banquet honoring the children of club members who would soon graduate from high school and go to college, Jason decided it would be a good idea to thaw their relationship, at least for a night.

Years of reading and writing stepped forward with a brilliant idea, one that would depend on his father's arrogance, the one thing he could always count on. It only took a couple of hours to concoct a plan, a plan not only to take advantage of his father's invitation but his father as well.

To minimize father-son time, Jason arrived at his father's country club as late as he could. When his father met him at the steps of the clubhouse, both acted as if they were best friends. As the night went on, his father's toasts became brasher. When a round of drinks finally replaced dinner, everyone prepared for the show that was about to commence.

The protocol for the remainder of the night was simple. Each future graduate would stand and announce the name of the college he or she would be attending, followed by a modest toast and/or boast from his or her proud father.

Whether by design or fate, Jason was the last to address the country clubs inebriated. As he stood, he sensed the room was his. He began by toasting all the graduates, their selections, and their fathers. He then struggled, as if trying to find words to say something painfully personal.

When silence told him his audience was ready, he announced that even though he had a scholarship offer from Wichita State University, he would not be able to accept it and follow his dream of attending WSU.

Like a veteran thespian, he allowed a pregnant pause to fall upon the room, before quickly looking up and down, as if trying to find control. He breathed deeply, straightened, and spoke softly as if reporting a death.

His explanation was simple. Immediately after his high school graduation, according to the divorce papers, his father insisted his mother sign, his mother would lose child support. Lacking child support, his mother would then have to downsize from her two-bedroom rental to a one-bedroom studio. Long story short, he would be homeless, and would therefore have to forgo college.

His father stood and reminded Jason of his scholarship. Jason, in turn, reminded his dad it was for books and tuition only. His father's lack of knowledge reminded the room of his father's lack of interest.

After giving a thank-you smile to his father, he took partial blame for his situation, confessing a lack of foresight. In the same breath, he asked them not to worry, since he had found a solution.

He straightened and with all the showmanship he could muster, he boldly announced he was joining the United States Army. After spilled drinks were dabbed, and coughing controlled, he went on to explain his reason.

Not only would the Army give him room and board for the next four years, but he would also be eligible for hazard-duty pay and the GI Bill that is if he survived his hazard-duty assignments.

Decorum prevented his father from being lynched. Whether the emergency meeting called by club members, was out of concern for Jason's scholastic future, to save him from future loss of life or limb, or their general dislike for his father, he didn't know and frankly didn't care.

The room immediately took his side, which he knew they would, and by the end of the night his future was secure, and the house he was presently parked in front of, was part of that security.

Jason's memory of that night, faded as he glanced at his watch. His mother's church would begin in fifteen minutes. If he waited thirty minutes to call, he would probably get her voice mail. He decided to wait forty.

While waiting to call, he tried to reconstruct the accident he had been in. It bothered him he couldn't remember much more than rear-ending a car on I-235, south of the Central Street exit. He did recall seeing the back of the vehicle seconds before the collision, but that was all he could recall.

He also recollected telling the police officer he was driving the speed limit, and the car he struck had swerved into his lane. However, the ticket resting on his dashboard exhibited his failure to convince him.

He instinctively tried to justify his mother's invitation to attend church as the reason for his accident, but he knew church wasn't the reason; Charlie was the reason, or what Charlie had to sell, was the reason.

Charlie Ziermer, except for blond hair and an extra twenty pounds, resembled Jason in more ways than Jason wanted to admit. They had met at his father's country club when they were fourteen and had been best friends ever since.

Charlie was at "Sam's Roast," as that night became known in Country Club lore, and although Charlie had chosen Kansas State as his first choice, the excitement that followed Jason's announcement prompted him to change his selection to Wichita State University.

Although they entered college the same year, at the present time, Jason had no idea, nor did he care if Charlie was attending school. Charlie's small apartment on the south side of Wichita, an apartment where he could get smashed in safety, was Jason's only affinity for Charlie.

He looked at his watch, which told him it was time. He contemplated whether to drive his car into the garage or leave it in the driveway. If he put his car in the garage; his mother would either offer him a ride to Charlie's or wait until Charlie came to pick him up. Since Jason knew no one was going or coming, he decided to leave it in the driveway.

Jason looked at his watch again, and decided to put an end to this nightmare, and phone his mother. He was so nervous it took him two tries to complete the number.

"Hi mom, it's me."

He waited for his mother to finish.

"I'm fine mom. I—"

He rolled his eyes in disbelief.

"No mom. I'm sorry."

When he couldn't see an end to her inquiries, he decided to take control.

"No mom. I've been in a car accident."

Before she could continue, Jason hurriedly said, "Mom, the police officer is telling me I have to leave the scene of the accident. I know you're upset, so here are the conditions you have to meet if we're going to see each other today. Because I love you and don't want you to get hurt, I want you to calm down before leaving the church. It's been raining, and I don't want you to get into an accident. I want you to chill out for five minutes before driving to my house. I know it takes about twenty-five minutes to get to my house from your church, so if you get to my house sooner than thirty minutes, I know you've only thought of yourself, and I won't see you."

As he took a big breath, he waited for her to go ballistic. When silence was all that came through the speaker, he continued.

"I'm doing this for your own safety, and my peace of mind. I'm also hanging up now, because the officer wants me to leave, and I don't think he wants me to drive and talk on the phone at the same time. See you in thirty minutes." He ended the phone call.

Jason knew his mother would make the twenty-five-minute drive in twenty minutes, if not sooner. That's why he wanted her to think he was just leaving the scene of the accident. He needed time to prepare his charade.

Exhaustion held him back on his first attempt to get out of his car. He succeeded on his second attempt but had trouble when he tried to unlock the front door. Fatigue and anxiety made his fingers thick, and uncooperative, causing him to drop his keys twice before a vision of his mother's impending visit forced him to focus and engage the lock.

Once inside he went straight to the lower level of his triplex, where he retrieved a small suitcase. Bringing it up two flights of stairs, he placed it on his bed, opened it, and haphazardly filled it with underwear, socks, a pair of jeans, and a couple of shirts.

Next, he stripped to his underwear, grabbed the first pair of slacks he found in his closet and fought to put them on. Once on, he put one dress sock on, leaving the other foot bare. It was imperative that he give his mother the appearance of changing from his "Sunday best," a normal act he would be doing if he had been driving to attend church at the time of the accident.

He then went downstairs to the kitchen and got rid of everything that didn't advertise recent activities. He thought about staging an early morning breakfast but abandoned that idea when he realized she would want to clean it up.

When the doorbell rang, he looked at his watch and realized she had made the trip in seventeen minutes. When he heard her unlocking the front door, he also realized she had a key.

"I need to get that lock changed," he quietly said to himself as he headed up the stairs.

While racing up the stairs he yelled, "Hold on mom, I'm coming down the stairs!"

CHAPTER SIX

Kerry was aware she was under Jason's thirty-minute warning as she got out of her car and headed toward his house. As she turned her key to unlock his front door, she was conscious of the fact that she should have knocked. She also knew she was his mother, a fact she was counting on as she opened the front door, catching her son running down the stairs.

"Hi, Mothe—" His mother's hug took his breath away. "Mother, I'm all right. That is if you let me breathe."

She let go of him and stepped back.

"You have to take better care of yourself, Jason. Now tell me what happened."

"Happy Mother's Day," he said with some civility.

He waited for a response that didn't come.

"Mom, I'm not hurt! When we leave, I'll show you the damage to my car, which will prove I'm not hurt."

Jason, what's wrong with your eyes," she said as she grabbed his face with both hands.

Nothing, other than seeing you, is what he wanted to say. Instead, he replied with the hope she would turn loose of his face, "What do you mean, they've always been brown."

The anger in his mother's face, accompanied by her silence, fueled his anger. He instantly realized that in order to control the conversation; he had to take control of his mother.

Removing her hands from his face he leaned into her and said in a whisper, "Look Mom, I'm tired. I've been in a car accident as you know, and I'm headed over to Charlie's house. From there we are going to a cabin in Lake of the Ozarks for about a week to get ready for finals." His glare said more than his words.

"I thought finals were at the end of the semester. Isn't this the middle of the semester?" Her question was accompanied by a mocking attitude.

"I mean midterms," he recovered.

"Why are you going to Lake of the Ozarks, and why with Charlie?" Remembering her promise not to inquire about his personal life, she quickly asked a safer question. "Are you sure you're not hurt?"

"For the last time Mom, I'm alright," he said wanting to change his mother as well as the subject.

"Let me explain. Charlie and I have been given an assignment by our English instructor, an assignment we have to complete in two weeks. We need to be alone so we can complete it. Charlie has access to a cabin, and we thought going there would give us a break, as well as be productive."

He took an exaggerated breath. "I know you're upset, but if you want to help me, you need to calm down, and let me get ready. You can see you caught me in the middle of undressing. Why don't you leave now, so I can finish dressing and packing? I promise I'll call you when I get back."

"There's something wrong with your eyes."

"No there's not," he said as he looked at his reflection in the hall mirror.

"You might have a concussion."

Wanting to concuss her, he spoke softly instead. "I love you Mom, but I need to finish dressing, grab my suitcase and coat, show you my car, and leave."

He paused, and when she didn't move, he said in a low, *slow* commanding tone, "I need to finish dressing. Either sit on the couch, so I can get ready, or leave."

Like a whipped dog, she found the couch, sat down, and tried to figure out what she was going to do next.

When Jason was finished dressing, he grabbed his coat, suitcase, and backpack, and went downstairs to complete his misrepresentation.

As he walked into the living room she said, "You weren't going to have lunch with me today, were you?"

If he hadn't laughed, he would have screamed.

"I said I would go to a Sacrament meeting with you. I didn't say anything about lunch. That's your dream, and I'm beginning to regret accepting your invitation to go to a Sacrament meeting."

He could see he had hurt her but wanting to get rid of her more than console her, he continued. "I need to go to Charlie's so we can finish our political science assignment. We—"

"I thought it was an English assignment," she interrupted with a look of discovery.

"It's a writing assignment about a political science subject. Okay! I've been in an accident!"

Anticipating further inquiries, he quickly added, "You don't need a phone number because the cabin doesn't have a phone, and if the cabin did have a phone, we would disconnect it. Why? Because privacy is the reason we're going to the cabin. Thank goodness there's no cell phone connection."

You made your point Jason," she said with conviction. She knew she wasn't wanted and didn't need further proof.

"I'll call when I get back next week. Let me grab my stuff and show you why you don't need to worry."

Kerry knew he wasn't going to call, and right now, that was fine with her.

When he started to leave, she tried to hug him, but he stopped her. "You're not helping. Let me show you my car, and when you see there's no damage, you'll stop worrying."

She turned and went out the front door. The fact that she failed to hold the screen door, wasn't lost on Jason.

After Jason muscled his way out the front door, he went to his car, threw his coat and backpack in the backseat, and put his suitcase in the trunk. He then gave her a don't touch-me smile, before pointing to the front bumper.

"There! As you can see there's not even a dent. You can't get hurt in a car accident if there's not even a dent on the bumper."

She pretended to scan the bumper as she turned to leave.

"Be safe," she said as she got into her car.

He wanted to say something but didn't.

As she drove off, she managed a waive while mumbling, "So much for prayers. I think I'll get some coffee."

As she rounded the corner, she didn't know he would raise the garage door and drive his car into his garage.

She didn't know he would leave all his belongings in the car as he entered his house. Or that he would disconnect the wall phone and turn his cell phone off before throwing it on the couch.

She didn't know he would almost fall, as he climbed the stairs to his bedroom, and upon entering, collapse on his bed without disrobing.

She didn't know why he would succumb to sleep so quickly.

She just didn't know.

CHAPTER SEVEN

Kerry wasn't home twenty minutes when someone came knocking at her front door. Still numb from her encounter with Jason, she sat on her couch hoping whoever it was would go away. However, not only did the knocks continue, but the doorbell also joined in. *I'll hide in my bedroom,* she thought as she robotically opened the front door.

"Come in Jean," Kerry said as she walked away from the door. "I bet you're concerned about my exit from the chapel."

"You could say that," Jean said as she stepped inside and closed the door. "One minute you were sitting beside me, and the next minute, you're running into the foyer, like someone died."

Hearing her own statement, Jean suddenly lowered her voice, and asked, "No one died, did they?"

"Just a relationship," Kerry replied. "I'm going to have a cup of coffee; is there anything I can get you?"

"No thanks."

After getting her coffee, Kerry sat down, hoping for a quick visit.

"Kerry, what happened? I tried to catch you, but by the time I got to the foyer, you were in your car."

"Jason was in an accident."

"Oh no! Is he all right?"

"I guess he is. I would be the last to know. When I went to his house and asked if he was hurt, he assured me he was all right, even showing me his car. However, every time I wanted details, he blew me off as it if was none of my business; as if he was hiding something."

"At least he wasn't hurt."

"That's just it. I think he was and still is. There was certainly something different about him, and it was clear, he definitely didn't want me there."

"You don't know if he didn't want you there," Jean said, trying to repair any possible damage Jason might have done. "How do you know he didn't want you there?"

"Come on Jean. I need a friend. If you're going to humor me, let's talk about something else."

"I understand. I wasn't trying to humor you. I'm just trying to help."

Kerry ignored Jean's attempt to apologize. "Jason said I needed to leave, so he could go with a friend to Lake of the Ozarks for some school assignment. So, I left, even though I knew he was lying."

Kerry stopped talking as emotion overcame her.

Jean waited for Kerry to get control of herself.

Kerry, trying to control herself said, "I don't think he wanted to see me today. In fact, I don't think he cares if he ever sees me again."

Both sat in silence.

"Jean, I'm sorry to bore you with my troubles. Would you like something to drink? Oh! I already asked you that didn't I?"

Jean, seeing an opportunity to rescue her friend, asked, "Could I have a cup of hot water with a slice of lemon, that is, if you have a slice of lemon?"

"A cup of hot water and a slice of lemon? Are you okay?"

"Yes," Jean laughed. "I understand it's good for whatever bothers you, and it seems to settle me."

"If hot water with a slice of lemon has a settling effect, maybe I should be drinking that instead of coffee."

Both smiled.

"I know you don't approve of me drinking coffee, but coffee helps me at work, and I know that's not an excuse, but—"

"Kerry, I try to judge actions, not actors."

"You're a good person Jean."

"For not drinking coffee, or for not judging?" Jean said wanting to make the room more comfortable.

"Both," Kerry said appreciating Jean's gesture.

"If I, were you…" Jean paused and began again, "If I were you, with your strengths and weaknesses, history, and circumstances, I'm positive I would be living your life in the same way you are."

"Thanks again for not judging me. I wish Jason wouldn't judge me."

"Aren't you judging Jason? You don't know if he's judging you, and if he is, you don't know what his judgment is. He might be judging himself, and his conclusion might be the reason for his actions. He was coming to Church to meet you, wasn't he? I'm sure you were the only reason he was coming to church. And remember, it *is* Mother's Day. That should say something. Anyway, you said he had just been in an accident. Maybe his actions were the result of his accident?"

"I hope you're right. Still, since he left home, our relationship if you could say we had one, has deteriorated."

Relationships take *work*," Jean said emphasizing the word work. "What are you working on to better your relationship with him?"

"Are you kidding? I call him during the week! I ask him to come over all the time! I—"

"Whoa horsy," Jean said with a laugh. "I'm not the bad guy here. I just asked the question. Let me ask a better question. Do you two have anything in common?"

"Yes. He's, my son."

"Besides being his mother, do you have anything else in common?"

As Kerry searched for an answer to Jean's question, a question she hadn't considered before, Jean prayed for direction in her attempt to help her friend. She was about to answer her own question, when Kerry blurted out, "Reading and writing! When he was little, I got him interested in reading and writing. I read to him all the time," her last sentence losing credibility with each word.

She paused. "I know I read to him from time to time," she said, seeming to question her own memory. "And writing...I'm an avid journal writer; have been ever since I can remember. Something my father drilled into me. As soon as Jason could write I gave him a journal. During the divorce, I think writing became a therapy for him. Did you know he's majoring in journalism at WSU?"

Pleased Kerry was focusing on something other than her own self-pity, Jean asked, "Do you still write?"

"Only bad poetry," she said with a slight blush of modesty.

"Why don't you join a poetry club, and ask Jason for some help with your poetry?"

"I don't need to join a club, to ask him for help."

"So, you've already asked him for help?"

"No."

"Let me get this straight. Either you don't need help, he's not talented enough to help you, or he won't help you."

Before Kerry could respond, Jean said, "Am I right in saying, you don't have much in common at the present time?"

Kerry's silence said everything.

"I suggest joining a writing club for this reason alone. In my opinion, compared to asking him about his personal life, it will be less intrusive to ask him to help you with a writing assignment, and far more productive than asking him to go to church or dinner."

"Jean, I don't think he has the time, or the desire to help me."

"You don't think he would help you! Is that what you're saying?"

"I don't think he would."

"Well, I guess there's no reason to consider my suggestion."

"Do you think he would help me?" Kerry asked with trepidation.

"I don't know Kerry. I know he won't if you don't ask. I think I'm safe in saying he would rather talk to you about your writing, than your church, or his life. Look at it this way Kerry. If your poems are as bad as you say, he'll feel sorry for you, and *sorry* is better than contempt."

"Okay Jean, let's say you're right. I don't know any writing clubs I could join."

"Raise your right hand," Jean said, as she raised her right hand. With a grin and some hesitation, Kerry raised her right hand.

"All in favor of the formation of the Sisters Writing Club of Wichita raise your right hand. Good! All in favor of Jean Atlee for president of the Sisters Writing Club of Wichita, keep your hands in the air. Congratulations Jean Atlee. You are now president of the Sisters Writing Club of Wichita.

Jean dropped her hand. "As my first act as president...Kerry you can lower your hand...as my first act as president, I assign Kerry Howells to present a poem she has written, a poem that has been critiqued by a relative attending Journalism School at WSU."

Kerry's eyes watered, as she laughed a laugh that had hope in it.

"Mrs. Howells, will you take this assignment?"

"Yes, Madam President. Let me retreat to my bedroom and see if I have a poem worthy of this prestigious club. I'll be right back."

"Wait a minute," Jean said as Kerry started to get up. "Madam President isn't a writer, and even if she was, she's not a relative, and even if she was, she's not going to WSU, nor is she the object of the exercise in question."

"Of course," Kerry said with awkwardness.

Jean leaned toward Kerry. "Can I run something by you before I leave?"

"Sure."

"Maybe Jason isn't the one you should be helping right now."

"What do you mean?"

"Maybe Kerry is the one you should focus on. Sometimes I focus on everything but myself. Only when I humble myself and go to the Lord in prayer, do I begin to see the weaknesses I bring to my problems. Only then does the Lord show me how to turn my weaknesses into strengths."

"Thank you, Jean. I needed to hear that."

"We all need to hear that, and I need to get out of here and let you write a poem."

"I've already written one."

"Why am I not surprised? I'll be looking forward to reading that poem," Jean said as she rose to leave. "That is after Jason has critiqued it!"

At the door, Jean looked at Kerry for a brief moment before hugging her, and whispering in her ear, "I love you honey, and so does your son."

Kerry could only smile as she watched Jean head toward her car.

CHAPTER EIGHT

The minute or two it took Jean to walk to her car and drive out of the driveway seemed like a month to Kerry. Out of respect for their friendship, she kept waving until her car drove out of sight. As soon as it did, she quickly closed the front door and raced to her bedroom computer to find the poem she was going to send to Jason.

When she turned her computer on, the computer screen revealed an array of familiar folders, folders named, 2 do, address/phone #, receipts, utilities, and so on, but the poem she was looking for was in a folder labeled VAULT.

She quickly opened it and was stunned at how many other folders it contained. She was grateful she had stored them in alphabetical order, allowing her to quickly find the folder labeled POEMS. After opening it, she found the WOULDN'T IT BE icon she was looking for.

However, a memory prevented her from opening the icon right away; a memory of her writing the very poem she was about to read. She saw herself as a sixteen-year-old, watching the mesmerizing movement of clothes in the drier in her mother's basement, wondering how her life would turn out; would she go to college, and if so, which college; who would she marry, and how many children would she have. These realistic questions led to wouldn't-it-be fantasies, fantasies that made her world fun and optimistic, a world she sorely missed. In fact, the few questions she was presently asking, were questions of hope, not fantasy. As she remembered the prophetic message of the poem's last stanza, she decided it was time to read.

As she began to read, the poem's length both surprised and pleased her. But what surprised her most was the curiosity she brought to her reading; it was as if she was reading someone else's poem.

WOULDN'T IT BE

One day, while thinking of when, why, and what's,
This and that, and a whole bunch of nots,
I gave birth to a thought, of devilish deeds,
A thought my mind often heeds.

A thought to challenge the great expanse,
And send one's mind into a dance.
Not one of reality but one that couldn't be;
A lump full of imagination covered with fantasy.

Just say "what if" or maybe "Why not,"
A person with imagination couldn't create a plot,
A plot to devise things that would never be,
Things that only my mind can see.

With this goal in mind, or maybe wherever,
I took up the task, or is it the endeavor,
Got a pen and sat under the trees,
And started to think of wouldn't-it-bees.

Wouldn't it be strange if bees made money?
And parking meters took only honey?

Wouldn't it be funny if a cow barked "bow wow?"
And the Lone Ranger rode Silver the sow?

Wouldn't it be weird if flies couldn't fly?
And lie detectors could only lie?
Wouldn't it be something if the sun shone black,
And one changed a tire with a "Bob" instead of a jack?

While feeding on the success of this incredible find,
One wouldn't it be, came bursting to mind.
So, daring, so colossal was this impossibility,
I passed from thought into a laughing spree.

But short-lived was this for sadness intervened,
Not even my genius had seen the foreseen.
A thought, a possibility, of what couldn't be,
Started to unfold for my mind to see.

As fear rushed in filling up to the brim,
My face gained hardness and lost its grin.
The thought was crazy, insane, and dumb
But to the world, insanity was the rule of thumb.

I wiped my eye and found a tear.
In my mind the thought was clear.
A thought I hope no one ever sees,
Of a world without wouldn't-it-bees.

Kerry was very impressed after her first reading. Not because it was an exceptionally good poem, but because it wasn't an exceptionally bad poem. She found it pleasant to read; there was some humor to be found, but more importantly, the poem needed help, meeting the necessary criteria for the purpose of submitting it to Jason.

A thought suddenly grabbed her. *I definitely need some wouldn't-it-bees in my life right now, such as, wouldn't it be wonderful if my future included Jason?*

After several minutes of reflection, she wrote four more lines on a separate piece of paper.

Wouldn't it be great if families were forever?

Always one, never to part and never to sever?

Where poems are strings to tie and bind,

And a mother's treasure is a son's love to find?

The ease with which she wrote those lines begged investigation, but her immediate problem wasn't their origin, but their location in the poem. It only took her seconds for a thought to resolve her dilemma. *The purpose of sending Jason this poem is to unite us in a common cause. He will have to read the entire poem and this latest entry to determine its placement, and hopefully, when he does, he will feel my love for him.*

She gave herself instruction as she searched for an envelope. "That's what I'll do. I'll send Jason a letter explaining my assignment and request his help, not only with the poem but where I should insert these four lines."

After preparing the envelope for mailing, she began to write a letter, but after a couple of sentences, she stopped. She decided to forego the letter and just include the poem, and her new addition with a request for his help at the bottom.

Once the letter was ready for delivery, all that was left to do was to determine whether to mail it or deliver it. Mailing would avoid confrontation, while the delivery would get a faster response. Fearing confrontation, she went to the front door, and clipped Jason's letter to the mailbox, ready for pick up the next day by the mailman.

Kerry then went back to her computer and closed the WOULDN'T IT BE icon and POEMS folder. She was about to exit the VAULT folder, when she noticed, next to the poem folder, a folder labeled PEARLS OF WISDOM. She immediately remembered it contained her father's mantras—personal inspirations her father felt the need to share with anyone, whether they were interested or not, mantras her dad said were instrumental in helping him overcome his faults.

Reflecting on her recent conversation with Jean, Kerry concluded she could use all the wisdom she could get. After opening the folder, she perused its contents, and found a favorite mantra of her dad's:

> When in doubt, and I mean any doubt, even if you doubt there's doubt, for Heaven's sake, your sake, and everybody's sake, even for Pete's sake, don't analyze, rationalize, or any IZE, just be nice and shut up.

Kerry could hear her dad's voice as she read the mantra. Although she had heard him rehearse this mantra many times during her life, new wisdom accompanied this reading. She certainly wished she had read this before going to see Jason. Realizing there might be another pearl of wisdom, she quickly printed a copy of the mantra she had just read and resumed her search for another mantra. Her search didn't take long:

> There is a real difference between wanting and desiring, both of which can become the other. A want is a fleeting wish whose productivity is comparable to that of grabbing smoke. On the other hand, a desire is a dominating thought that becomes tangible with persistence and time. No wonder it's rare when you get what you want, and rarer yet when you don't get what you desire. Remember, the only thing harder

than getting what you want is not getting what you desire.

Although this mantra might have been applicable to her dad's life, it wasn't relevant to her present situation. She certainly didn't attract that which she wanted, or Jason would be in her life. And yes, their relationship was like smoke, however, he dominated her thoughts making a mother/son relationship with him a desire not a want.

Maybe you've spent too much time focusing on a future without Jason, instead of a future with Jason. The thought made her read the mantra again. Her second reading brought an epiphany that forced her to search for a mantra often used by her dad as a disciplinary tactic.

When she found it, she immediately printed it, but for some reason let it lay in the tray. When she finally retrieved it, she didn't read it at first, she just looked at it as if she knew she wasn't going to like what it had to offer. Finally, she read it silently before rereading it out aloud.

"Circumstances don't make me they reveal me, allowing me the opportunity to remake myself. Because circumstances program the mind, overcoming a bad circumstance isn't as important as overcoming a bad program, and the Lord is the only one that can change a bad program."

Three thoughts came to Kerry's mind. One, she had no doubt that her life with Sam had given her a bad program. Two, computers don't reprogram themselves, technicians do. Three, the Lord was the only technician who could reprogram her.

She sat back and slowly read the mantra two more times. She was glad she had gone into this folder. As she was about to close it, she caught sight of her personal favorite:

This is my time on this earth. I'm here for a special purpose, part of which is to help others find their special purpose. I've been given so many days in which to fulfill my purpose, and I act accordingly. I don't waste a minute visiting regrets for what I have or haven't done. I repent and/or move on. Remember, information isn't as important as identifying its source.

Tears came to Kerry's eyes as she felt her dad's presence. She exited the folder and turned off the computer. For some reason, she felt drained. She said a short but purposeful prayer before going downstairs. Once downstairs, she went outside and retrieved Jason's letter from her mailbox, got into her car, and drove to his house to stick the envelope in his door.

CHAPTER NINE

J ason opened his eyes and stared at the ceiling for a few seconds before fear grabbed his attention. He quickly sat up and tried to figure out where he was, or if he was alone. He listened for signs of life, but only heard his own heart. His eyes frantically swept the room from one object to another, looking for familiarity. Only when he was convinced, he was in his own room, did he try to figure out how he got there.

Observing he was fully clothed, he quickly concluded he had "fallen out"; a vernacular used to describe the sequence of events a meth-addict undergoes when, after an extended period of drug use and sleep deprivation, the body succumbs to sleep. The awareness of this fact told him it would take him about thirty minutes before he could put his world back together.

Jason got out of bed, undressed, and headed for the shower. As he showered, his mind seemed to clear. He remembered he was in a car wreck but couldn't understand why he was even in a car, let alone where he was headed at the time of the accident. He remembered being at Charlie's house for a number of days, but how many days was a question he couldn't answer. These thoughts were on his mind as he toweled off.

He dressed and began to search his bedroom for his phone. Unable to find it, he headed downstairs. At the bottom of the stairs, he spotted his phone on the couch, and when he went to retrieve it, he noticed his cell phone was turned off, and the wall phone was disconnected.

"Mother," he said with a sudden hint of accomplishment.

"Mother's Day." Things were beginning to fall in place.

"Charlie…party…church, wreck, I'm back!"

His euphoria disappeared when he remembered his mother's visit.

He went to the front window to see if his mother's car was anywhere in sight. He didn't see her car, but he did see an envelope protruding from the edge of the screen door. Finding no sign of his mother, he opened the front door, grabbed the envelope, and quickly retreated into his house, closing the door behind him.

When he saw the writing on the envelope, he knew it was from his mother. He thought about throwing the envelope in the trash basket, as he passed through the kitchen on his way to the garage, but he didn't. Nor did he trash it when he returned to the kitchen after retrieving his coat, suitcase, and backpack.

After placing his coat and suitcase on a chair, and his backpack on the kitchen table, he sat down and calmly turned his cell phone on to check his messages. There were four, one from his mother wishing him well, two from his car insurance company asking him to come in and fill out a report concerning his accident, and one from a professor wanting a meeting.

He laid his phone on the table and opened his mother's letter. He was happy to find a note, and a one-sheet poem, instead of a letter, but why a poem?

"You want me to help you with your poem? The Sisters Writing Club of Wichita! Give me a break." Jason said after reading his mother's note.

Jason crammed the note, and the poem, back into the envelope. However, instead of throwing the envelope in the trash, he stuck it in his backpack. He didn't know why, he just felt like he should.

Remembering Mother's Day was the day he crashed, he went to the calendar on his cell phone in order to calculate how many days he'd been asleep.

"Two days! I've been asleep for two days," he said as if to argue the point! "How many days was I awake for my body to demand two days of sleep?"

Charlie was the only person who could answer that question, and luckily for Jason, Charlie answered his phone on the sixth ring.

"Hi, Charlie. How long did I party this time?"

"You're awake. How did Mother's Day go with mom? I have to give it to you. When you left here, I thought you were too wiped to meet anyone," Charlie mocked.

"I got in a wreck going—"

"You got in a wreck," Charlie said before Jason could finish his sentence!

"Yes, a wreck, and if you keep interrupting me, I'll just hang up."

"Listen, my friend, I didn't cause your wreck."

"Didn't you?"

"Are we feeling sorry for ourselves? Quickly tell me what you want, so I won't *interrupt* you again."

"Just let me tell you what I can remember, while I can remember what I can remember. I rear-ended a car on the way to the church building. I think a family was in the car I hit. I got a ticket, and other than that, I can't tell you what happened. I think I went to sleep while driving."

"Was your car totaled?"

"Just a small dent. I went home and called my mother, and you know my mother. She left church and came over to my house."

"Awesome. Don't miss a detail. She came over to your house and...."

"There's nothing to tell. By the way, how many days did we party?"

"Ten and some change."

"Ten!"

After a moment of thought, Jason said, "I have to give up meth. It's killing me."

As if digesting what had been said, neither spoke for a short period. It was Charlie who finally broke the silence.

"Jason, why did you and Cynthia break up? Was it because Cynthia got you hooked on meth?"

"It's simple. I was trying to get clean, and she wasn't."

"Didn't you both try to quit once?"

"Yes, and that's when we split up. When we were high, we were good, and when we weren't high, we weren't so good."

"Why don't you just quit," Charlie said in an irritated tone. "Didn't you say, 'I have to give up meth, it's killing me'?"

Jason didn't answer.

"Jason, I know something about chasing the dragon, chasing the intensity of that first high, and take it from me and every addict I know, the dragon can't be caught. Just enjoy what you get."

"I thought I could talk to you. I—"

"Buddy, you know we won't get off meth, so why don't you enjoy your highs instead of torturing us both?"

"Thanks for your support and understanding," Jason said with self-disgust. "There are two reasons why I don't walk away from you. One, I need some meth, and two, I need some meth."

"You're always welcome my friend. Aren't we classmates? Grab your wallet and come over anytime."

"I'll see you, Charlie," Jason said trying to remember if they were ever friends.

After he hung up, he sat with his hands in his lap. He knew his addiction was ruining his life. He knew most addicts come off meth only to return. He knew the only way out of this nightmare was the Lord, and they weren't speaking to each other at the moment. He also knew he wanted some meth. He'd go back to Charlie's, but not today.

Jason turned his cell phone off, threw it on the couch, and headed upstairs for more sleep.

CHAPTER TEN

Lee Richards was a forty-five-year-old lawyer with aging red hair. He stood six foot one, had a straight and commanding posture, but walked with a slight limp. When he wanted your attention, his blue eyes grabbed it.

When trying a case, he *tried* to look like a farmer wearing a suit. He liked that image. He knew juries trusted and warmed to farmers in suits, while plaintiff attorneys took farmers in suits for granted until it was too late.

Today the courtroom saw him in scuffed cowboy boots, wearing a brown suit, brown tie, plastered with flying geese, which unsuccessfully tried to cover a missing button on a worn white shirt.

"Objection. Hearsay," Lee said halfway rising to show respect as well as let the jury know he was still in the courtroom.

"Sustained," said the judge, happy to get to participate.

This wasn't Lee's first personal injury trial. He had lost count of the times he had witnessed a well-orchestrated dialog between a plaintiff's counsel and a treating chiropractor. He knew their questions and answers before they were asked or answered. He also knew that wading through this tandem of boring dialog between lawyer and chiropractor, was a necessary evil in defending his client, and more important, attacking a representative of the health care system, a system he loathed. Fortunately for him, he knew how to use boredom to his advantage.

Deciding to play with his opponent, he scooted his chair away from his table, filling every corner of the room with a grating sound that would make a dog howl. Having captured the attention of everyone, he retrieved his briefcase from under his table with more effort than necessary, placing it upon his desk, and slowly opened it as though it was booby-trapped.

After a brief search of its contents, he pulled out a yellow legal notepad and stared at it as though he had made a mistake. When his stare started to lose its value, he turned his attention back to an interested jury, confused chiropractor, and scowling attorney.

"Your Honor." pleaded the plaintiff's counsel in an attempt to have the judge intervene.

Lee looked bewildered.

"Continue, Mr. Gentry," the judge replied with a wave of dismissal, and a stifled smile.

When questioning resumed, Lee began to write. However, instead of writing notes pertaining to the direct examination he was ignoring, he started to outline his life.

> born April 27, 1945, in Stafford, KS
> dad and mom were farmers
> moved to Hays, KS
> went from high school to Vietnam
> estranged brother
> Vietnam to K State
> married Gayle Williams, an art
> student from Missoula MT

Writing Gayle's name caused him to pause, but only for a moment before continuing.

> Washburn Law

He paused for a moment, remembering his journey from the seat of a tractor to a seat on a graduation stand as class magna cum laude. *Good times.*

> Sed

A strong cough from the jury forced Lee to look up and smile as if he knew the cause. When the plaintiff's attorney continued his direct examination, Lee continued writing.

> Sedgwick County District
> Attorney's Office Wichita

While cocking his head, he looked at the plaintiff's attorney, as if puzzled by a question he had just heard. He held this pose until he saw several jurors noticing his concern. This pleased him. He scanned the jury once again before continuing his writing.

> assistant DA
>
> Gayle's death

The writing of Gayle's death caused him to reflect on his overnight climb to an assistant DA. He felt his common sense, and work ethic were the reasons for his climb, and when politics came calling, he began to see himself as the District Attorney of Sedgwick County, in fact, Attorney General for the State of Kansas.

However, when he lost his wife to cancer, he lost his desire for the DA's office, for any office; he lost his desire for everything except revenge. Needing to attack the medical establishment, he left the DA's office and accepted a position in a large plaintiff's medical malpractice firm.

Success in his new field was quick but painful. Although he loved revenge, each case was a painful reminder of his wife's death. It was then he remembered a car accident he had been in a year before his wife's demise.

While driving his wife to a doctor's appointment, he accidentally drove into the back of a car, which was stopped at a red light. The damage to the vehicle he struck was minimal, and the driver appeared to be uninjured, at least that's what he thought. Confident any claim would be minimal; he labeled the accident an unfortunate event and turned his attention back to Gayle's doctor appointment.

Months later, he received a letter from his insurance company, notifying him he was the defendant in a lawsuit. It seemed the plaintiff's chiropractic bill was in the thousands.

As he remembered the small dent in the bumper of the car he had struck, he also remembered the occupant saying she wasn't hurt. A sense of injustice settled on him, like a balloon losing air.

He went to a medical library and read a large number of peer-review articles dealing with the physics of low-impact, rear-end car collisions. To his surprise, the victims in low-speed accidents were sometimes subjected to tons of force; the severity of which, being inversely proportional to the amount of damage their vehicles sustained. This research also showed soft-tissue damage to be the common injury in such accidents.

This discovery prompted him to read articles dealing with the treatment of soft-tissue damage, some even suggesting chiropractic treatment as the treatment of choice.

Realizing his case wasn't as strong as he first thought, he went to trial expecting to lose. He wasn't disappointed. But what did surprise him was how he lost.

Throughout his trial, the plaintiff's attorney, as well as the treating chiropractor, failed to mention any of the articles he had discovered. Instead, both gave the jury a plate full of disorganized inconsistencies presented in a sloppy, incredulous, and inept way. He was surprised the judge didn't call for a mistrial. To make matters worse, his defense attorney, either out of ignorance or disinterest, allowed without objection, the introduction of this impotent presentation.

Sure, that what he had witnessed was an anomaly, he visited similar trials only to realize, with few exceptions, his trial represented the norm.

At the time, he didn't realize the gold mine he had stumbled on. "Whiplash" would become the perfect vehicle to exact revenge on the health care system. He would never again have a client who had been injured because of medical malpractice. Even if the chiropractic profession wasn't the medical profession, it represented health care, and that was close enough.

Once Lee decided to switch careers, he applied to every law firm that represented an insurance company. Although the response was immediate and overwhelming, his choice was easily made when the law firm of Bullock, Barth, and Hodge, promised him he would be their primary litigator in all automobile accident trials, involving a chiropractor.

Another cough from the jury box broke Lee's trance. He looked at the plaintiff's attorney and smiled. Mr. Gentry was in his later thirties and demanded to be referred to as Mr. Gentry, in and out of the courtroom. He was on TV more than he was in court, and it showed. His personality was that of a circus barker, a barker who didn't know the difference between selling a side-show and trying a case. His spiked hair topped a slender body of average height. His skin color was the product of Wichita's best tanning salons. Today he was advertising a classy European-cut blue suit; finished with shoes so new, they affected his walk. He wasn't a bad attorney. He knew his way around a courtroom. His biggest flaws were his obsession with money, looking good, and money.

Dr. Bradley, his partner in crime, was a skinny, six-foot, know-it-all chiropractor dressed in the best suits Wal-Mart had to of-fer. Outside the courtroom, he smoked like a chimney, and inside the courtroom, he smelled like a chimney. Having been a chiro-practor for hire, he was on a first-name basis with half the bailiffs in the county.

Lee smiled as he looked at Dr. Bailey. *You're being paid four hundred dollars an hour to bore us. Enjoy your money and your mo-ment, because I'm up next, and you're going to earn every dollar, and suffer while earning it.* The thought got his juices going.

Realizing he needed to make his presence known, he looked at the jury until his stare was noticed. Having captured their at-tention, he then slowly looked at his notepad, and made an entry, pausing to look at the jury after each word.

> Get Ready I'm Up Next

While keeping his attention on his notepad, he slowly started to stand, but quickly sat down. Once down, he stared at Mr. Gentry, as if trying to send a telepathic message. When plain-tiff's counsel turned to look at him, he quickly started to write, as if a revelation had joined him at his table.

> boring trial—will soon change

> boring plaintiff's counsel—REALLY
> boring plaintiff's counsel.

Turning to look at the plaintiff sitting at the next table, Lee made a note:

> Interesting plaintiff—Will be more interesting before the day's over.

He then looked at his client, Mr. Petri, who, at five feet eleven, one hundred ten pounds, housing a tinny voice that would challenge a high-pitched parakeet, sat like a dog knowing he was about to be fed. Lee didn't like him. He was a bully who didn't care about anyone. *How he got a driver's license, should be the subject of this trial*, a thought Lee almost wrote.

Upon realizing Lee was looking at him, Mr. Petri looked back, with a smile that would make a blind date call home.

Lee smiled and winked to give confidence. Then made another entry:

> What an idiot

For the past hour and seven minutes, Dr. Bradley, with the assistance of Mr. Gentry, had put the jury to sleep with monotone accounts of overkill. But Mr. Gentry's verbal cadence told Lee it would soon be his time to wake them up; it would soon be his opportunity to expose the plaintiff and her doctor. It would soon be "showtime."

CHAPTER ELEVEN

"I have no further questions, your Honor," said Mr. Gentry, as if he had just given the state of the union address.

"Thank you, Mr. Gentry," said the judge as he looked at Lee. "Mr. Richards, you may cross-examine the witness."

Lee shuffled his notes with a look of confusion. His non-response to the judge's invitation was a calculated risk to win the jury's attention. His peripheral vision confirmed the brilliance of this strategy, as he watched each juror slowly turn his way. The jurors weren't the only ones interested in his lack of response.

"Mr. Richards, are you ready to begin your cross-examination?" the judge questioned, in a tone of irritation.

Failing to meet the judge's stare, Lee replied with a bit of annoyance. "One moment, your honor."

This remark caused the judge to straighten in his chair.

Still shuffling papers as if trying to understand the obvious, Lee suddenly stopped and stared as if he had found what he was searching for. Pretending to read what he had found, he waited for the judge's patience to run out. He didn't have long to wait.

The judge, in an attempt to get Lee to begin his cross-examination, slowly leaned toward his microphone. However, as the judge leaned forward, Lee, in unison, slowly began to rise from his chair. The judge stopped his advancement, and fell back into his chair, only to see Lee freeze halfway out of his chair. After a couple of seconds, the judge wrinkled his forehead, and once again moved toward his microphone, only to witness Lee's movement to a standing position. Skeptical, the judge refrained from saying anything but failed to recline as well. When Lee just stood at his desk reading the paper he held in his hand, the judge's patience was gone.

"Mr. Richards, I'm sure you will agree that it would be most beneficial to *you*, as well as the rest of us if you would begin your cross-examination."

"Of course, your Honor," Lee said as if pleased the judge was looking out for his welfare. "I was somewhat confused about counsel's direct, but I'm ready to begin my cross-examination."

Upon reaching the podium, Lee paused. *Use questions to ID the source*, he reminded himself, a favorite mantra Lee used before every confrontation, whether friend or foe.

Lee smiled at the doctor as though he was surprised to still find him on the stand. "Good morning, doctor! I found your testimony to be very interesting."

Lee loved this introduction. He could just imagine a fact-weary jury trying to figure out why he thought Dr. Bradley's testimony was interesting.

"During your testimony, I saw you refer to your records quite often. Records are very important to a doctor, aren't they?"

"Yes. It would be impossible for a doctor to remember, with accuracy, the examination and treatment of any patient, weeks after a visit, let alone months."

"Am I correct in saying, after each procedure, be it gathering information, performing examinations, or providing treatment, you make notes concerning what you found and did?"

"You're correct. I then give my notes and records to my front office for billing and scheduling."

"Thank you for that clarification. Am I correct in assuming all treatment dates have corresponding billing dates?"

"Yes. All examinations and treatments should have complimentary billings dates. For example, if you came into my office on the first of April, and I examined and treated you, the billing date for that examination and treatment would be the first of April."

"Thank you, doctor."

Lee left the podium, went back to his table, and retrieved a portable Elmo visual presenter—a projector used to reflect the image of whatever is placed upon its display glass. He took the Elmo back to a small table beside the podium, where he turned it on, placing a copy of a billing statement on its display glass. He then focused the image on the screen. When pleased with the sharpness of the presented image, he turned the projector off and turned his attention to Dr. Bradley.

"I would like to ask you about your records, and in order for the jury to see those records I'm questioning, I would like to project an image of *my* copy onto a large screen. You don't have a problem with me doing that do you, doctor?"

"Of course not."

"Have you provided me with a copy of all your records, concerning the plaintiff's treatment of the accident in question?"

"Yes."

"Do you keep good records?"

"I would say so."

"Dr. Bradley, according to your billing records, you took five x-rays of the plaintiff, on October the fourth. Yet your examination records for October the fourth show only four x-rays being taken. Since billing records should complement examinations re-cords, could you explain this discrepancy?"

Dr. Bradley began to search his records for the date in question.

While Dr. Bradley was searching his records, Lee turned the Elmo on and placed side-by-side, copies of the billing and exam-ination records for October the fourth.

After a brief search, Dr. Bradley explained, "Yes. I see what you mean. I only took four x-rays. Obviously, there was a mistake by the front office. They're only human."

"They, meaning the employees in your billing department."

"Yes."

"Dr. Bradley, you wouldn't want Mr. Petri to pay for an exam-ination he didn't receive, would you?"

"Of course not," replied the doctor. "My front office simply made a mistake."

"Of course. Mistakes happen."

"Doctor, you billed Mr. Petri for a muscle-testing examina-tion, dated November the fourteenth. Could you find that exam-ination in your records"

As Dr. Bradley rustled through his records, Lee replaced his previous display, with copies of billing and examination records for the entire month of November. After he arranged them side-by-side, he waited as Dr. Bradley frantically tried to find the re-quested record. He allowed a full two minutes of silence, before interrupting Dr. Bradley's futile search.

"Dr. Bradley, you won't find a muscle testing examination for that date or any date in your records."

Dr. Bradley shot a quick look at his attorney, a look which was answered with a don't-look-at-me-you've-been-in-court-more-times-than-I-have stare.

"I take it that this is another departmental error?"

Before Dr. Bradley could respond, Lee said, "Dr. Bradley, you wouldn't want Mr. Petri to pay for an examination he didn't receive, would you?"

"No," he quietly said, shooting a nervous glance toward the jury.

Again, Lee cleared the display glass and introduced a billing record.

"Dr. Bradley, as you can see, I have displayed an image of the plaintiff's bill for December the third. Could you find a record for treatment on December the third?"

Dr. Bradley searched his treatment records with no expectation of success. However, when he did find the requested treatment entry, he proudly declared, "My records show I treated Mrs. Wilson on December the third, and as you can see from your copy, my front office billed her for treatment on December the third."

The jury almost applauded.

"GOOD," Lee said with such enthusiasm as to draw smirks throughout the courtroom.

Lee then used a laser-pointer; to draw attention to the billing entry directly below the billing entry just discussed.

"Dr. Bradley, look at the billing entry directly below the December the third entry we've just discussed, and tell us what you find."

Dr. Bradley, along with the jury, did as Lee said, and went to the billing entry directly below the *December the third* entry, only to find a second December the third entry.

"I think this is called *double billing*? You wouldn't want my client to—"

"No," he interrupted with authority.

For the next fifteen minutes, Lee, mistake by mistake, reduced Dr. Bradley's bill, as well as his credibility.

"Doctor, to be fair, mistakes happen, and we have discussed the mistakes of others. Even though you are ultimately responsible for such mistakes, you didn't create them. I pointed them out because, as you have repeatedly stated, you wouldn't want Mr. Petri to pay for examinations that weren't given, for treatments that weren't given, or to pay twice for examinations and treatments that were given. However, I would now like to ask you about the records you did create, records your front office had nothing to do with. Doctor, why did you x-ray the plaintiff?"

"Due to the traumatic nature of any automobile accident, I always x-ray vulnerable areas, as well as those areas producing fracture-like complaints."

"Dr. Bradley, let me see if I can paraphrase what you just said. Due to the traumatic nature of an automobile accident, certain areas of the body are vulnerable, and should always be x-rayed. On the other hand, those areas that aren't vulnerable shouldn't be x-rayed, unless they produce fracture-like complaints. Is that what you wanted to say?"

"That's correct. For example, because the neck is always vulnerable in an automobile accident, I always take x-rays of the neck, regardless of symptoms."

"Doctor, how about the chest. You took x-rays of the plaintiff's chest. Was that because her chest was vulnerable?"

"Yes, but only because she was the driver. The driver's chest is always in close proximity to the steering wheel, and thus always vulnerable. In these types of accidents, I always x-ray the chest of the driver."

"Would the lower back be an area you would normally x-ray?"

"Since the lower back is not a vulnerable area in these types of accidents, I x-ray the lower back, only if fracture-like symptoms are reported."

Dr. Bradley's confidence disappeared as he watched Lee place two copies on the Elmo—one complaint record and one incoming x-ray bill.

"Doctor, as we all can see, your records show you took x-rays of the plaintiff's lower back. However, I can't find a record of the plaintiff complaining of lower back pain. Since the lower back isn't a vulnerable area, and the patient didn't complain of fracture-like symptoms, why did you x-ray her lower back?"

Dr. Bradley ignored the screen as he searched his own records.

Lee didn't want to waste any more time. "Dr. Bradley I can't find a complaint of low back pain or any symptoms of low back pain anywhere in your notes."

Dr. Bradley stopped his search and said, "Sometimes a doctor has to follow his instincts. My instincts told me I should x-ray his lower back."

"Don't you mean *her* lower back?"

"*Her* lower back," Dr. Bradley said with a tight mouth.

Lee removed his copy of Dr. Bradley's x-ray records, leaving the copy of his patient's incoming complaints on the display glass.

"While I have your complaint records for the jury to see, let me ask you some questions concerning them. I noticed each complaint is followed by a number," Lee said as he pointed to several numbers. "Could you explain these numbers?"

"I would be glad to. I always ask the patient if they have any complaints, and if they have complaints, like numbness or restricted movement, or pain, I record them. Then I ask the patient to grade each *pain-complaint,* with a number between zero and ten, zero representing no pain, and ten representing the worst pain you can have."

"I think I understand," said Lee as if he were interested. "The higher the number, the worse the pain, and vice versa."

"That is correct."

"Does a number determine how you treat, or how long you treat?"

"It can. If I can't reduce the pain-complaint numbers, in a certain amount of time, I change my treatment, or refer the patient out to another doctor."

"What if the pain worsens; the number goes higher?"

"I discontinue the kind of treatment I'm giving, and either treat differently or refer to another doctor."

"Doctor, if the patient is getting better, and the numbers are going down, how do you know when to stop treating?"

"I stop treating and release the patient when the decreasing number plateaus for two consecutive months."

"Two months," Lee said with a look of confusion. "When the number levels out and stays the same for two months?"

"Yes."

After clearing the projector, Lee placed a copy of the plaintiff's treatment record on the display glass. "Doctor, would you use my copy of the plaintiff's treatment record, to help us understand what you just said, and how it applies to the plaintiff?"

"Certainly. As you can see from Mrs. Wilson's records, when she first came in, her initial pain-complaint number was a ten. However, I reduced that ten to a five, by the end of her first month of treatment, and that five to a one, by the end of her second month."

"Doctor, that's quite an accomplishment in two months," he said wanting to keep Dr. Bradley's attention on his success. "You must be quite a chiropractor to take a patient from a pain-complaint number of ten, to a pain-complaint number of one, in just two months. What treatment did you use to obtain that success?"

"Just chiropractic adjustments."

"Could you explain what a chiropractic adjustment is?"

"A chiropractic adjustment is a specifically directed, high-speed-low-thrust force, to a hypo-mobile joint, by hand or instrument."

"Wow! Could you say that again in English?"

"Sure. Let me give you an example. If a patient has neck pain, the source of that pain is usually a muscle spasm. This muscle spasm also restricts or prevents the movement of that joint in which it is attached. I find this restricted joint and apply a high-speed-low-thrust force to it. This force restores normal movement of the joint, which results in a reduction of pain in the area."

"Do you use an instrument to apply this force, or do you just use your hands?"

"I use my hands. I find I have more control with my hands."

"How can you be sure you don't give too much force? Wouldn't an instrument, because it would give the same amount of force every time, be more accurate?"

"After thousands of adjustments, you become very skilled at giving an adjustment, and I have given thousands of adjustments."

"How would another chiropractor, less skilled than you, know if he had applied too much force?"

"Since I haven't experienced that, I can only guess."

"Guess."

"I would think the patient would experience an increase in pain."

"If that doctor was using a numbering system as you use, would he expect his patient to report a higher number on her next visit?"

"Yes, a higher number would be consistent with an injury."

"Let's get back to your patient's treatment record. Your records show you kept your patient's pain-complaint number to one, through the month of December. Is that correct?"

"Yes."

"As well as throughout January, February, March, and April?"

"Yes."

"All the way through May until the eleventh day. Am I reading your records correctly?"

"Yes."

"Am I correct in stating that your patient had a pain-complaint number of one, for over five months?"

"Yes."

"What happened to your two-month rule?"

The jury, in unison, turned to await the doctor's response.

"There are always exceptions to a rule. This was Mrs. Wilson's fourth accident in the past four years. I was worried she might have a relapse."

"The plaintiff's fourth accident!" Lee repeated, "And you have been her doctor in all four accidents?"

"Yes, and we've had good results in all her accidents until now. However, you must know, each accident predisposed her to a future injury. That's why April, I mean Mrs. Wilson's treatment didn't hold this time," the doctor said in a hurried pace.

"The records show you got April, I mean Mrs. Wilson, to a pain-complaint number of one, but they don't explain why you never varied your frequency of treatment, or why you kept treating her for months after her pain-complaint numbers told you to release her."

"I don't understand?"

"Your records show you treated the plaintiff three times a week beginning the fourth of October until the eleventh of May, regardless of her complaints or pain-complaint numbers. Shouldn't your two-month rule have told you to release her after two consecutive months of pain-complaint numbers of one?"

"Her previous accidents waived the two-month rule. We both felt we had to keep her neck stable so it could heal properly."

"WE BOTH FELT," Lee let his statement hang over the jury! "Dr. Bradley, did the plaintiff have a say in the frequency of her treatment?"

"It's her neck. Of course, she had a say...I mean she didn't have a total say. I'm the doctor."

"Doctor, do you get paid for each adjustment you give?"

"Of course! Why shouldn't I? I don't see what you're getting at."

Lee smiled. *You're the only one.*

Lee didn't ask another question for a full minute. Only when he saw the judge lean toward his microphone did he continue.

"Your patient didn't have a relapse for over five months. Then on May the eleventh she got worse. Why the relapse on May the eleventh?"

"As I said, things like this happen," he said as he looked for a clock.

Lee placed his copy of May's complaint sheet on the display glass.

"You adjusted the plaintiff's neck on May the ninth, didn't you?"

"Yes."

"The number she reported for her neck pain on that day, before your adjustment, was a *one*, wasn't it?"

"Yes."

"When the plaintiff came to your office on May the eleventh, two days after your adjustment on May the ninth, the pain-complaint number she chose for her neck pain, before your adjustment, was a *seven* wasn't it?"

"Yes," he said with no emotion.

"The plaintiff's pain-complaint number on May the ninth was a *one*, and two days later it was a *seven*. Am I reading your records correctly?"

"Yes."

"Dr. Bradley, since your notes fail to mention any trauma to the plaintiff from the time, she left your office on May the ninth, and her return on May the eleventh, can you explain the increase of her pain-complaint number from a one to a seven?"

The courtroom waited for his answer, which was slow coming.

"No. Nevertheless, I must point out, my adjustment on May the ninth, was the same type of adjustment I had given her throughout her four accidents. Things like this happen. People have relapses during the course of treatment. That's why I didn't release her earlier."

"Yes or no, are you saying as far as you know, the only force your patient's neck received between the ninth of May and the eleventh of May, was a force from an adjustment you gave?"

Dr. Bradley didn't respond.

"Yes or no Dr. Bradley."

"Yes. But— "

"Why, did your patient stop coming in?"

"You would have to ask her that question."

"I intend to Dr. Bradley. I'm looking forward to it."

Lee looked at the judge. "Your Honor, I'm through with this witness"

When Mr. Gentry declined to re-direct, the judge dismissed the doctor, repeated his earlier admonitions to the jury, and adjourned court until two-thirty that afternoon.

With success crowding every thought, there was only one place he needed to go. Lee handed his briefcase to his paralegal, gave his client a things-are-great speech, and left the courtroom feeling invincible.

CHAPTER TWELVE

L ee ignored peers and strangers alike, as he left the courtroom. While walking to the parking garage, he drew
stares from passersby, as he verbally rehearsed his upcoming cross-examination of the plaintiff.

Once he reached his car, he got in, buckled up, and rolled all
the windows down as far as they would go. After inserting a Willie Nelson tape, and turning the volume up to "uncomfortable,"
he fled the parking garage, heading toward the northwest side of
Wichita.

As downtown turned into familiar neighborhoods, the lure of
Jose's Mexican Restaurant, or Jose's as he referred to it, began to
compete with the exhilaration of his morning success. It wasn't
the food he loved, but a blueprint established years prior.

Lee's association with Jose's began by accident. While trying
to find a place to eat during a trial, a trial that he was losing, he
came upon the shopping center that housed Jose's. After an average lunch, he returned to court only to find a settlement request
from the opposing counsel. Lee took this turn of events as a sign,
thus incorporating a visit to Jose's as a mid-trial routine.

This ritual wasn't the only reason Lee went to Jose's. Jose's
was a restaurant whose first language was foreign to his ear, thus

providing an indistinguishable background of romantic conversation that didn't demand his attention, and since none of his friends were aware of the location, it also functioned as a culinary sanctuary, bringing Lee an uninterrupted environment in which to strategize.

Lee pulled into Jose's parking lot, parked his car, and listened to the end of Willie's song, before ejecting the tape to the delight of everyone who still had hearing. Upon stepping out of his car, he was somewhat startled by a familiar voice.

"Hi, Mr. Richards," Jimmy said hoping his interruption was welcomed.

"Jimmy! Jimmy Bullock. I thought you were taking the Bar exam."

"Nope. Finished the bar two weeks ago. I should get the results in about a month."

"You'll pass," Lee said. "Are you going to represent the needy, or get rich like your dad?"

"Get rich I hope," Jimmy shot back with a smile.

Jimmy was the only son of Wayne Bullock, the senior partner of Lee's present employer Bullock, Barth, and Hodge. He sported red hair, freckles, and blue eyes. He packed one hundred and ninety listless pounds on a five-six frame, making him look more like a student than an athlete. His suit, which clashed with the rest of his apparel, was "off the rack" and looked as much. Fortunately for Jimmy, his personality and grin made everything he wore, superfluous.

"Do you come to Jose's often," Lee asked as he opened the front door to the restaurant.

"No. I was in court today, and when I got back to the office to tell my dad how great you were doing, he told me to go back and tell *you* how great you were doing. He knows about your ritual, so here I am, and by the way, you're doing great."

"Your dad has always been a great judge of trial attorneys," Lee said with a wink.

"I know this is a time for you to gather your thoughts about this afternoon's trial, so I'll go now. I just wanted to tell you you're doing great," Jimmy said hoping to be invited to stay.

"No, you don't! I need the praise, as well as advice on how I should handle the plaintiff this afternoon."

Jimmy knew Lee was being kind, and he also knew he should go, but he couldn't refuse lunch with the best trial attorney in his father's law firm, or Wichita, for that matter.

Once inside the restaurant, a middle-aged oriental woman, silently grabbed two menus, and shuffled toward a secluded table in the back corner of the restaurant. When they reached the table, the woman seated them, laid the menus on the table, and turned to Lee. "Hi, Pelly! You want usual?"

"Yes Stella, we both want the usual."

What's the usual?" Jimmy said in a whisper.

"You don't want to know," Lee whispered back.

"I'll take what Pelly is having," Jimmy said trying to fit in.

"Thank you, Stella," Lee said handing her both unopened menus.

As the waitress shuffled away from the table, Jimmy leaned forward and said, "Who was that and what's the deal with her calling you Pelly?"

"That's Ming, the owner. She happens to be a former client I represented in a medical malpractice suit. Pelly is her attempt to pronounce Perry, TV's Perry Mason. She likes to refer to me as Perry since I was her lawyer. I play along by calling her Stella,

Perry's secretary. She has a hard time pronouncing the letter (r), which makes me Pelly instead of Perry."

"How did an Oriental come to be the owner of a Mexican restaurant?"

"This restaurant used to be a struggling clothing store owned by her husband, Jose. After his death, Ming purchased it with the money she received from his life insurance and turned it into a Mexican restaurant in order to make a living. To honor his memory, she put his name on the window."

"Isn't it quite a leap from *wife* to the *manager* of a restaurant?"

"The way I heard it, Ming, on a weekly basis, used to cook for Jose and his expanded family. After he died, she probably thought she might as well get paid for it. Changing the subject Jimmy, what are your plans? Are you going to work for the firm?"

"I think I will, at least for a while, and you're the reason."

Surprised, Lee put his coffee down. "Why would I be the reason you're coming back to work for your dad?"

"Listen, Mr. Richards, coming from a family of lawyers, I knew, whether I liked it or not, I was destined to become one. Fortunately, my dad didn't care what kind of law I wanted to practice, and neither did I as long as I didn't have to go to court. That is until I saw you whip my dad in a medical malpractice case four years ago."

"Are you saying you enjoyed seeing your dad lose a case?" Lee said with amusement.

"He didn't lose his case. He got it handed to him; he got crushed. You made the trial personal for each juror. By the end of the trial, those jurors, including myself, felt like we were the ones that had been injured. I walked out of that courtroom knowing I wanted to be a trial lawyer just like you."

"Jimmy, your dad is one of the best litigators I've ever seen."

"And don't think I didn't hear that every day of my life, especially throughout law school," said Jimmy too quickly.

Embarrassed by what had slipped out, Jimmy wanted to
change the subject. "Why did you leave malpractice litigation for
personal injury litigation?"

"Jimmy, ever since I was little, I had a dream to be a criminal
lawyer and work in the District Attorney's Office; I even wanted
to be the DA. My dream became a reality right out of law school,
and it seemed my goal would be my destiny. Then my wife died
of cancer. I came out of that ordeal hating the medical society
so much; I decided to sue them for a living, and it wasn't long
before I left the DA's office and joined a medical malpractice
firm. It also wasn't long before I realized I was reliving my wife's
death with every case. Fortunately, I stumbled into personal injury litigation, which showed me how I could painlessly exact my
revenge."

Lee's honesty made Jimmy uneasy. Wishing he could disap-
pear, he looked toward the kitchen, hoping to find Ming bringing
their order. When Ming was nowhere to be seen, he looked at
Lee with a smile and said, "Do you say fender-bender in court?"

"Absolutely! Then I apologize for misleading the jury since the
plaintiff's car didn't even have a bent fender."

Both laughed.

"Mr. Richards, since I will be defending these types of cases
one day, what's the most important thing I should remember
during a trial?"

"The most powerful tool in a courtroom, or anywhere for that
matter, is a question. Questions control the mind. What was the
first name of your best friend in law school?"

"Bob," Jimmy responded.

"Do you see how quickly a question moved your mind from our conversation to the name of your best friend in law school? Court credibility for your client is what you want. If your client, has it, he or she wins, and if he or she doesn't have it, he or she loses. Your questions can expose testimonial *inconsistencies* making plaintiff information and its source less credible. On the other hand, well-crafted questions can make a guilty defendant credible. Give me your analysis of Gentry's case so far."

"I think he's lost his case."

"Why?"

"One, the plaintiff couldn't have been injured, because the car she was in only had a small dent. Two, if she was injured, she would have gone to a medical doctor instead of a chiropractor. Three, a good doctor is credible, and Dr. Bradley wasn't credible, so he isn't a good doctor."

Lee was quick to reply. "Great. I hope the jury has your rules."

"What do you mean," Jimmy said somewhat offended.

"I'm sure the jury came into the courtroom with the same rules you just expressed. With that said, in order for the plaintiff to win, the plaintiff's attorney, Gentry, must present evidence that proves the juror's rules are either wrong or wrong pertaining to the case in question. On the other hand, I only have to enforce the rules the jury walked in with. Think about it. Dr. Bradley said nothing today that would make the jury question their rules. If anything, he strengthened their rules with his incompetence, incompetence that was accentuated by the inconsistencies of his evidence. We all have rules, and we judge everything by those rules. When a story is consistent with our rules, we find that story and the storyteller to be credible. When the facts are inconsistent with our rules, we find both the story and storyteller to lack credibility. I'll say it again in a different way; when you discredit the evidence, you also discredit the source of that evidence."

Lee took a breath. "If I was Gentry, I would have given the jury an exception to their first rule. I would have put a high school physics teacher on the stand to explain that a force going into something, is either absorbed by that something, or causes that something to move. Next, I would have another expert, by way of peer review articles, testify that the energy transmitted from a striking vehicle into a struck vehicle, would either damage the struck vehicle or accelerate that vehicle and its occupants. In language the jury could understand, he would testify that given the physics of the collision in question, the patient should have been injured in the accident."

"How will you attack the plaintiff this afternoon?"

"The same way I attacked Dr. Bradley. I'll let her tell her story to the jury, and then I'll juxtapose her story with the facts, pointing out all the inconsistencies in the process."

Lee paused to let his pupil catch up. When he did, the lecture resumed. "Let's talk about your second rule. You and the jury think if she was suffering from soft tissue injuries, she would have gone to a medical doctor instead of a chiropractor; you believe chiropractors aren't real doctors."

"I didn't say that!"

"To be fair, you didn't. But that's what you inferred. I'm sure the jury thinks the same way you do, and fortunately for me, Gentry reinforced their prejudices. On the other hand, I would've had Dr. Bradley show the close comparison, concerning the subjects taught and the number of hours needed to graduate, between a local medical school and the chiropractic school he attended. Then I would have him present scientific evidence regarding the effectiveness of addressing soft tissue injuries with chiropractic treatment. By the way, most "whiplash" injuries are predominately soft tissue in nature."

Jimmy leaned forward, and said with a smile, "I'm waiting to see how you're going to change my third rule concerning Dr. Bradley."

Lee returned the smile. "Your third rule is probably the most prevalent rule I find with jurors. They associate a good doctor with good notes, and I can't blame them. Most doctors take good notes. On the flip side, would you rather have a good doctor that took bad notes or a bad doctor who took good notes? The answer is obvious. Anyone in their right mind would choose a good doctor over a bad doctor, regardless of their note-taking skills. I think Dr. Bradley is an adequate chiropractor. Fortunately for us, he takes dubious notes. If I was Gentry, I would either show Dr. Bradley how to take better notes, or I would settle more of his cases."

"But the plaintiff didn't take notes. How are you going to discredit her?"

"I'm going to let her give me the evidence I can compare with the facts, making the jury aware of all the inconsistencies in the process. That isn't all I'm going to do this afternoon. I have a little surprise for Gentry and the judge; something I've never done in a personal injury trial."

"Wow! What are you going to do?"

"You'll have to come and see. I can tell you this, it will confuse the judge and worry Gentry."

"Pelly, here two usuals," Stella said as she placed their orders on the table and shuffled away.

Jimmy stared at his plate, while Lee dug in.

CHAPTER THIRTEEN

Mrs. Wilson had above-average looks, and an athletic body to match. Her speech was clear, and her delivery was straightforward. Her dress suit was appropriate for court, which was no surprise to Lee, considering the number of times she had been in court. She was comfortable in comfortable surroundings.

The jury was interested in meeting her, that is, for the first ten minutes of Mr. Gentry's direct examination. After that, boredom stole their attention causing them to search the courtroom for a distraction. They weren't bored with Mrs. Wilson, they were bored with her lawyer's direct examination, an examination that barely mentioned her chiropractic treatment, something Lee didn't do when Mr. Gentry concluded his direct examination.

"Mrs. Wilson, since Dr. Bradley has been your chiropractor in your previous car accidents, I'm sure you're familiar with his numbering system; a ten representing the worst pain you can imagine, and a zero representing no pain," Lee said with an expression of urgency as he walked to the podium.

"Yes, I'm familiar with his numbering system. I like his numbering system. I think it makes sense. Dr. Bradley is a good doctor, and I trust him."

Lee was glad her answer strayed from the boundaries of his question. Her arrogance and disinterest, products of previous successes in her previous trials, would lower her guard, and allow Lee the freedom he wanted.

"Mrs. Wilson, did your chiropractor choose those numbers at the beginning of each visit, or did you?"

"I'm the one who chose those numbers, and he is the one who wrote them down," said Mrs. Wilson, her jaw set, eyes narrowed, and voice unmistakably defensive.

"Thank you for that clarification."

He looked at his notes. "Did you also select the treatment?"

"No," she replied with resentment.

"Did you prescribe the length of treatment?"

"Of course not. The doctor does that."

"Did Dr. Bradley decide when you were well?"

"As I understand it, you never get *well* from a soft tissue injury, just better."

"Is that a yes, or no?"

"Yes. That's his job."

"You don't have any input in his decision, do you?"

Mrs. Wilson smelled a trap. "It's a team decision. When Dr. Bradley gets me to a place where my complaints have either disappeared or have plateaued, he releases me. There's no reason for him to keep treating me when a plateau is reached."

"Your treatment records, concerning *this* accident, showed that he treated you for over five months after your pain-complaint number had reached a one. Why?"

"This accident was an exception. Dr. Bradley decided, because it was my third accident, he needed to make sure my treatment would hold."

"It was your fourth, but who's counting."

Smirks caused the judge to admonish Lee and the courtroom. Only when decorum was regained, did Lee continue.

"From May the ninth to May the eleventh, you went from a pain-complaint number of one, with no other complaints, to a seven with new complaints. Could you tell us what happened during that time frame?"

"Nothing happened. I just had a relapse."

"If it was just a relapse, why did you stop seeing Dr. Bradley after May the eleventh?"

"We decided I had reached a plateau in my treatment, and it was time for me to be released."

"After Dr. Bradley injured you on May the ninth, why did he decide to stop treating you on May the eleventh, or did you make that decision?"

"I don't know what you're talking about. He didn't injure me. The last injury I experienced, was from your client when he rammed his car into mine."

"Something must have happened between May the ninth, when you were a one, with no new complaints just before your adjustment, and May the eleventh, when you were a seven, with new complaints when you came to his office. Unless I'm told differently, the only force to your neck during that period, came from the adjustment Dr. Bradley gave you on May the ninth."

"He didn't hurt me on May the ninth, or I wouldn't have come back on the eleventh. I must have slept wrong or something after the adjustment. I can't remember that far back."

"Could you explain why there is no mention of "sleeping wrong" in his notes? Never mind, I withdraw my question.

"Concerning your treatment schedule, it seems complaint-pain numbers of one, without other complaints, didn't mean anything to you, or Dr. Bradley. Did you and Dr. Bradley conspire to run up your chiropractic bill, only to have your plan backfire when Dr. Bradley accidentally hurt you?"

"No! That's absurd."

"Thank you, Mrs. Wilson. I have no further questions."

Lee's abrupt closure of his cross-examination caught Gentry by surprise. However, since he wanted her off the stand, as much as she wanted off the stand, he stood and announced, "Your Honor, the plaintiff rests."

After Mrs. Wilson left the stand, the judge once again leaned toward his microphone, looked at Lee, and said, "Are you ready to present your case?"

"Your Honor, the defense rests as well."

Lee's announcement got the attention of the judge as well as Gentry. In fact, everyone in the courtroom was surprised.

"Mr. Richards, are you sure you don't want to present a defense?" the judge said as if he was trying to bend his mind around what he had just heard.

"Yes, Your Honor. I don't think I need to."

The judge was bewildered by Lee's decision. Nevertheless, he repeated his regular admonition to the jury and dismissed them until nine o'clock the next morning.

After the jury vacated the courtroom, the judge looked at both attorneys and said, "Tomorrow, both of you will get forty minutes for closing arguments. Mr. Gentry you may give your entire closing before Mr. Richards gives his, or bifurcate your closing, giving a portion before, and a portion after Mr. Richard's closing argument. Regardless of your decision, I will notify both of you, when you have five minutes remaining in each of your presentations."

Gentry replied in a pre-rehearsed script, "Judge, I will divide my forty minutes into a twenty-five-minute presentation prior to defense's closing, and a fifteen-minute presentation immediately following Mr. Richards remarks."

While the judge was gathering his prepared jury instructions, Gentry looked at Lee and said, "Richards, declining to present a case is pretty bold."

"When you know you're going to lose, why put on a defense," Lee said with a smile.

Gentry didn't like the look on Lee's face. On the other hand, Lee liked the look on Gentry's face.

CHAPTER FOURTEEN

After closing arguments, it took the jury less than an hour to come back with a verdict. Not only wasn't the plaintiff going to be compensated for past treatment but future treatment as well. In fact, she wasn't even getting money for pain and suffering. Lee had to admit he was somewhat surprised by the jury's decision. He had never heard of such a finding in his short career in the personal injury field.

As he shook hands with those favorably affected by the outcome, he managed to scan the courtroom for a strange face he had seen throughout the trial, a face he had wanted to meet but failed to do so for one reason or another. Failing to find that face, he slipped out of the room and the building.

Because foot traffic around the courthouse was light, it didn't take Lee long to find a vacant park bench. He sat down and placed his briefcase beside him. After getting as comfortable as you can get on a park bench, he stared at the city before him and saw nothing but the city before him. He should have been ecstatic. Instead, he wasn't anything, depressed, concerned, curious, anything.

The vibration of his cell phone brought him out of his daze. The text from his boss read: Congrats. Import visitor meet at the office. Waiting.

The text annoyed him. He texted back: Will walk thru door when walk thru door.

After sending the text, he turned his phone off and dropped it into his briefcase. He didn't know what he wanted, but he certainly knew what he didn't want, and that was communication with anyone at the moment.

It took him a moment to get control of his emotions, and when he did, he began to analyze his life. He knew he was the best attorney in Wichita, and today's verdict had confirmed that fact. He also realized that in the past year, his life had become a routine of various routines. Every day that he wasn't in court, his thinking was robotic at best.

This realization made him stand up, but only for a moment before sitting back down with a possible solution to get him out of his funk.

In law school when life seemed to trip him, he would pick himself up by seeking a sanctuary where he could present, to imaginary fact finders, successful briefs, legal summaries, or mock trial presentations of his making. Regardless of its construction, revisiting one of his successful creations always left him with a feeling of invincibility, invincibility he presently needed to pick him up off his floor of redundancy.

A thought came to him. *Why not give the closing argument you just gave?*

Noticing a pigeon perched on the ground in front of him, he addressed this skittish juror. "Mr. Pigeon, and all future fowl, I have only two things to tell you before you are allowed to deliberate the evidence you have been given. The first being the reason we didn't call an expert to challenge the plaintiff's injuries and treatment, and the second, to explain why you must reject the plaintiff's request for money."

He paused to let two more pigeons join the one.

"First of all, let me correct what I just said. We did call two experts; the plaintiff's car and common sense."

He pointed at a tall tree. "This is a blowup picture of the plaintiff's car. You have to have good eyesight to find any evidence of this so-called *crash*, so let me help you."

He took an ink pen out of his pocket.

"With my laser pointer, I will help you find the small dent in the bumper of the plaintiff's car. Looking at that dent, don't you think the word *crash* should be replaced with the word *bump*? If a picture is worth a thousand words, and each word is worth a dollar, the worth of this picture, or this accident, would be valued in cents, not a dollar, and certainly not dollars. I'll come back to this *dent* in a couple of minutes."

A chuckle from a passerby temporarily interrupted his summation. He smiled, acknowledged her interest with a nod, and continued as one more pigeon joined the jury.

"We didn't need another expert to tell you, Dr. Bradley billed for far more examinations than he performed. He told you. We didn't need an expert to tell you Dr. Bradley billed for treatment he didn't do. His records told you. I thought about putting an expert on the stand to explain why Dr. Bradley treated his patient for over four months, with pain-complaint numbers of one and no complaints, but since Dr. Bradley couldn't explain it, I didn't think another expert could. I didn't think I needed an expert to tell you Dr. Bradley injured his own patient. The plaintiff told you when she chose a pain-complaint number of one with no complaints on May the ninth, and then on May the eleventh chose a pain-complaint number of seven with new complaints. Remember, both Dr. Bradley and the plaintiff both agreed there had been no other force to her neck between those two dates: no force other than the doctor's adjustment. I didn't think you needed an expert to assist you with the obvious." He looked to his right. "I apologize to Mr. Petri if I was mistaken."

One pigeon took flight.

"Second, you must reject the plaintiff's request for lifetime payments. None of you witnessed the bump in question. None of you witnessed the treatment given. Thus, you can only rely on what the plaintiff and her chiropractor told you. On the other hand, you have a right to demand from the plaintiff and her chiropractor, a story that makes sense, a story that is consistent with their facts. If they can't deliver such a story, they have no right to ask Mr. Petri to give them anything. Common sense should prevail in court, not inconsistent stories."

He stopped while three attorneys entered the building.

"Remember the dent. You're probably asking yourself how a small dent could produce an injury, let alone an injury that was treated for as long as Dr. Bradley treated the plaintiff; especially when Dr. Bradley's own protocol called for her to be released after two months. You don't have to ask, just use common sense, and follow the money. Mr. Petri accidentally put a dent in the plaintiff's car; a dent so small I had to blow up a picture of that dent, so you could see it. Dr. Bradley and his patient, the plaintiff, in this case, both familiar with the "whiplash" game, took advantage of this *dent* and conspired to get as much money from Mr. Petri as possible. Their plan failed when Mr. Petri brought his case to me, and we brought it to you."

He smiled as three pigeons joined his jury.

"Remember, Mr. Petri has fixed the dent. He just doesn't feel it's fair that he should have to pay for treatment that wasn't needed or given in the past; treatment that won't be needed or given in the future. When you place the plaintiff's theory beside the facts, all you have are inconsistencies and greed. And when you see these inconsistencies and greed, give them nothing. Tell them you don't appreciate being used."

Lee's jury took flight as Jimmy clapped.

"It's just as good the second time, Mr. Richards. However, I was instructed to tell you, there is a very important person waiting to speak with you. In other words, you are wanted immediately."

Even though Lee was glad it was Jimmy's voice he heard, he wasn't very successful at hiding his irritation. "Jimmy. Like I said in my text, I will walk through the door when I walk through the door."

"But Mr. Richards, my dad wants you to walk through the door now," Jimmy pleaded. "There is a very important man who saw the trial and he is waiting to meet you."

Jimmy's information about 'a very important man who saw the trial', caught Lee's attention.

"All right," Lee said sensing Jimmy's anxiety. "Go back and tell your dad I'm on my way."

"Thank you, Mr. Richards," Jimmy said with relief.

Not waiting for Lee to get up, Jimmy walked away.

Lee slowly got up and followed him, the distance between them increasing with each step.

Life is about to change.

Lee, trying to figure out why he would think such a thing, stopped walking. When recognition failed to join him, he proceeded with a smile and a quicker pace.

CHAPTER FIFTEEN

The fact that everyone in the office building was smiling as though they had been given the rest of the day off, was evidence Lee's victory had preceded him. He was appreciative of the many accolades he received as he hurried toward his meeting.

As soon as he entered the conference room, Wayne Bullock, senior partner of the firm, asked, "Did you think you would get a zero verdict?"

"Only after it was given," Lee replied with all the modesty he could find, which wasn't much.

Lee turned his attention to the man standing to the right of Wayne and saw the face he had seen in the courtroom for the past week. When their eyes met, the man shook Lee's hand and said, "Well done Mr. Richards. I'm Frank Watt, president of Farmer's Alternative Insurance Company. I've heard a lot about you, and after watching you in court this week, I'm even more impressed."

Frank Watt was somewhere under short. What he lacked in height, he made up in girth. At four eleven and two hundred pounds plus, his appearance drew your attention. So did his dress and pronunciation. He wore a smart blue, pinstriped suit, with expensive jewelry that fit his office. His voice had authority, which was transported in a British accent, making him interesting to listen to.

"Mr. Richards, I've come to ask you for your help in getting rid of a chiropractor, a chiropractor who has plagued my company for years."

"I hope you didn't choose me because of today's verdict. You have to give a lot of credit to the plaintiff, her attorney, and Dr. Bradley."

Lee's remark brought laughter.

As Jimmy was leaving the room, his father asked him to close the door on his way out.

"Wait a minute," Lee said with some urgency. "When the president of an insurance company, comes to its defense firm for help, I assume that help will be in a courtroom, and not in an alley. And if I'm going to court on a big case, I need help from someone right out of law school, someone who has studied the latest appellate rulings. Jimmy fits that bill, and I need him to help me on whatever case we're going to defend."

"No problem," said Frank.

"Close your mouth son," said Wayne with pride.

Wayne motioned for Lee to take a seat. "Mr. Richards, how would you like to put Dwight Fitzmore out of business?"

"Dwight Fitzmore, the chiropractor who has five offices in Wichita, as well as a couple of offices within a twenty-mile radius? Dwight Fitzmore, the chiropractor who gouges his patients for every penny he can get? Never heard of him."

"That Dwight Fitzmore, and by the way he has six offices in Wichita, not five. We know you've cross-examined chiropractors Grant, Green, Powell, Clayton, and of course Bradley, but did you know they all work for Fitzmore?"

"No, I didn't."

"How many times have you gone up against Fitzmore?"

"Once, maybe twice."

"Three times. Can you guess why it hasn't been more?"

"Because I'm good," Lee said in jest.

Frank ignored Lee's attempt at humor. "His bills are usually just under our treatment radar. Consequently, he rarely goes to court. I think he makes so much money from his other doctors, he doesn't have to over-treat his own patients. I've had enough of Dr. Fitzmore. This company is not only ready to question all of his bills in a court of law; we're considering talking to the district attorney about possible fraud allegations. And that's not all. Whether the district attorney goes after him or not, I'm going to ask the Kansas Board of Chiropractors to jerk his license."

"You're serious?"

"Quite serious, "said Wayne, wanting to get into the conversation. "And Farmer's Alternative Insurance isn't just focusing on Fitzmore. If this case goes the way Mr. Watt wants it to go, other chiropractors in the area, besides those who work for Fitzmore, will be attacked in like manner. Do you realize, all you have to do to win this case is to expose Fitzmore?"

Frank cut in, "If you expose him, and I know you will, we want to litigate other cases in the surrounding areas of Kansas City, Kansas, and Kansas City, Missouri. Who knows, there could be a Kansas City branch of Bullock, Barth, Hodge, and Richards, to spearhead those litigations.

Wayne wanted to rejoin the excitement. "And those chiropractors, who are treating their patients as patients and not traveler's checks, will benefit as well. Like you told me once, people in small accidents can be seriously hurt, and if their chiropractors would take good notes, peer-review research would put them out of our reach."

Frank picked up a small pile of files and handed them to Lee. "I've selected three accidents I think would represent Fitzmore's incompetence. All three took place in the Wichita area, and are still being treated, only because we haven't stopped paying for their treatment. In each of these accidents, Fitzmore's bill is extremely high, especially for him. For once, I don't think he's concerned about going to court. Either his bill is so high, he can make money even if it's cut, or he thinks the case is so solid, a jury would find for his patient."

Frank selected the top file and laid the remaining files on a nearby desk. "The first accident took place at the intersection of Twenty-First and Maze Road. Our insured is a twenty-nine-year-old construction worker who ran a red light, ramming his panel truck into a midsize Chevy, driven by a fifty-year-old Sister from a nunnery in Wichita. Both vehicles were totaled, and both drivers went to Via Christi Hospital where they were both diagnosed with sprain/strain injuries and released on the same day. Our insured, John Smith, if you can believe that name, maintains his stoplight was still on yellow when he entered the intersection, and the police report had one witness out of three, who corroborated his story. Our insured, prior to this accident, had a clean driving record."

Lee asked, "Did the nun treat with any other doctor, other than Fitzmore?"

"No."

"Did our insured seek treatment after he visited the ER?"

"No."

"How does our insured look in person, and does he have a family?"

"He's a divorcee with a son who lives with his ex-wife, has a high school diploma, and is pleasant to talk to. As far as looks go, he's presentable."

"Was there anyone in either car who wasn't wearing a seatbelt?"

"No."

"Were there any airbag deployments in the accident?"

"I don't know. I'll check this accident, as well as the other two accidents for airbag deployment. Are there any other questions before I go to the second accident?"

Lee shook his head.

"The second accident is a typical rear-end collision at a stoplight, the intersection being Second Street and Main. Our insured, Jerri Snider, a thirty-five-year-old female teacher, driving a late midsize Ford, hit the back of a Corvette, carrying Fitzmore's two patients; boys aged twenty and seventeen. Our insured's car sustained three hundred- and ten-dollars' worth of damage, while the Corvette sustained four thousand, four hundred dollars in damages. No one went to the ER or sought treatment of any kind, except for Fitzmore's patients, which were only treated by Fitzmore. By the way, the driver of the Corvette was legally drunk, and went to jail."

"What are the boys like?"

"Spoiled. They alone would be reason enough for us to go to court. Still, if it weren't for the extremely high chiropractic bill, over ten thousand dollars, we would have settled by now. By the way, each boy's chiropractic bill is the same amount. That doesn't look right to me."

"It won't look right to a jury either. What is our teacher like?"

"Very professional, and likable."

"Is she married?"

"Yes. She got married last year and is three months pregnant. Her husband is also a teacher at another school and is just as presentable as his wife."

"What are the boy's parents like?"

"I don't know. Is it important to know?"

"Could be. Sometimes character witnesses are needed, even if they only sit in the gallery and don't testify."

"I'll get on it."

"What about the third accident?"

"The third accident took place on I-235, on Mother's Day, just one and a half months ago. Fitzmore already has a bill ahead of his usual amount because of the number of patients the accident brought him. His patients are a family of five, made up of a forty-two-year-old male driver, and his thirty-seven-year-old wife, who was a front-seat passenger; a thirteen-year-old boy, a nine-year-old girl, and a two-year-old girl who was in a car seat. Except for the father and the mother, all were sitting in the backseat. Strangely enough, there was no damage to the patient's 1999 Dodge minivan and only a small dent to our insured's 1990 Toyota. Again, occupants of both cars refused the ER. Only Fitzmore's patients received treatment, and their treatment was only with him."

"Talk to me about the family."

"They are a lovely Mexican family. I think a jury would be sympathetic toward them. They wait to be spoken too, and then offer only what is required."

"And our insured?"

"Jason Howells is hard to figure out. He has an attitude that turns you off. He comes from a broken home, is a full-time student at WSU, and doesn't have any means of employment that we know of. This is his first accident. His father is Sam Howells. Have you heard of him?"

"No. Should I?"

"Not necessarily. His father is a contract attorney in Wichita."

"The name Howells seems familiar. What is his mother's name?"

"His mother's name is Kerry Howells. She is a school nurse at North Side Middle School. Fitzmore's twenty-five-thousand-dollar chiropractic bill is the only reason we considered this case."

Lee heard nothing Frank said after Kerry Howells. Lee's decision was already made. If Kerry was his late wife's nurse, he had to meet her again.

Frank waited for another question. When one didn't come, he asked, "Which case is the best case for us?"

Lee didn't respond right away. He was still looking at Kerry's name. Suddenly he circled it and closed the file.

"Frank, am I right in thinking this trial is about getting Fitzmore's incompetence on record, not minimizing what we might have to pay a plaintiff or plaintiffs?"

Frank started to speak but stopped. After a brief moment, he smiled and said, "You're right. The object of this trail is Fitzmore, not the outcome."

"Getting Fitzmore's incompetence on record?"

"That's correct."

"And the more incompetent records he gives us, the better our odds?"

Frank smiled. "Exactly!"

"This is the way I see these cases," Lee said with increasing respect for Frank.

"The first accident is a she-said-he-said accident, and the "she" is a nun who went to the ER. Because she's the only plaintiff, it's not a good case for what we want to do. Still, if you want to go to the District Attorney, and/or the chiropractic licensing board, we can use this case along with the other two, to demonstrate a pattern of unnecessary treatment. We should deny treatment immediately and give the case to someone in the firm."

Lee got out of his chair and began to pace. "In the second accident, most of the energy from the striking vehicle was directed into the Corvette. I think it would be easy to prove the two boys weren't hurt as much as Fitzmore's records report. This case is better than the first case because there are two patient records to attack, instead of one. The more patients an accident has, the more examination, treatment, and billing records there are to attack. I would wait a couple of weeks before denying treatment, and then again give the case to a different lawyer in the firm, but have the lawyers in these two cases, work together on their defenses."

Lee sat back down. "The third accident is our best accident. Right off the bat, it gives us five patient records to question. There is also a bonus, in that these records deal with bodies of different ages, gender, and accident vulnerability. They should have different degrees of injury, if not different injuries and healing periods. One should also expect different diagnoses, treatment schedules, results, and prognoses. I'll bet anything; his records are the same for each patient. Don't deny treatment. I'll let you know when to pull the plug."

"He's everything you said he was," Frank said as he grabbed his briefcase. "I'll let you two do whatever you do. I'm confident we couldn't have given this case to a better attorney."

Walking toward Lee, Frank continued. "Don't get up. It was nice to finally meet you, Lee. I will be looking forward to our trial. I wouldn't miss it for the world."

As Frank and Wayne were exiting the room, Lee turned to Jimmy. "Contact Luis Proctor, the personal injury investigator we use and get him to find out everything he can concerning Jason's mother. I'll find out about his father. I want that information Monday morning by eight o'clock. Tell Luis it's urgent. And then try to set up a time for Jason Howells to come in next week."

Lee went back to his office and closed the door. He sat on the edge of his desk, and opened Jason Howell's file, wondering if Jason's mother could be the nurse, he had met the day his wife died.

CHAPTER SIXTEEN

For Lee, the weekend lasted a month, and every clock said it wasn't Monday. When he tried to visualize Kerry Howells, he only saw his own impatience. Was Kerry Howells, Gayle's nurse, or was she some other Kerry Howells?

When Monday morning finally arrived, even though Lee was sleep-deprived, he greeted it with energy and apprehension. Breakfast was touched, but only out of habit. He had no memory of the drive from his house to his firm's parking garage. He knew he should be doing something besides waiting for Jimmy, but he waited anyway.

It was five minutes past eight when Jimmy knocked on Lee's open door.

The frustration of Lee's weekend came out.

"Well, you're late!"

"I'm sorry," Jimmy said as he laid the folder on Lee's desk, and quickly left.

When Jimmy closed the door, Lee told his secretary to hold all calls. He opened Jason's file as if it was a prize-winning envelope from Publisher's Clearing House. He frantically searched the file for Jason's personal information, and upon finding it, immediately closed the file only to reopen it.

Looking through Jason's brief history and contact information, Lee finally found her. This Kerry Howells was Gayle's nurse at Wesley Hospital, or at least she was a nurse employed by Wesley when his wife died. He paged Jimmy.

"Did you want to see me?" Jimmy said, as he hesitantly stood at Lee's door.

Lee, wanting to apologize for his earlier conduct, began to verbally dance. "Jimmy, well done. Don't mind my impatience. I'm always like this at the beginning of a case I know will end up in trial."

"I just want to help, not hinder," Jimmy said with little confidence.

"Would you call Jason Howells, and have him come in as soon as he can? Also, contact his mother and make an appointment."

"Why his mother?"

"Like I said earlier, we might need her for a character witness."

"Do you want me to call his father as well?"

"No. Mothers are always more observant and believable when it concerns their sons. The same is true with fathers and their daughters."

* * * * * * *

When Lee got back from lunch he found a note on his desk, notifying him of Jimmy's need to see him as soon as possible.

"Jimmy, what's up," Lee said with a hint of apprehension in his voice.

"Jason Howells doesn't want to see you. He told me he isn't going to go to court."

"Did he say why?"

"He just said he didn't want to go court. What do we do now?"

"Call him back and tell him you gave me the message and I understand."

"You understand!"

"You need to tell him I know how intimidating going to court must sound, but I just need to find out what happened in the accident, and how's he doing. Tell him I'm certain I won't call him to testify. Then tell him, he needs to realize, the people he injured want him to pay their chiropractic bill of approximately twenty thousand dollars, as well as another twenty-five thousand for the pain and suffering he has caused them. If he wants protection from his insurance company, protection he has already paid for, he needs to come in and let us help him. If he doesn't want our help, help he's already paid for, I need for him to at least come to my office, and sign some papers releasing us from our responsibility to protect him from the people he injured, and the law firm who is suing him. If he still doesn't want to make an appointment, thank him for taking your call, wish him the best, and then quickly hang up; do not entertain any further conversation. If he calls back and gets belligerent, transfer the call to me."

"Do you think he'll call?"

"Jimmy, the plaintiff is suing him. Not his insurance company or this firm. We represent Jason only if he wants us to represent him. The contract Jason signed is with Farmer's Alternative Insurance, not us, and that contract is contingent on his cooperation. If he doesn't cooperate, then the contract he signed is void, and he will have to represent himself in court. I'm betting when he realizes he's going to court, no matter what; when he realizes the bind, he's in, he'll call. Now go make his day. And when he calls back, make an appointment for him to see me as soon as possible, even if you have to move a previous appointment of mine."

It took Lee most of an hour to get back into a normal flow. Lunch came and went without a word from Jimmy. Just when he was rethinking his strategy, there was a rapid knock on his office door.

"Come in," Lee said with confusion.

Jimmy's smile divulged success.

"His appointment is for tomorrow morning at nine-thirty."

"Was he happy?"

"Of course, he was. And I'm due to make senior partner this week," Jimmy said with a laugh. "Do you want me to set up an appointment with his mother?"

Lee thought for a moment. "Yes. Make it for eleven-thirty, any day this week. If eleven-thirty doesn't work, make it for four-thirty, but make it for this week if possible."

"Why those times? Don't they cut into lunch and dinner?"

"Jimmy, ask any question you want about trial procedures, techniques, or strategy; any questions about rulings or points of law, any questions you want to ask, but ask them after you have done what I want done. When I ask, or tell you to do something, the only questions I want from you, are questions pertaining to the completion of what I have asked you to do. By the way, I think you're doing a great job."

Jimmy left Lee's office trying to figure out whether he had been complimented or scolded.

Two hours later when Lee was with another client, Jimmy slowly entered the conference room and handed Lee a sticky note.

> Kerry Howells tomorrow morning at eleven-thirty. There's a slight problem.

"Excuse me, John," Lee said as he got up and headed toward the door. "I have to instruct Jimmy on something important. It'll only take a minute. Please excuse me."

"What's the problem?" Lee said as he and Jimmy stepped into the hall.

"She works at a middle school and has to be back by one o'clock."

"Great."

"Great? Doesn't that cramp your meeting time?" Jimmy questioned.

"Nope," said Lee with a smile. "And Jason's appointment is at nine-thirty?"

"Correct."

"Great," said Lee as if he had won another battle in court.

CHAPTER SEVENTEEN

Jason showed up for his appointment wearing faded jeans with well-placed holes, a blue dress shirt that wasn't tucked in, dirty tennis shoes, and a chip on each shoulder.

Due to Jason's demeanor, Lee skipped pleasantries and got down to business. He had no intention of putting him on the stand and immediately conveyed this. His tactic worked, at least until he told him he was going to interview his parents at a later time.

"What do my parents have to do with this?" Jason's question being louder than called for.

Realizing the need to take control of the meeting, and Jason, Lee continuously stared at him as he slowly leaned forward as if getting ready to slap him upside the head. After a couple of seconds of saying nothing, he quietly spoke. "Your attitude troubles me, Jason. It suggests you haven't told anyone…everything. Is that true?"

"I've told you everything, sir," said Jason as he tried to escape Lee's stare.

"Good. Let me summarize our situation. You, or someone else, have paid Farmer's Alternative Insurance Company a lot of money to protect you in a scenario just like the one you are presently in. Farmers Alternative Insurance has hired me to provide you with the protection you need when your case goes to court, and your case is going to court. I need your help to help me protect you, as much as you can be protected. If you don't help me, according to the contract you signed with Farmers, I can, and will walk away leaving you to defend yourself. However, before you walk away from my help, you should remember that my help has already been paid for, and if you fire me, it will probably cost you approximately fifty thousand dollars. Now, if you have fifty thousand dollars lying around, or think you can do a better job than I can, tell me. If not, you'll sign a waiver, we'll shake hands, and you can be on your way. However, if you want my help, you will help me *any way* I need you to help me. Any questions?"

"No questions," Jason said with disdain.

Lee leaned back and relaxed.

"As far as you know, was anyone hurt in this accident?"

"No."

"If no one was hurt, help me prove it by telling me what happened."

As Jason told his story, Lee noticed several inconsistencies, inconsistencies that gave him the impression Jason was either withholding information or was uncertain as to what really happened. However, Lee reminded himself that this case was about Dr. Fitzmore, and a nurse he hadn't seen since his wife died.

"Did the driver of the vehicle your car ran into, give you any indication that he was turning into your lane?"

"I can't remember. That's why I can't take the stand."

"I understand Jason, but you need to know, I'm asking you these questions to prepare *me* for court, not so I can prepare you for court. So, hang in there. We're close to being done, at least for today."

"At least for today!"

"I don't see us having to meet more than one or two more times before trial. That is if you don't want to testify. If you want to testify, we'll have to meet more often. One more time, do you remember the car in front of you, giving any type of signal before pulling into your lane?"

"All I can remember is hitting the car in front of me. One minute the car wasn't there, the next minute it was. I don't remember whether they signaled or not."

Lee thought for a moment. "Is it possible you simply rear-ended a car that was always in front of you? It's no problem if you did. I just need to know."

"The car came out of nowhere. What can I say?"

"It was raining that morning…" Lee stopped. He realized he didn't want to find out any more than he already knew.

Changing direction he asked, "What kind of relationship do you have with your father?"

"What does my father have to do with this?" Jason said with a new sense of alarm.

"You might need to have a character reference, and I was thinking of interviewing him."

"If I'm not taking the stand, why do I need a reference? You said you weren't going to put me on the stand."

"Good point. But what happens if the other side wants to put you on the stand? What if they think you were intoxicated, or on drugs?"

Jason studied Lee and then stood as if to leave. "First, I don't think too much of my dad, and I know he doesn't think too much of me. In other words, counselor, I would think twice about having him as my character witness. Second, I wasn't tested for any impairment at the scene. I would think any attempt to introduce such a theory, could easily be kept out of court. Am I reading the situation correctly?"

"Impressive," Lee said motioning for Jason to sit down. "I don't know what the other side will do. It has been my experience they won't call you to testify if we stipulated negligence on your part. However, it's been my experience not to totally rely upon my experience. In other words, I want to be ready for anything. If your father wouldn't be a good character witness, how about your mother? Do you and your mother have a good relationship?"

"We're not close."

"If you had to have a character witness, would your mother be a better character witness than your dad?"

"I don't know. You're the lawyer. Isn't that why you get paid the big bucks?"

"Did your mother see you after the accident, and if so, how long after the accident was it before she saw you?"

"A couple of hours?"

"I'm going to talk to your mother because she might have observed something I need to know. Not going to a doctor after an accident just means you didn't go to a doctor after an accident, it doesn't mean you weren't hurt. If she saw you shortly after the accident, she might have noticed a difference that might be important to our case."

Jason pondered Lee's thinking, nodded his head in agreement, and said, "Are we through?"

"We're through. This office will keep in touch."

When Jason left Lee's office, Lee began to organize his notes but stopped after several unsuccessful attempts. All he could think about was a reunion with Kerry Howells, a reunion that would happen in one hour and fifty-one minutes.

CHAPTER EIGHTEEN

"Mrs. Howells is here for her eleven-thirty appointment," Vicki said, pausing to let Lee drink her in.

"Thank you, Miss. Courtney" Lee emphasized her last name, hoping Vicki would realize her hopes of impressing her boss, were going to stay hopes.

Lee didn't want to show Kerry he was anxious to meet her, so instead of following Vicki to the reception area, he went to the restroom instead.

He stood in front of the restroom mirror trying to find something to fix, and when he couldn't, he whispered "show time" to his reflection, and walked out to meet Mrs. Howells.

"Hello Mr. Richards," Kerry said as she offered her hand long before Lee was able to accept it.

"Please, call me Lee," he said as they shook hands. "It's been a long time since we last saw each other. Did you remember who I was when my assistant called?"

"No. Did you make the connection when you saw my name?"

"Not at first," he lied.

They both laughed more than their responses called for.

"Mrs. Howells, thank you for coming in on such short notice. Would you like anything to drink?" Lee offered as they entered his office.

"No thank you, and by the way it's Ms. Howells and I would appreciate you referring to me as Kerry."

"No problem, Kerry. Were you a *Ms.* when my wife died?" he said, showing her a seat in front of his desk.

"No, in fact, I was served divorce papers the day your wife died. My divorce followed shortly thereafter, and it's been Ms. ever since."

"I'm sorry to hear about your divorce. I hope things have gotten better?" Lee said as he took his position behind his desk. "I've never forgotten how nice you were to my wife and me. The personal attention you showed us was certainly appreciated."

"Thank you," she said glancing at her hands, before looking at Lee. "Both of you were great to me as well. You made my job easy, which wasn't always the case. I envied how much you cared about each other."

Wanting to change subjects, Kerry leaned back in her chair and said, "I was surprised to hear from anyone concerning my son's accident. Since Jason said no one was hurt, I thought his case would be settled out of court."

"Kerry, the reason we're going to court is money. It's what happens in today's world. When anyone makes a mistake, a mistake that's covered by insurance, litigation is a possibility. With that said, the chances Jason will take the stand are slim. However, I would still like to know him better. Could you describe Jason from *mom's* point of view; some background, what he was like before the accident and after the accident? I understand you saw him hours after the collision."

"Yes, I did, and he did seem different after the accident."

Lee, noticing Kerry looking at her watch said, "Kerry, I need to apologize for my law clerk making this eleven-thirty appointment. When do you have to be back at work?"

"I have to be back at one o'clock," Kerry said, grateful for Lee's concern.

"We could postpone this meeting until next week, or we could go to a small restaurant near here and kill two stones with one bird."

"Isn't it two birds with one stone?"

Lee smiled, somewhat embarrassed. "I take it we have a "yes" for lunch."

* * * * * *

"When you discovered your assistant's mistake, why didn't you just rebook my appointment?" Kerry asked as they walked toward the restaurant.

"You know, I never thought of that." Lee knew she wouldn't believe him, and her look confirmed his suspicions.

"I thought we would eat at the old Lasen Hotel. Have you ever been to the Lasen?"

"You mean Lassen," Kerry said with a giggle. She couldn't believe how comfortable she felt with this man, and how uncomfortable he was.

"Sorry. Lassen."

"I've never heard of it," she said as if hearing the name for the first time.

Lee noticed her wit. "The Lassen Hotel, which you might know as the Market Centre, was built in 1918. It used to be a hotel in downtown Wichita. In 1983, it was turned into an office building, and in 1984 it was listed on the National Register of Historic Places. It houses a restaurant called The Silver Spoon. I recommend it because it's close to us, and it's close to one o'clock. Are you game?"

"Are we headed that way?"

"We are," he replied somewhat embarrassed.

"Then I'm game."

As they walked, Kerry hesitantly said, "To tell the truth, I'm nervous. But not about Jason's case. I trust you with my son."

"Then what's the problem?"

"I'm nervous about being with you."

"Why am I making you nervous," he said as if he was defending himself.

"I don't know. It was a stupid remark. Let's just forget it."

After several steps, Lee said with concern in his voice, "If you want something to worry about, I haven't eaten at this restaurant before."

Kerry's laugh was a "thank you" as much as it was a laugh. She was beginning to appreciate Lee's humor, and the small banter they were having.

The walk to the Lassen took only minutes. After finding the restaurant, Lee requested a table in the corner.

A hairy-armed waiter, holding a pad in his hand, and the precise time his shift was over in his head, came to their table and asked, "To drink?"

Both ordered coffees, as well as the specialty, not because they wanted meatloaf, but because they both wanted "hairy arms" to leave while they still had an appetite.

"What do you think the trial will be like?" Kerry asked when their waiter disappeared.

"This case is about the plaintiff's injuries. I won't contest liability, but even if I did, the whole case will revolve around the chiropractic treatment received by the plaintiffs."

Kerry, without being asked, eagerly offered, "Jason's a good boy. He's enrolled in college, has a clean record, and as far as I know, doesn't drink."

"Does he do drugs?"

"No!" Kerry quickly responded.

Lee could tell Kerry didn't have a clue as to her son's habits, nor did she want to know.

"Nothing against Jason. It's a common question I ask all my clients. Let's change the subject and talk about you. Tell me about Kerry Howells."

"Well, you know about the divorce. I worked at Wesley Hospital for a number of years after your wife died, then I took my present job as a school nurse."

"Why did you leave Wesley?

"Work schedule, duties, stress, and I didn't want to be around dying people anymore."

The meatloaf arrived quicker than both would have liked. After exchanging the ketchup bottle, and a few topics of little interest, Lee said, "I have a request, if I may?"

"You may."

"In summary, give me a quick synopsis of your son. Be general. Just let it come."

"There are really two Jason's. The Jason before I was served divorce papers, and the Jason after service. The before-Jason and I were quite close. He was a typical kid who got good grades, never talked back, and his word was his bond. However, after I was served, and his father left us, Jason's world seemed to crumble. He was mad at me for his dad leaving, and I must say, his dad did everything to feed that anger. I honestly think Jason didn't think it was my fault, but he had to blame someone. As the years passed, he became self-centered, if not reclusive. To my knowledge, Charlie Zimmer is the only person he has anything to do with."

"Who's Charlie Zimmer?"

"He's a son of one the members of my ex-husband's country club. My ex-husband used to run with a group of attorneys, whose sons also ran as a group. Charlie's one of those boys."

Lee referred to his notes.

"At the time of the accident, wasn't your son attending Wichita State University?"

"Yes."

Lee checked his notes again. "I have him living at 1717 Athenian Street, on the northwest side of Wichita."

"That's correct."

"How can he afford to live in a house? I don't have him employed."

"Good question," Kerry laughed as she quit playing with her spoon. She looked to the ceiling and paused as if excited about what she was going to say.

"What I'm about to tell you, will say as much about your client as anything I could say. You see my ex-husband and his attorney friends, are a group of individuals who preoccupy themselves with one-up-man ship, whether embellishing trial results or using their children's accomplishments to improve their status. As the story goes, they, infatuated with their perceived status as the elite, decided to hold a dinner honoring their children's high school graduation. The dinner was to be held at their country club, and money was not to be an issue. The way I heard it, after the banquet, each boy or girl, stood and reported what college they were going to, as well as the name of the law school that would follow their college graduation. Toasts and cheers followed each announcement, that is until my son made his."

Kerry was enjoying the expression on Lee's face. "I was told, Jason announced he was going to join the Army. When asked why, he said that although he had a scholarship, his parent's divorce decree didn't provide money for his living quarters after high school. He also reported the child support his mother had been receiving, would stop when he graduated, which had forced his mother to downsize from a two-bedroom to a studio rental, rendering him homeless come graduation, thus one of the reasons he was joining the Army. When asked why he had picked the Army, and not a safer branch of the Armed Forces, such as the Coast Guard, he pointed out the Army offered hazard-duty pay to everyone assigned to a war zone. By volunteering for a war zone, providing he survived his hazard-duty assignment, he could bank his hazard-duty pay for college. He assured them the hazard-duty pay, plus the GI Bill benefits, plus the money from a part-time job, would be enough to allow him to go to college, that is, if he survived his hazard-duty assignment. Now, I don't know how accurate that story is, because I heard it second hand, but if it isn't I don't want to know," Kerry said with amusement.

"He said if he survived his hazard-duty assignment, twice?"

"He's good isn't he," Kerry said with pride.

"He's good," Lee said as they both grinned.

"Of course, everyone who hadn't passed out by then, looked to his father expecting an explanation. Not wanting to lose face, his dad pointed out that the absence of an educational provision in the divorce decree had been a clerical mistake, one he would take care of first thing Monday morning. His moment of redemption was shattered when Jason asked if he could live with him so he could go to college. His dad countered by suggesting a dorm. I guess boos filled the room, even from the soon-to-be high school graduates. Someone suggested a rental, which gained momentum. His dad thinking all "the talk" would be nothing more than a Monday morning hangover, agreed to the rental. However, his *hope* became his *hangover*, when a divorce lawyer drew up a contract and had all the attorneys sign it, including "poor old dad." When the dust settled, Jason had free college, a free house, as long as he maintained a "C" average, his dad's hatred, and a small monthly stipend to boot. I would have given almost anything to have seen his dad's face when the room toasted Jason's good fortune."

"How do you know all this?"

"The wives of these pretentious idiots despise my ex-husband as much as I do. They used to report to me if they heard anything concerning my son or my ex-husband."

"Did they get back to you about this accident?"

"No. In fact, I haven't gotten a report from them in a long time."

When Kerry looked at her watch, Lee raised his hand to get the waiter's attention and bill.

"I have enjoyed our talk," Kerry said while gathering her belongings.

"Me too."

* * * * *

Not much was said as they walked back to Lee's office. As they approached the office door, Kerry said, "If it's alright with you, I'll go to my car instead of coming in. I need to get back to work."

"I understand. This might be out of line, but I really enjoyed being with you today."

"Why is enjoying being with me out of line?" she asked, with a grin, her teasing surprising her as much as it did Lee.

"What I mean is, I haven't enjoyed being with someone this much for many years. To be honest, the main reason I wanted to see you, is to thank you for Gayle's care."

"You could have done that over the phone," Kerry said with a twinkle in her eye.

"I think I should shut up, say goodbye, and let you get back to work."

"I hope you're better in court," Kerry said, with amusement.

"So do I," he laughed. "I'm going to do something now I certainly wouldn't do in court."

"Kiss me! You're going to kiss me?" Kerry said as she laughed at the startled look on Lee's face. She was just as surprised about her remark as he was.

"No!" said Lee flustered.

"You don't want to kiss me?"

"Yes! I mean no," Lee said, surprised at how much he was enjoying her.

"Please tell me you're better in court."

"You're mean," Lee said as he stepped back, smiling to let Kerry know he was enjoying her kidding. "I hope I get a kinder jury."

He stepped closer, "Would you like to go to dinner with me? I mean we could—"

"No," Kerry abruptly interrupted.

Lee immediately sobered.

"After the Silver Spoon, I don't trust your choice of restaurants. I would rather make us a picnic lunch, and go to the park," Kerry said enjoying her control.

"That sounds great."

"How about picking me up Saturday at eleven?"

"Saturday at eleven."

Their departing handshake was slightly longer than their initial handshake.

CHAPTER NINETEEN

"Goodbye Miss Chung," Lee said to his client as she walked out of his office. "Remember, our trial begins Monday morning at 8:30. I'll meet you in room three, on the second floor of the Court House at eight o'clock. See you then.

Miss Chung was still talking as Lee closed the door. He immediately looked at his watch. "Only twenty minutes." He wrung his hands as he circled his desk twice before he sat down. "Thank you, thank you, thank you," he said wishing he knew who he was thanking.

Since his picnic with Kerry, a picnic packed with homemade food, contagious humor, and unpredictable excitement, his world seemed different. Either it had changed, or he was looking at it for the first time, in a very long while.

The last five months had been remarkable. It didn't matter whether they ate in or out, watch television or a movie, went for walks, or sat on the couch—she made his world safe, fun, and hopeful. Only when he wasn't with her, did he slip into comparisons of the past, analyses of the present, and doubts about the future.

He looked at his desk clock, picked up his phone, and dialed the front desk. "Miss Courtney, this is Lee. I have—"

"Hello Mr. Richards," Vickie's intentions dripping from the receiver, "Can I—"

"Miss Courtney," Lee quickly interrupted while writing a memo to fire her at the next partner's meeting, "I have an appointment with Mr. Bullock in ten minutes. Make sure you don't allow anyone to meet with him before that time."

"Yes, Mr. Richards. I—" Lee hung up the phone and circled his memo.

Lee didn't know why he was so nervous about his meeting with Wayne, and yet he did; he didn't want to look like a fool to a friend who had counseled him after his wife's death.

"You mind if we have this meeting in your office?" Wayne's voice startled Lee. "I have to get out of mine at least once a day."

"Wayne, you didn't have to come to my office, I would have come to yours."

Wayne waved him off. "What's up Lee? This must be serious. You're not quitting the firm, are you?" Wayne asked with a glare that was replaced with a smile as he sat down.

"No Wayne. I'm not quitting," he replied as he leaned forward on his desk and studied him, trying to decide if he really wanted to do this.

"What I want to talk to you about has nothing to do with law or this firm. In fact, I don't know what it has to do with…and then I do."

"You're better in court, aren't you?" Wayne sarcastically asked.

"That's funny. I've been asked that same question by someone you know *of*."

"I know, or know of?"

"Know *of.* About five months ago I went on a picnic with a lady who has turned my life around. I can't remember enjoying life this much for…let's just say for a long time. Meeting Kerry has also brought some problems, problems you counseled me on when my wife died. To be blunt, I'm scared."

"I wish I had that kind of *scared* in my life," said Wayne as he sat back and interlocked his hands behind his head. When Lee didn't smile, Wayne unlocked his hands and sat up. "It sounds like you're in love."

"I am."

It took a couple of seconds for Wayne to realize Lee was serious.

"Great! Why the unhappy face? Do I know her?"

"You know *of* her."

"There's that know *of* her thing. What do you mean I know *of* her?"

"Do you remember me talking about the nurse Gayle had when she was in Wesley?"

Wayne searched his mind. "Don't take this personally, but I don't. Wait a minute; I do remember you talking to me about a nurse, a nurse that was really nice to both of you. Is that what you mean by I know *of* her'?"

"Yes and no. Does the name Kerry Howells, connected with Dr. Fitzmore's case, ring a bell?

"Kerry Howells? No."

"Kerry Howells is the mother of Jason Howells, who is the driver of the car who hit a car filled with Dr. Fitzmore's patients."

"The plaintiffs we are litigating?

"The plaintiffs we are litigating," Lee echoed.

"Lee, do we have an ethical problem here?" Wayne said with concern.

"I don't think so. She isn't a client, just the mother of a client."

"Are you sure you're in love with this woman?"

"Yes."

"So, what's the problem? Do you feel guilty about loving someone besides your late wife?"

"I did at first. But that quickly went. No, it has to do with her profession and religion."

Wayne didn't say anything. He just sat looking at Lee with his mouth slightly open.

Lee realized he had to be more explicit. "Do you remember why I went from being the assistant district attorney, to a medical malpractice litigator?" He didn't give Wayne time to answer. "I was trying to bring the medical profession to its knees. I was searching for medical doctors to sue. Nothing has changed, I'm still gunning for the health care system."

"Is this *Kerry* in the health care system?"

"A nurse."

"I see. Why would you date the health care system?"

"I shouldn't have, but it's too late now."

"Are you thinking of…" he paused, "you are thinking about getting married!"

"You're beginning to see the problem," Lee said as he put his hands into a praying position, with the tips of both index fingers pressed to his lips.

"Lee, I'm confused. When you marry this nurse, won't she stop being a nurse?"

"I hope so."

"Problem solved."

"I think she's religious as well."

"She's religious?" Wayne asked for clarification.

"I think she is, and I know you find that amusing, but I don't."

"Oh, you bet I find that amusing. I know you hate the religious community but are you listening to yourself? Why do you think she's religious? Don't you know?"

"I think she says a silent prayer before each meal. When we go out to dinner, she never orders any alcoholic drinks, her language is clean, and she declines all Sunday morning invitations."

Wayne stifled a laugh. This was his friend, a friend he helped in years past, and would help again.

"I know you're concerned Lee, but I have one opinion, one question, and one piece of advice. In order for you to hear any of them, you have to give me your word you will listen and consider each one before dismissing any one of them."

"You have my word."

"This is my opinion. I'm sure you could find atheists, in this building alone, who have private conversations before eating, don't drink or cuss, and stay home all day on Sunday, let alone Sunday morning."

Lee started to say something, but Wayne's look kept him quiet.

"This is my one question. Why haven't you asked her if she's religious?"

"I agree with your opinion, and the answer to your question is, I'm afraid she's religious. I know my thinking is stupid, and that's why I need you to set me straight on what to do. I can get by the medical thing. As you said, that can change when we get married, but her religion won't, and I don't want to marry someone who's religious."

"Do you want to marry this girl?"

"With all my heart."

"There must be some part of your heart that doesn't want to marry her. You loved your late wife, didn't you?"

"You know I did."

"Just answer the question."

"Yes, I did."

"Was she religious?"

"Yes, especially after she got sick."

Wayne's look, made Lee re-answer, "Yes."

"Do you regret marrying your late wife?"

"No."

"Think about my questions and your answers." Wayne didn't give Lee long to think. "Are you ready for my one piece of advice?"

"Yes. I'm ready. I really am. I don't know if I'll follow it, but I'll give it a lot of thought, I promise."

"Good enough.

"Lee, you are the best litigator we have, and I think the reason is simple; you don't come across as a litigator in court. When you kicked my tail in court some years back, it wasn't because you were a better litigator, it was because the jury saw you as their advocate. You asked the questions the jury wanted to ask; questions that brought out the inconsistencies in the stories and explanations they were hearing. More importantly, you asked the jury questions as if you were as confused as they were. By doing so, you created *doubt*. You made them *doubt*. Take your own advice. *Identify* a major tenet of her faith, then kindly *discredit* that tenet by making her common sense answers contradict what she believes. Make her doubt her beliefs. Don't question Kerry. Let Kerry question Kerry."

Wayne gave Lee a minute to consider what he had just said.

"Do you know what her faith is?"

"I have no idea. She's probably a Christian."

"Then find a major tenet of the Christian faith, write a list of questions, and then question her as if you're confused and want to know the answers."

Wayne stood up. "Have I helped?"

Lee stood as well. "Tremendously!"

As soon as Wayne left his office, Lee began jotting down a crude outline. By reviewing his experience with Gayle and her religion, he knew exactly what areas to attack. He would ask her to explain the discrepancy between the Trinity and Christ's baptism, his prayer in the garden and on the cross, and Stephen's vision while being stoned.

When he looked at his list, he didn't see his writing but the hurt on Kerry's face.

"Do I want to do this?" he said to the paper he was holding.

It didn't take him long to answer his question. "You have an obligation to save her from herself, if not for yourself."

CHAPTER TWENTY

Lee's arms gently encircled Kerry, as he kissed her soft lips. But for a stuffy nose and his body's need for air, he would have prolonged this exquisite salutation for the rest of the day.

"Do you think you might be rushing our relationship," Kerry said as she stood in her doorway.

"Listen, lady, it took me over eight years to get to your front door."

Kerry gave him a squeeze and stepped back to let him come in.

"Your timing is great," Kerry said as she went into the kitchen to check the dinner she was cooking, "I've already done the hard work."

"That's why I've been sitting in the car for the past twenty minutes."

Kerry just smiled as she checked the chicken she was frying. She loved Lee's sense of humor. It made the room lighter; it made her life lighter.

"Wow, my timing is good. The table is set; the food looks like it's almost cooked. Am I good or am I good?" Lee said hovering over the stove.

"For what, is the question," her witty response causing Lee to beam.

Nervous about what he was planning to say, he took a seat at the kitchen table and vacillated between a head-on and a round-about approach. He had just convinced himself to abandon his interrogation altogether when he saw her lips moving as she stirred the gravy.

"Sweetheart, are you praying?"

"Just a small one," she said, not looking at Lee. "I like to give thanks for the food and you."

"I never thought of you as a religious person. I don't mean praying makes a person religious, I mean; well, you know what I meant?"

"No, I don't. What does a religious person look or act like?

"Unless they're a nun, I don't know what they look like. But praying is what religious people do, don't they?"

"I think I know what you mean," Kerry said dreading where this conversation could go.

"You don't have a problem with me being religious, do you?"

She thought her question was harmless until Lee said. "I might."

Kerry turned and looked at him. "What do you mean 'I might'?"

"I'm sorry, that didn't come out right. It's just that I have a knee-jerk reaction concerning religion. It stems from all I went through with my late wife. The problem is my past, not us, not the present."

After a short silence, Lee nonchalantly asked, "Are you a Christian?"

"Yes. I'm a Christian. Are you a Christian?"

This line of inquiry wasn't' going the way Lee would have liked. "No, I'm not religious. You might say, when my wife was dying, I had a run-in with religion."

"I do remember you having a problem with the clergy who visited your wife, but Lee, not all Christians are smothering."

Wanting to change subjects, Lee asked, "What's with all the different interpretations on what a Christian should be like. If they all follow the same God, why do they all believe so differently?"

"Good point," she said, purposely not answering his question.

"What they teach is so confusing to me," Lee said as if reflecting. "For example, the Trinity has always confused me. Isn't the Trinity the belief that God, Jesus, and the Holy Ghost are all one being or entity or something, yet they're separate, yet they don't have form, or they're one form or something like that?"

Glad Lee was concentrating on his problem instead of her religion, she emptied the pan of cooked chicken onto a large serving plate. "How Christendom views the Trinity is just as confusing to me as it is to you, and probably Christians as a whole. However, if we're going to talk, you have to help me with the food while we're talking."

Relieved that Kerry was willing to talk, Lee responded quickly, "No problem. I might have this wrong, but when it comes to Christians, isn't the Trinity one of their core beliefs?"

"I believe so. Would you fill our glasses with water?"

Lee got up, grabbed the water pitcher, and began filling the glasses on the table. "I'm going to leave the Holy Ghost out of my questioning, and just center on God and Jesus being one and yet two. And again, I'm not arguing or putting Christianity down, I'm just confused. How can they both be *one*, if a voice from God said he was pleased with Jesus being baptized? If they're one, is Jesus doing a ventriloquist act?"

The second he said ventriloquist, he was sorry. He waited for her anger.

"That makes sense to me. Could you put some bread on the table? The bread is in the pantry."

Lee stood silent, not sure what had just happened.

"Lee. The bread."

Maybe she wasn't listening, was Lee's only thought as he went to get the bread. He would make sure she heard the next couple of questions.

"If Jesus prayed to God in the Garden of Gethsemane, and to God on the Cross, how could they be one? Why would he be praying to himself?"

"I agree. I think we're ready to sit down," Kerry said looking at Lee with a smile.

Lee was dumbfounded.

"One more thing," Lee said as he sat down, "When they stoned Stephen, he said he saw Jesus on the right hand of God?"

"I believe you're right. Would you pass the chicken?"

While passing the chicken, Lee said in frustration, "How can they be one, if they're standing next to each other?"

"I agree with everything you've said. Do you want gravy?"

Beaten like an abused dog, Lee ate half his chicken before he asked, "Kerry, what type of Christian are you?"

"Mediocre at best. I think the question you want to ask, is how can I agree with you, and still be a Christian. There are some Christians who believe God, Jesus, and The Holy Ghost are separate personages, and I'm one of them."

No longer trying to educate Kerry, as to the foolishness of Christianity, Lee asked, "Which faith do you belong to?"

"I'm a Mormon. Would you pass the peas?"

Lee picked up the peas; with no awareness of picking up the peas. "I thought Mormons wore bonnets and drove horse-drawn buggies?"

Kerry laughed as she took the peas from Lee. "I think you have us mixed up with the Mennonites and the Amish."

"When did you become a Mormon?"

"I was born into the Mormon faith."

Each looked at each other as if sensing a "crossroads" moment. Kerry took the initiative.

"My religion seems to be very important to you. Why don't we finish eating, and talk about it after we have dessert? I've put a lot of time into this meal, and who knows, it may be our last, so let's enjoy it if we can."

Lee laid his fork beside his plate and took her hand. "I love you, Kerry. I know it's not romantic hearing me say that for the first time over a plate of chicken, but I want you to know, I love you with all my heart."

Kerry's tears said what the lump in her throat wouldn't let her say.

Lee wished he hadn't told her he loved her, at least not under these circumstances. He also wished she would have responded in kind.

Both struggled to be normal, not only because of what was said but what might be said after peach pie and ice cream.

* * * * * * *

After dishes were gathered and put into the dishwasher, Kerry took Lee's hand and led him to the living room couch, where they both sat down. Kerry facing Lee, with her hands holding his, looked directly into his eyes.

"Let me tell you about how I came to be a Mormon. My great, great grandfather, Timothy Hourrigan Howells, received a Book of Mormon from a missionary named Dan Jones in 1846, in a town in Wales called Merthyr Tydfil. After reading the Book of Mormon, Timothy and his family ended up joining the Church in 1847. At that time, Jones was urging all new converts to migrate to the Salt Lake Basin. Although Timothy was sold on Dan Jones and the gospel, he wasn't sold on leaving Merthyr Tydfil. He had a good job in the local iron works and wanted to stay and retire where he had been born. On the other hand, his wife, Mary Jane Compton, wanted to escape Merthyr's pollution, and move to Ireland where her ailing father had a potato farm that had been hit by what was later named the Irish Potato Famine; a famine started when a fungus-like organism ruined up to one-half the potato crops in Ireland. She must have been a strong-willed person, for they ended up doing just that in 1849. And that's not the end of the story. A year after the famine ended, her father up and died. It took them until 1854 before they could sell the farm for enough money to board a ship bound for New York."

She stopped for questions, or any response such pause would elicit. When none came, she resumed.

"Of all the stories my dad has told me over the years, my favorites are the stories of his twenty-eight-year-old great, great grandfather and his family of two, crossing the ocean on a ship, crossing the plains pushing a handcart, and finally arriving in the Salt Lake Basin in 1855. But it gets better. Timothy and his family were only in Salt Lake for two weeks, when Brigham Young, he was the leader of the Church at that time, asked Timothy to help with the iron works in a location in Southern Utah; a location which later became Cedar City. He accepted Brigham

Young's challenge, went to the prescribed area, and built a log cabin for them to live in."

Kerry was surprised at Lee's attention to her story. "Bored yet?"

"Not in the least."

"Cedar City is where my great grandfather, Mack Cavander, my grandfather, Roy Michael, and my father James Richard, were born. At the beginning of the Korean War, my father joined the Air Force. When the war ended, he and my mother decided to make the Air Force a career. That decision eventually led us to McConnell Air Force Base in Wichita, Kansas. When my dad retired, he and Mom, Lois Fay, returned to Cedar City. A year later, to the day, both my father and mother were killed in a car accident. I was married and living in Wichita at the time of their death."

Lee immediately straightened. "I'm sorry. I—"

"No problem," said Kerry with gratitude. "My father gave me everything I have that is good. My mother loved me and was ahead of her time in anything she tackled."

Kerry choked up, and Lee kept silent.

"I'm looking forward to the day when I can thank them both for being the best parents a girl could have. I told you about my divorce. Have I told you about this great guy I met five months ago? I hear he's a magnificent lawyer named Lee Richards."

When Lee smiled, Kerry asked. "Do you know anything about the Mormon Church?"

"I've heard about Brigham Young. He was a Mormon, wasn't he?"

"Yes. As I said earlier, he was an early leader in the Church. Are we through?"

"I don't' know. You're the one telling the story."

Kerry smiled. "I mean are we through as a couple?"

"No! No! No! Didn't you hear me when I said I loved you, and by the way, do you feel the same?"

"Lee, after Sam, I don't trust myself. I think I'm in love with you, no, I know I'm in love with you, but we haven't dated that long, and I thought I knew Sam… I'm…."

Lee squeezed her hand, which made Kerry stop talking. When they both smiled, Kerry continued, "Would you like me to send some missionaries over to tell you about my church?"

"I love you Kerry, but I'm done talking to preachers. Don't you have something I could read?"

"I have something better. Do you know Russell Cruz? He isn't a preacher, and by the way, we don't have preachers. He's an attorney. You, being an attorney and all, you might feel more comfortable speaking with him."

"I don't know him, but I think that's a good idea. But Kerry, and I mean this in a kind way, I want you and him to know, I'm going to be honest and open about my questioning. You need to inform him I'll be there to ask questions, not listen to propaganda."

Lee pulled Kerry to him. "Let me tell you, if my actions haven't, I love you, Kerry Howells."

CHAPTER TWENTY-ONE

I f you have a drug habit, and *money* is needed to support that habit, a Wal-Mart parking lot is a good place to find some. One only has to find a receipt for a cash or debit purchase, return to the store, collect the merchandise recorded on the receipt, and take both receipt and merchandise to Customer Care where cash will be refunded. This exercise is very simple and lucrative if you find a receipt. If you don't, this exercise is humiliating and frustrating. Jason was experiencing the latter when he received a text message reminding him of an appointment with his English Professor.

* * * * * *

As Jason sat in the professor's office, he could only focus on the receipts he hadn't found that morning. He made up his mind that as soon as his meeting was over, he would leave Wichita, and resume his search in the Wal-Mart parking lot, in nearby El Dorado.

"Dr. Hurley will see you now," the secretary said with a glance and a required smile. Jason got up, grabbed his backpack, and went into Dr. Hurley's office.

Dr. Hurley, Jason's English professor and advisor, was six-one, with a long torso, making him appear as if he was sitting on something when seated behind his desk. He wore ten-year-old clothes that were a size too big for his build. His attempted ducktail had gray streaks advertising the other end of prime. His thick glasses teetered on the end of his nose, ready to fall with the slightest movement on his part. He advertised intelligence instead of common sense, with mannerisms always pointing to the past.

"Hi Dr. Hurley," Jason said as he shook hands and took a seat.

Hurley shoved the report he had been reading to Jason. "As you can see, these records have you missing classes, off and on, for the past six months, with an increase in frequency in the last two months. Can you explain this? Is something wrong?"

"Wow! I didn't think mom had been that sick. I'd like to tell you what's wrong with her, but no one knows. I think it's depression, dementia, or both, but when she gets it, it throws her for a loop. When that happens, she's almost bedridden. Since she's alone, I go over and do-little things; clean, cook, get groceries, you know, little things, so she can get back on her feet. I try to stagger which classes I miss, but I can see I have to do a better job."

Hurley didn't believe a word he had heard. "Maybe you should quit school until she gets better."

Jason could read Hurley as well as Hurley could read Jason. "Maybe I should. I'll think about it. Quitting school would certainly set mom back, mentally that is, but attendance should come first."

Give me a break, Hurley thought. "Let me switch hats. As one of your professors, I gave you an assignment last week, an assignment you were supposed to turn in Monday. This is Friday and no assignment. You just gave me a creative story explaining why you keep missing classes; by any chance did you write it down so you could give it to me, and therefore get credit for something pertaining to *creative storytelling*?"

Jason was glad Hurley was annoyed. He was interested to see how he was going to react to his next charade.

"I have a writing with me," Jason said, enjoying a subdued expression of surprise on Hurley's face. "With mom's care and all, I just forgot Monday altogether, but I have a writing. I hope I didn't leave it at mom's house."

Jason, knowing he had nothing to hand in, pretended to search his backpack. He tried to stifle his surprise when he found his mother's envelope. Remembering it contained a poem and an addition; he searched the poem for his mother's signature, and when none was found, handed the poem to his professor.

"I wanted to complete my assignment and write a story, but I found it difficult, with all the care she required. So, I wrote a poem instead. I even came up with another idea for a different poem, sort of a play-with-words poem, if there is such a thing. I hope under the circumstances it would be acceptable. If this isn't, I'll get you whatever you want by this coming Monday, even if mom has to go to the hospital."

Dr. Hurley was on to Jason's ruse. "A play-with-words poem. I can't wait to read it."

Jason ignored him. "Now the poem I'm giving you today isn't the play-with-words poem I'm working on. It's just a poem; a poem that needs some work. I didn't think I was going to turn it in today, or it would be ready to grade."

"Really! I thought you knew you were bringing it today, and if you were going to turn it in today, why does it need work?"

"Aren't all poems a work in progress?" Jason said avoiding answering his question.

To Jason, it seemed as if it took Hurley an hour to read his mother's two-page poem. He wished he had read the poem before handing it to him, but that ship had already sailed; he just hoped it wouldn't sink with him on it.

"Not bad. I liked the play on words, the flies-that-couldn't-fly, and lie-detectors-that-could-only-lie lines. I'm looking forward to reading the next one, the play-with-words poem."

"The next one?"

Hurley rested both elbows on his desk, and said with a hint of amusement, "Remember that other poem you're working on; the play-with-words poem?"

"Oh, that poem," Jason said, knowing neither believed the other.

* * * * * * *

Jason called his mother as soon as he left Hurley's office. "Hi, Mom. Sorry I'm late getting back to you on the poem. I thought it was so good, I took it to one of my professors."

"You took it to a professor! You liked it that much!" What did you think of the addition I made? Do you know where you're going to put it in the poem?"

Jason had no idea what *addition* his mother was talking about, but if he could dance with his professor, he could dance with his mother. "Where do you think it should go?"

"I think it should be the fifth stanza."

"Hey, that was the same conclusion the professor and I reached. Mom, I can't talk now. I'm as busy as ever. I think you should write me another poem, but this time, write a play-with-words poem."

"What do you mean?"

"Write a poem that plays with words. For example, what you did with the flies and lie detector stuff."

"A play-with-words poem. Okay, I'll try it. Maybe we could have dinner after I write it?"

"Sure Mom. Could you write it sooner than later, say maybe in a week? My professor would like to review it before finals start."

"Why does he want to review it?"

"I don't know. Maybe he'll use it in a test or a lecture."

"I'll try. How are you doing?"

"Mom, I've got to go. I'll be in touch."

"Can we meet after I write it?"

"Sure Mom. Remember, a week."

"Bye Jason. I love you," she said to a dial tone.

CHAPTER TWENTY-TWO

"Hi. I'm Lee Richards. I have an appointment with Mr. Cruz."

"Yes, Mr. Richards. I'll let him know you're here," said the receptionist. "Would you like a bottle of water?"

"No thank you," he politely declined.

The receptionist lightly knocked on her boss's door, and when invited in, opened the door wide enough to say, "Lee Richards is here for his appointment."

"Give me about five minutes. I'll buzz you when I'm ready," Russell said with some anxiety.

When his receptionist closed the door, Russell got on his knees and said a quick prayer. Ever since Kerry's call, he had prayed to know how to handle Lee's obvious agenda of gathering information about the church in order to show Kerry its fallacies. Although the plan Heavenly Father had given him was confusing, with the Lord's help he knew it would work; he just didn't know how or why.

After his prayer, and minimal preparation, Russell buzzed the front desk.

"Mr. Richards, you can go in now," the receptionist said as she pointed to the door behind her.

Lee grabbed his clipboard, smiled, and said nothing as he entered Russell's office.

"Hi Mr. Richards," Russell said shaking Lee's hand. "Can I call you Lee?"

"Only if I can call you Russell."

Both smiled as they took their respective seats.

Lee immediately measured Russell and found an athletic body, average looks, and black-trimmed hair. His blue long-sleeve shirt, red tie, gray slacks, and black wingtip shoes were conservative yet stylish. He was Lee's height, which surprised him, since there weren't too many attorneys in Wichita, over six feet. But what surprised him the most was the comfort he felt in his presence. It was like they had always been friends, which in itself was discomforting since he was there under false pretenses.

Russell spoke first, "I've talked to Kerry. She told me you have some questions pertaining to our faith."

"Your faith and the name of your church," Lee quickly replied. "What's with The-Church-of-Jesus-Christ-of-Latter-Day-Saints name?" Not waiting for an answer, he continued, "When I found out Kerry was a Mormon, I went to the yellow pages, and tried to find a Mormon church I could visit. The only churches under "M" were three Methodist churches and one Mennonite church."

Russell broke out in laughter. "That's funny! I never thought about that."

Regaining his composure, Russell spoke. "Lee, a church is usually named by well-meaning people who see the need to worship Christ in a different way. With good intentions, and the Bible as their guide, they name their church after a biblical figure, purposeful ordnance, or a principle they adhere to. On the other hand, Mormons believe Christ's ancient church, with the same organization, authority, and direct revelation, was restored to the earth in 1830; thus, the name, *The Church of Jesus Christ of Latter-Day Saints*, the-latter-day-saints name distinguishing His present church from His ancient church."

"Do you call yourselves saints, because you're in *His* church?"

"No. Members of Christ's ancient church were called saints"

"And the name Mormon?"

"The nickname *Mormon* comes from The Book of Mormon, one of our standard books of scripture. Just as the Old and New Testaments are testaments that Jesus is the Christ, The Book of Mormon is another testament that Jesus is the Christ. The book is made up of the writings of ancient prophet-historians, most of the writings being abridged by an ancient American prophet named Mormon."

Lee was sorry he asked. "Before we begin, Russell, I'd like to thank you for your time. I also want to apologize up front for any discomfort my questions might bring. I'm not interested in joining your religion or attacking it, so if you can't answer a question, just say so. This isn't a deposition. My problem isn't with *your* religion; it's with *any* religion."

Russell let a couple of seconds go by before responding. "I appreciate your statement more than you think. On my mission, more times than not, people were interested in arguing their point of view or gathering information so they could use it to talk their friends into leaving the Church. It's rare when someone truly wants to know about our faith."

Lee didn't miss Russell's intended remark.

"Let me be upfront as well. I find it hard to explain an infinite subject with my finite mind. In other words, there are some questions whose answers we, as a people, are not ready for. However, with that said, I'll try my best to answer any questions you might have. But remember, the conviction of a believer, doesn't make his belief true. His belief is either true, or it isn't. If there is a God, it's immaterial whether we all believe He exists, or no one believes He exists."

Lee sarcastically replied, "And pray tell, how does one know?"

"You've answered your own question. Prayer. If you're sincere and pray about the information I give you, you'll know whether what I say is true or false. I wish I could explain how you'll know, but I can't. It's a personal experience that, frankly, has to be experienced. However, I can promise you, you'll know when that experience comes."

Russell decided it was time to put his plan into action. "Kerry told me you had some questions concerning the Trinity."

"Yes, I have some questions about the Trinity, but today I would like to inquire about some of the policies of your Church."

"I bet you have a list," Russell said trying to be nice.

Lee took a piece of paper out of his pocket and handed it to Russell without comment.

Russell took the paper and looked at it, reading each question out loud. "What is the priesthood? Why did it take so long for Blacks to get it? Why don't women have it? Why did your church practice polygamy? Why am I not allowed to go into your temples? And finally, what do you do in your temples?"

Russell, still holding the paper, looked at Lee. "I've heard these questions before. I wish I had had this list prior to your arrival. I thought we were going to talk about the questions you had for Kerry...the Trinity questions."

"If you don't mind, I would like to discuss—"

Russell interrupted. "Let me answer the questions Kerry didn't answer, and I'll answer these questions next time. But before I answer questions concerning the Trinity, let's rehearse the power and importance of a question. You are aware that once a question is received, it has to be entertained by the one receiving it, even if only for a brief moment. The question dictates the answer we search for, the answer we get, and the answer we don't get. Questions are the biggest contributor to our learning, and yet the least investigated form of inquiry. Are questions better than answers? I don't know. I do know I can always question an answer, but I can't always answer a question."

Russell was beginning to relax as the Spirit took over.

"I don't have to tell you how important questions are in our line of work. Other than the opening and closing arguments, all the evidence that comes into a courtroom is in response to a question. The question asked will determine the evidence received, and some questions are more important than others; some are primary, and some are secondary, and some are setup questions if you know what I mean."

Lee was getting frustrated, and Russell could sense it. "Please don't be offended, Lee. Although questions concerning women, Blacks, and the priesthood are intriguing, any question concerning our faith, is glaringly unimportant if the answer to any one of the following four primary questions is false."

This statement had Lee's attention, and Russell knew it.

"One, is there a god who is our father? Two, is Jesus Christ the son of this god, the savior of the world? Three, is the Church of Jesus Christ of Latter-Day Saints, Christ's restored church? Four, is the Plan of Salvation true?"

Lee smiled. He saw his advantage. "I see what you mean. In fact, if there isn't a God, all the questions about your faith, in fact, all faiths concerning God, are irrelevant."

Russell returned Lee's smile. "Precisely. That is unless those questions are for personal gain."

Lee ignored Russell's last comment. "Let me save us both some time. I've known for a long time that God, or father as you call him, doesn't exist. I discovered that before my wife died. Thus, by deduction, there can't be a son; no son, no Christ; no Christ, no Christ's church, restored or otherwise. Concerning this plan of salvation, I've never heard of it. It sounds like propaganda from a faith, which is nothing more than a bunch of people wanting to have faith in something."

Lee's analogy didn't surprise Russell. Kerry had told him about her interaction with Lee at his wife's deathbed. That information was, in fact, the foundation of his plan.

As if contemplating something new, Russell commented, "That makes sense. As far as you're concerned, there is no god, no Christ, thus no Christ's church, past or present.

"Right," Lee emphasized.

"And you know this because you found it out for yourself."

"You are correct."

"And you can't comment on the Plan of Salvation because you've never heard of the Plan of Salvation. Right!"

"Right!"

Russell suddenly realized why he had been inspired to do what he was about to do. He reached inside his desk and pulled out a pamphlet with the heading—"The Plan of Salvation."

"I used to hand this pamphlet out when I was on my mission. They don't print it anymore, but it was one of my favorites. I'm sure reading it would please Kerry and give you the information needed to answer my fourth question."

Russell waited for Lee's comeback.

Lee, with his mouth, slightly opened, looked at Russell in astonishment. He couldn't believe what he was witnessing. Finally, he took the pamphlet.

"Let's be honest Lee, you're here to get information that will help you navigate your relationship with Kerry. Reading the Plan of Salvation might give you that information. If anything, reading it will demonstrate your respect for her."

Realizing he had something in writing which he could research, he couldn't help but feel Russell's arrogance had just backfired on him. "You got a point," Lee said. "I'll read it. What's it about?"

"You'll find out when you read it. I'll say this. It will answer three questions—where we came from, why we're here, and where we're going after we leave here. God has a plan for the entire human race, and that includes you and Kerry; a plan that will allow each of us the opportunity to have all He has."

"Wow! That sounds big."

"You don't have a clue," Russell said with a smirk growing into a grin.

"Thanks again for your time," Lee said as he began to get out of his chair.

"Hold on, I'm not quite through."

"Oh please," Lee said with fatigue in his voice.

"I'll make a recommendation that will help you better understand the pamphlet, as well as make a lot of points with Kerry?"

Lee was getting tired of Russell but making points with Kerry was enticing. "This needs to be short," he said as he resumed his seat.

"This dispensation was opened up when a young boy got on his knees and prayed to find out which church he should join. If you will get on your knees before reading the pamphlet, and sincerely pray to find out if what the pamphlet says is true, God will tell you whether it's true or not."

Russell couldn't believe what he had just suggested. It certainly wasn't his idea. It just came out of his mouth. Not knowing how Lee was going to react, he held his breath, wishing he had let Lee leave.

After what seemed like a lifetime of silence, Lee spoke, "Okay I'll get on my knees and say a prayer before I read the pamphlet."

Russell was stunned. He couldn't believe what he had just heard. Lee's next comment brought him back to earth.

"Anything else? Shave my head maybe?"

Russell was disappointed, but he still felt good about his challenge.

Both stood.

"When you find answers to my list of questions, give me a call. Don't worry. I'll read your pamphlet as you asked. I keep my word, and in return I expect you to keep yours and get back to me about my questions."

Both shook hands in silence before parting.

* * * * * *

Once in his car, Lee started to put the pamphlet in the glove compartment, but instead put it in his briefcase. He didn't know why, he just did.

Upon backing his car out of his parking space, he caught sight of himself in the rearview mirror. "Lee, why did you commit to reading that stupid pamphlet?"

Because Kerry's worth it, the mirror responded.

CHAPTER TWENTY-THREE

"Hello!" Kerry yelled through the screen door for the third time. Because Jean's car was in the driveway, and there had been no response to the doorbell or her verbal requests, she was contemplating entering Jean's house.

"Is anyone home?" she yelled again.

"I'm coming! I'm coming!" Jean called out as she came into view and headed down the hallway toward the screen door. Upon reaching the door, she opened it and invited Kerry in.

"When you didn't come to the door, I didn't know whether you had died or left town," Kerry said as she entered the house.

"I would have told you either way," Jean commented as they both laughed and hugged.

"Sorry. I was in the busy room, which at my age, is the busiest room in the house," Jean said hoping Kerry would get her humor.

What isn't there to like about this woman, a thought that brought a smile to Kerry's face.

"Were you in church yesterday? If you were, I didn't see you. In fact, I haven't seen you in church this past month," Jean said, like a mother concerned about her child.

"I've taken the sacrament every week this month. I just sneak out afterward."

Expecting the other one to speak, they both looked at each other until Jean broke the stalemate, "I'm waiting," Jean said with an open grin, head cocked, and eyes wide.

"I'll explain in a minute, but I have to tell you the best news ever. I did the assignment!"

Jean showed her confusion when she asked, "The assignment?"

"Madam President of the Sisters Writing Club of Wichita, have you forgotten the *assignment!*"

"No. I mean yes, I had. I mean no, I haven't."

Kerry laughed. "Jason, not only read my poem but took it to his professor to read."

"You're kidding?"

"That's not all the good news. Jason wants me to write another poem. He challenged me to write a play-with-words poem, and before you ask me, it's a poem that plays with words. For example, wouldn't it be weird if flies couldn't fly and lie detectors could only lie?"

"Can you, do it?"

"I've already done it. It was easy. Since there's so much, I want, and yet I don't know what I want, I wrote a long poem about *wanting*. I can certainly see the Lord's hand in all this."

Knowing Kerry would have the poem with her, Jean held her hand out.

Kerry presented the poem and then retrieved it before Jean could look at it. "Read it first, and then I'll explain it. No, you tell me what you get out of it, and then I'll tell you what my intentions were."

Jean got up and headed toward the kitchen. "I need a cup of hot water. I don't have coffee, but would you like—"

"I'll take a cup of hot water as well," Kerry interrupted with pride.

"Two hot ones in a cup!" Jean called out to an imaginary short-order cook.

After cups were prepared and places taken, Jean began to read:

What WANT Wanted
By Kerry Howells

Jean stopped reading. "Your title's confusing."

"You're right. Let me explain some things before you read the poem. The poem is a play on words, at least, that's what I intended it to be. It is supposed to say a lot about all of us. The words that are capitalized represent people that dwell on the meaning of the word I've capitalized. For example, REMEMBER would represent a person whose life centers on remembering. HATE would represent someone whose life is consumed with hate. ENVY is someone who is filled with envy. I'm WANT in this poem because I've gone through life always wanting to be someone else; always wanting what others had, when all along, with the Lord's help, I'm enough; I already have what everyone wants, and that is to be happy with who I am."

Jean kept silent as she unconsciously tilted her head to the side. Finally, she smiled, looked at the poem, and continued to read Kerry's poem:

WANT, trying to be unemotional about
something emotional,
Sat under a tree by a brook of thought
flowing to nowhere,
Searching for a reflection of wisdom,
chewing on a twig of hope,
Enjoying a sanctuary often
visited but never occupied.

WANT wanted something a WANT
would want.
But WANT didn't know if WANTs
wanted, or what they wanted.
WANT just wanted to know what a
WANT would want.
That's all WANT ever wanted.

Feeling the wind of inevitable, WANT
cuddled LONG AGO,
A companion with stories of
REMEMBER and WHAT IF,
Adventurers traveling to ports of
emotion with cargos of dreams.
DESIRE looked desirable; something
WANT often wanted.
So much so, he briefly desired to be
DESIRE, but only briefly.
WANTs don't desire for long, shouted
DESIRE with a taunt,
DESIREs get their desires; WANTs
never get their wants.
WANT just wanted to know what a
WANT would want.
That's all WANT ever wanted.

A small storm of consideration blew in
for consideration,
A consideration to be considered, for
the hour was late,
And the first consideration WANT
considered was HATE.
Everyone hated HATE, that is, everyone
but HATE.
Even WANT wondered if HATE hated

being HATE.
He considered LOVE; he would love to
be loved,
But even though he loved the idea, he
didn't know how to love.
WANT just wanted to know what a
WANT would want.
That's all WANT ever wanted.

Confusion began to fall from
thunderous clouds of questions,
Filling ravines with doubt and raging
torrents of depression.
HOPE was something WANT hoped for
but soon gave up hope.
He was tired of wanting but not enough
to become TIRED.
He could search for SEARCH, but he
would always be searching.
To be HAPPY he'd have to be happy, or
content to be CONTENT,
Or jealous to be JEALOUS, or excited to
be EXCITED.
WANT just wanted to know what a
WANT would want.
That's all WANT ever wanted.

Clouds parted and MERCY smiled
exposing rays of courage,
Warming his imagination, filling his
lungs with endurance,
While RESOLVE centrifuged his
thoughts into an epiphany.
Why not THOUGHT he thought, a
thought he hadn't thought.

But he soon stopped thinking for he
got lost in thought.
What WANT wanted, was the reason
WANT thought.
To find what WANT wanted was the
battle he fought.
WANT just wanted to know what a
WANT would want.
That's all WANT ever wanted.

TIME whispered its time, and
SADNESS repeated the message.
DISAPPOINTMENT helped him up,
saying what was, was.
Then REALIZATION made him realize a
realization.
Everyone wants to want, even WANTs
want to want.
Being part of all wants was WANT's
blessing, his fate.
WANT had discovered his want before
it was too late.
It's true for all, the many, the few, let
alone me, and let alone you.
To want, you need WANT in order to
want, making him needed.
That's all WANT ever wanted.

Jean laid the poem in her lap, and looked at Kerry, trying to find words to express her thoughts. "The poem blows me away. I love the way you played with words. Not only did you play with them, but you also played with them in a thought-provoking way."

"You know Jean, when I began writing this poem, I was WANT, wanting to be wanted, but by the time I finished it, I realized I was NEED. I wanted to be needed, and Jean, I think I've found someone who not only wants me but needs me."

Jean was stunned. She put her cup of water on the table and sat back. "Are you talking about Jason?"

"No."

When Kerry didn't continue, Jean leaned forward with wide-eyed frustration, "Then who are you talking about?"

"Do you remember when we were in church on Mother's Day, and I got a call from Jason about an accident he had been in, causing me to abruptly leave the church?"

"I think *abruptly* would describe your departure quite well."

"Well, Jason needed an attorney to defend him, and I met Jason's attorney's and I, or we, have been going out for the past five months, the best five months of my entire life. I feel alive, and I mean alive!"

As if Kerry was looking at Lee, she raised her gaze and said, "He's about six-one, with red hair, some gray here and there, blue eyes, about a hundred and ninety pounds. I met him again at his office. We—"

"Wait a minute. You met him again?"

"I'll explain in a minute. Lee wanted to talk to me about Jason, but since his assistant messed up and made my appointment near lunchtime, we decided to have our meeting over lunch. We ended up going to the Silver Spoon in the old Lassen Hotel. After lunch, he asked me out, and every day since then we've been dating, talking on the phone, dating—"

"You've already mentioned dating," Jean interrupted with amusement.

"Sorry. For four weeks we've been dating. Whoops, I said it again. You get the idea. Jean, a day hasn't gone by that we haven't been in contact."

"It sounds wonderful."

Kerry's smile faded. After a brief period in which neither spoke, she looked at Jean. "I love him, Jean."

"You sure don't sound too happy about it."

"I'm not."

"You're not! Why?"

"Let me explain the "again" question you had. His name is Lee Richards. He's not only Jason's lawyer, but he was also the husband of a woman I cared for years ago. In fact, his wife died the day I was served divorce papers. I think I told you about her and her husband."

With surprise in her eyes, Jean remembered. "If I'm thinking of the same couple, their love for each other was life-changing for you. Am I talking about the same couple?"

"Yes."

"I also remember how he hated religion. Any religion. We are talking about the same person, are we not?"

"The same."

"Is he upset about your religion?"

"I don't know."

"What do you mean, 'I don't know'? Didn't you tell him you were a Mormon?"

"Not at first. Only when he caught me silently blessing the food, did questions take me to that confession."

"What happened then?"

"He asked me about the Trinity."

"The Trinity?"

"The Trinity. It surprised me too. But I think I did a good job keeping out of his trap. To be honest, I felt good about defending my beliefs. You might say I had a spiritual experience when

I stood up for what I believed. I gave him Russell Cruz's phone number, and he made an appointment to see him."

"Why Cruz?"

"Lee wouldn't see the missionaries, and Brother Cruz is a strong member, and an attorney as well."

Kerry looked at Jean. "What will I do when he ends our relationship, or worse, wants me to leave the Church?"

"What do you mean? Would you leave the Church?"

"No, and that's my problem."

Jean knew what Kerry meant, which made Jean proud and sad at the same time. "Maybe he'll check the Church out and join. Or, what if he doesn't join, but doesn't mind if you stay in the Church? Sam certainly didn't live the Gospel, and you stayed with him."

"That's right, and I never want to have another relationship like that again."

Jean grasped Kerry's hand but didn't speak.

"Russell called me and told me not to get my hopes up. It seems Lee was only there to keep his promise to me. I don't know Jean...."

"Losing with integrity is better than winning without it," Jean said. "And I don't think you're going to lose. I think I have more confidence in Lee than you do. He and his late wife were a special couple, and he was a major part of that special couple.

Kerry, would you like some cake?"

Jean's question caught Kerry off guard.

"Thanks, Jean. I would."

"I wished I had some to give you."

Jean's humor made Kerry feel safe again.

CHAPTER TWENTY-FOUR

Lee felt good as he left Russell's office. The pamphlet would, no doubt, give him some needed ammunition. Their exchange did nothing but solidify Lee's beliefs that Mormonism was a manufactured religion. However, to be honest, he was impressed with Russell's conviction, as well as his delivery. Even his primary questions made sense, that is, if you cared.

By the time he arrived back at his office, Lee had completely dismissed his interview with Russell, as well as his promise to read the pamphlet. Satisfied that his investigation with Mormonism was over, he attempted to get back into his routine. Nevertheless, failure accompanied every try, and after several hours of mistakes, he decided to call it quits and go home.

* * * * * * *

When he parked his car in his garage, he looked around trying to determine if something was different. Not finding anything, he went into his house to take a shower. While in the shower, he tried to come up with a plan, a procedure, something that would keep his relationship with Kerry, but nothing came.

Lee dressed, went into the living room, and turned the television on. All he found was noise and depression. Turning it off, he tried to review the meeting he had with Russell but couldn't focus. He tried to review his previous encounter with Kerry, but again he drew a blank. The only image he could focus on was the pamphlet Russell had given him.

Irritated, he left his house and went to a grocery store. Upon arrival, he tried to remember why he was there. When he couldn't remember, he went home and tried to fix himself something to eat, but nothing looked appetizing. Although it was late, he got in his car and set out to find a local restaurant. It didn't take him long to discover he couldn't decide which restaurant to go to. In frustration, he finally decided to go home and go to bed.

After a restless night, he woke Saturday morning at sunrise and headed for a small cemetery outside Stafford, Kansas. As he turned into the cemetery, the car seemed to automatically drive him to Gayle's gravesite. When he got out of his car, a slight breeze kissed his face, as his eyes beheld a deep blue sky with long strips of hazy clouds moving with the wind. Although these twenty-five acres of sanctuary had more residents than the town, there was only one resident he wanted to visit.

Lee sat down and rested his back against Gayle's headstone and waited for the experience he needed. It didn't come. He talked to Gayle but only heard himself. He wanted a response, something, but the wind was he all got. He planned on a longer stay, but after an hour, he gave up, got up, and went back to Wichita.

* * * * * *

Upon arriving in Wichita, he drove to the park where Kerry had taken him on their first date. However, after thirty minutes he went back to his car and drove home.

He was just as lost at home as he had been at the cemetery. Having no appetite, he went to bed. *Sunday would be different* he vowed to himself.

Sunday morning caused him to review the weekend. All he saw was a weekend of aware moments; *aware* he didn't remember the trip to a location; *aware* he was watching television, but not remembering sitting down to watch; *aware* he had driven to a supermarket instead of a restaurant. It also carried with it a reminder of his obligation to read the pamphlet Russell had given him.

He decided to take control and went into his home office, took the pamphlet out of his briefcase, but laid it on his desk, as he headed for the kitchen to get something to eat.

"Leeeeeee!" he yelled as he entered the kitchen, "Just read the pamphlet!" He pivoted and stormed back to this office, grabbed the pamphlet, sat on his couch, and said to the ceiling, "God, help me read this pamphlet. Amen. And thanks for the pamphlet. Amen."

He began to read, but after only a couple of paragraphs, gave up, laid the pamphlet down, and searched the ceiling trying to find a plan that would get him out of his commitment with Russell. The only thing he could find was his commitment.

Lee rolled off the couch and sat on the floor. "God, help me read this pamphlet, so I can keep my word to Russell. God, help me read this pamphlet, and if it's true, and I know it isn't, but if it is, tell me. Thanks, and amen in the name of God."

He got up, and picked up the pamphlet, and began to read. He only read three sentences before his cell phone rang, making him throw the pamphlet on the floor.

After finding the call to be a solicitation from a solar company, he turned his phone off, got on his knees, looked at the ceiling, and shouted, "God, if you want me in this Church, you've got one more shot! Amen!"

He sat on the couch and began to read with no expectation of success. In fact, he wanted to experience what he had already experienced, so he could abandon his attempt with a clear conscience.

As he began to read, familiarity met his eyes. It was as if he already *knew* what he was reading, and what he was *going* to read. Time and again, he heard himself proclaim, "I know this!"

When he finished reading, he got up and went out to his front porch. Lee didn't know why, he just did. He sat on the front steps for a second, then stood and looked at the maple tree in his front yard, as if he was seeing it for the first time. *This pamphlet's true* he thought. *It's answered so many questions, questions I didn't even know I had.*

Suddenly, the importance of his past, present, and future, came before him. He felt so insignificant; yet significant. He also felt foolish when he remembered how arrogant, pompous, and pretentious his manner had been with Russell.

After composing himself, he debated whom he should tell first, Russell or Kerry, and whether to tell them in person or by phone. He decided it had to be Kerry, and it had to be in person. He wanted to see her face and hear her accolades. She would be so pleased; so proud of him.

With the weight of the world off his shoulders, he went inside and turned on the television to watch Sunday football. As soon as it came on, he turned it off. "After the experience you've just had," Lee said to himself, " you know you shouldn't be watching football on Sunday. That's God's Day."

He went into the kitchen. However, it wasn't long before he returned and turned the football game back on. "I'm not a Mormon yet," he said as he took a bite out of his sandwich.

CHAPTER TWENTY-FIVE

Russell had brought Kerry up to date on his meeting with Lee. She was surprised when he told her he had challenged him to pray before reading a pamphlet he had given him. The news had left her anxious. He would be at her door in a matter of minutes, and she didn't know what to expect. Would it be their last time? Would she compromise? The meal was prepared, but was she prepared to lose Lee?

When Lee's car pulled into her driveway, she put on a positive attitude and met him at the door. "Hi, Lee."

"Hi, Kerry. I've got some great news." His words were full of excitement.

"So do I, and I want to tell you mine first," Kerry said, perplexed by what he meant by *great*.

"Not until I get a kiss," he said with a grin as he walked into her house.

Once Kerry closed the door, Lee spun her around and hugged her as if he was holding on to a life raft. After a prolonged hug, he softly kissed her on the cheek without relinquishing his hold.

Kerry broke away and said with some concern, "You act as though you're saying goodbye."

"Not a chance. Tell me your *great* news, so I can tell you mine."

Relief and excitement overcame her. "Jason is communicating with me again." Lee's look told her he didn't have a clue as to what she was talking about. "Let me tell you why that's a big deal. When Jason's father divorced me, Jason became somewhat distant. Jason and I have been okay since then, but the gap between us is getting wider, not closer. The fact that he tried to meet me at church this past Mother's Day, was huge. I think Jason promising to see me was a turning point in our relationship, as well as a turning point in my life. Although his car accident was unfortunate for him, it was fortunate for me, and I hope for us."

By now she was beginning to bounce.

"My great news is…Jason and I…we're collaborating on a poem I wrote!"

Lee smiled as he placed his hands on her shoulders in an attempt to reduce her bouncing,

"I'm starting to get my son back. Next to having you in my life, there's nothing more important to me than my son. I can't expect you to understand the value of what I'm saying."

Tears watered her eyes and cheeks as she laid her head on his chest. It took Kerry several minutes to compose herself. When she did, she looked up at him with some trepidation and said, "What's your *great* news?"

Lee took a deep breath, stepped back, and said, "I went to see Russell, and I want to thank you for arranging our meeting. He's a nice guy, and I mean that. If he weren't, I wouldn't tell you he was. He did a good job of not answering my questions."

Kerry's heart sank.

"He also gave me a pamphlet to read and asked me to get on my knees and pray about its truthfulness before reading it."

Kerry's heart sank even lower. Russell had informed her about the pamphlet and the prayer, but not about asking Lee to get on his knees before his prayer. With trepidation, she asked, "Did you get on your knees?"

"I did."

Again, tears came to Kerry. She used her sleeve to blot her eyes before asking a more important question, "Did you read the pamphlet?"

"I did."

"And what do you think?"

"I want to get baptized."

At first, she thought she must have misheard his answer. Then she summarized he had incorrectly heard her question. She stepped back, turned, and took a couple of steps before stopping. With her back to him, she asked again. "What did you think of the pamphlet?"

"I found it to be true, and I want to be baptized."

It took Kerry but seconds before her jaw tightened. She whipped around, and with a pointed finger and rancor in her voice said, "Lee, I don't think that's funny! This is serious to me! If you don't want to hear about my church, fine! But don't mock what I believe!"

Lee, expecting jubilation, was dumbfounded. "I'm serious! By the time I finished reading the pamphlet, I knew it was true! I want to meet the missionaries, take the discussions, and get baptized."

She didn't look at Lee as she walked the room, talking to the floor as she walked. Kerry shook her head as if trying to dislodge what she had just heard. "I'm sorry I'm not jumping for joy, but you have to admit this is unusual. If you did read the pamphlet, you would know how serious this is to me, and you."

"Did you say, 'if you did read the pamphlet'? You don't think I read it, do you?"

"I don't know what to think?"

"Let me ask you a question. Have you read the Plan of Salvation pamphlet?"

"No."

"Then why question me? You don't have enough information to find out if I'm lying."

Kerry stopped walking. There was an uncomfortable silence before she apologized. "I'm sorry. Here I expect you to have faith in my church when I don't have faith in you. Please forgive me."

"Since you haven't read the pamphlet, would you like to know what it's about? Please say yes. I want to tell someone. Maybe you can see if I'm correct in my understanding."

"Now I feel foolish."

"You should." Lee gave her a quick kiss before she could respond.

"I was impressed with how the pamphlet presented itself. The pamphlet didn't argue the beliefs of others; it used scripture references to present its message, which for me, gave it credibility. However, I must confess, I wouldn't know a scripture if it bit me."

His comment brought a snicker and a hug.

"Let me say, the pamphlet turned religious confusion into common sense. At least it did for me. That is if you believe in the King James Bible. Funny. I guess I'm beginning to believe in the Bible."

"How do you know what you read is true," Kerry said wanting to compare her religious experiences with his.

"I don't know how to explain it to you. I wish I could, but I can't. I just know it's true."

To Kerry, Lee's answer was the perfect answer. She stepped back and said, "May I give you a suggestion?"

"Oh, I don't know," he said as he rubbed his chin.

"I'm serious."

"Sorry. Of course, you can."

"Start writing a journal. Today! My father got me writing in one, right after I first learned to write. Every entry brought me closer to the Lord. If it was important in my life, good or bad, I put it in my journal. In my teens, writing in my journal became my version of a diary. During my marriage, it became my therapy, and after my divorce, it became my lifesaver."

She led him by the hand to a couch where they both sat down.

"When I have a spiritual experience, I try to capture it on paper. If you don't capture it, no matter how strong the experience, it will fade with time. I definitely suggest writing down your experience reading the pamphlet; what led up to reading it, your struggles in reading it, what you got out of reading it, and whether reading it has changed you. Write down what happened yesterday and what happens tomorrow. Write down what happens today if you think it's important. You will be surprised how writing stops time and allows you to reflect, learn, and grow. Even go back to the time we met in the hospital. In fact, that might be a good place to begin your journal. Let the Lord help you write it."

"Am I in your journal?" Lee asked with a slight smile.

"You are and will be as long as you're in my life."

"Will, what you just said, be in your journal?"

"You mean what we're talking about right now? Probably," said Kerry somewhat confused by Lee's question.

"Well, be sure and write this down. Do you have some chicken?" Lee enjoyed Kerry's expression.

"Chicken? What do you mean? Cooked chicken, frozen chicken, what are you talking about?"

"Any chicken. Do you have any chicken from the other night?"

"No. Why?"

"Since the first time I told you I loved you, was over a plate of chicken, I thought I would ask you to marry me over a plate of chicken."

Kerry's eyes widened more than her mouth dropped.

"I don't mean tomorrow. I know you love me, and I know we've only dated for a short time. I know you need to find out if I'm as sincere and wonderful as you think I am, and by the way, I'm really more wonderful than you think I am."

Lee quickly kissed her on the cheek. "I do love you Kerry, and someday I would like to marry you."

Without giving herself permission, Kerry heard her mouth say *yes*.

Her answer didn't faze Lee, because that's what he expected.

"But there's no hurry. Okay?" Kerry whispered in a weak voice.

"Okay."

Both held each other as if the other would vanish.

"Please give me a year," Kerry said to Lee's chest.

"A YEAR! Why a year?"

"Couldn't we date for a year?"

"Okay, we can date for a year," Lee said to Kerry's hair.

"Thank you, Lee."

"So, you agree to marry me?"

"Yes."

"Then, since we've already been dating for five months, we'll get married in seven months."

Kerry giggled. "You're a good lawyer. Seven months or thereabout."

"Thereabout," Lee repeated with a grin Kerry couldn't see.

CHAPTER TWENTY-SIX

Lee entered Russell's office, walked up to the receptionist, and waited for recognition. He didn't have to wait long. "Can I help you?"

Lee offered the pamphlet to the receptionist. "Would you give this to Russell?"

Before the receptionist could respond, Russell came into the area carrying several files. "Please give these to Linda when she comes back from her break," he said while placing the files on her desk.

"Hi, Russell."

Russell's disappointment was obvious. After their first meeting, Lee was the last person he expected to see in his office. "Lee, it's good to see you. What brings you here? We didn't have an appointment, did we?"

"No. I just wanted to bring your pamphlet back."

"Of course. Have a seat. Give me five minutes, and I'll be right with you. Emma Jane, will you hold all my calls?"

Russell went into his office, closed the door, and immediately got on his knees. Lee's attitude, the last time they had been together, was still fresh in his mind, making this visit a dreaded surprise. What's more, he hadn't researched Lee's questions like he said he would. He shook his head and immediately began to pray.

After his prayer, he stayed on his knees waiting for inspiration. All that came was discomfort. Finally, he had an idea. He didn't know if the idea was his or the Lord's, but it gave him enough courage to get off his knees and open the door.

"Lee," he said with all the optimism he could muster, "come on in."

After handshakes and seating, Russell began. "How's Kerry?"

"She's fine," was Lee's only response. He purposely didn't expand on his answer, for he was enjoying Russell's attempt to look comfortable.

Not knowing how to respond to Lee's silence, Russell decided to go with the plan he had just received. If he got in trouble, he could always use *lack of time* as his excuse for not researching Lee's questions and Lee's *unscheduled appointment* as an excuse to cut the meeting short.

"Have you read the pamphlet I gave you?"

"I did, and I found it very interesting."

Lee's comment, 'I found it very interesting,' made Russell wary. Knowing things were only going to get worse, he asked, "Did you pray before reading it?"

"I did."

Russell didn't respond right away because he didn't know if Lee had heard him correctly. After several seconds, he leaned forward hoping to ignite more dialog, and when it didn't come, he blurted out, "Well!"

Lee responded by leaning forward as well, and calmly said, "I found what I read to be true, and I would like to take the missionary lessons and be baptized."

Russell's countenance was expressionless. He stood without commenting and stared at Lee. Keeping his stare, he then sat back down. After several seconds, he finally spoke, his voice clothed with irritation. "Lee, this isn't something to be taken lightly. I was hoping you would have some questions, instead of the cavalier remark you just uttered."

Fighting to disguise his amusement, Lee sat back and feigned annoyance. "Are you kidding me? I don't believe this! What's with you Mormons? Do you guys ever have investigators join your church?"

Lee's remark surprised Russell. "What do you mean?"

"What do *you* mean? I read your pamphlet, had a spiritual experience, want to be baptized and join your church, and all I get is skepticism! Kerry doubted me, just as you're doubting me! Doesn't an investigator have the right to have a spiritual experience! Doesn't he have the right to want to be baptized!" Lee was laughing by now.

"I'm so sorry. I—"

"Forget it. I'm getting used to it. Will the missionaries be as dubious as you and Kerry?"

"No. I assure you the missionaries are a different kettle of fish. After they meet you, all they'll see is water."

"Water?"

"You'll understand soon enough."

Russell, like a boy wanting to hear an adventure, came around his desk and pulled up a chair next to Lee. "Don't just sit there, tell me everything."

"I have no questions concerning the pamphlet. As I said, I know what I read to be true. On the other hand, I do have a few questions about what happened to me as I was reading it."

"What do you mean?"

"Twice, I tried to read the pamphlet, and each attempt found disinterest after only a couple of paragraphs. If I hadn't given you my word, I would have given up after the second try. However, my third attempt brought familiarity to a pamphlet I had never read before. It was as if I was reading something I already knew. But that wasn't all. The feeling that accompanied the third reading was…I don't know what to say. I can't describe it. And if that isn't confusing enough, later, when I re-read the pamphlet, the first feeling didn't accompany my second reading. You might say the first reading was an unexplainable spiritual experience, while the second reading was just informative."

Russell was beside himself. "As you now know, we had the Plan of Salvation explained to us before we came to this earth. When you read the pamphlet the first time, the Holy Ghost brought this prior knowledge to your consciousness. That's where the *familiarity* came from. The *feeling* that you can't explain, was his presence. On the second reading that feeling was absent because the Holy Ghost was absent. Why? Maybe He wanted to teach you how to recognize Him. I can tell you this, recognizing his presence is more important than anything you read. As far as trying to explain that *feeling*, you can't. No one can. They have to experience it for themselves."

Lee sighed. "As you once told me, I have a lot to learn."

"Believe me, you have no idea how much. I was born into this church, and I'm still learning. I suppose you want me to address your questions," Russell said, ready to offer Lee his "lack of time" defense, as to why he wasn't ready.

"Not really. I don't want to hear anything that might get me off this high."

Russell began to tear up. "I would like to give you some advice if I may. If I've told you this before, forgive me because I'm going to tell you again. In today's world, Christians as well as non-Christians, look at happenings and practices in biblical times with leniency; it was God's will. They view a prophet leading his followers into the wilderness for forty years as understandable; not preaching the gospel to a class of people called *Gentiles*, a wise decision on the Savior's part; plural marriage as an accepted practice; restricted temple attendance as customary; an all-male priesthood as the norm. Yet today, a prophet leading his followers across the United States demonstrates domination; briefly withholding the priesthood from the black race as racism; plural marriage as carnal slavery; restricted temple attendance as manipulation; male priesthood bearers as sexist."

Russell could see Lee's interest, giving him the courage to continue.

"If it was God's decision in ancient times, why isn't it God's decision today? I sometimes wonder if His ancient Church went through the same scrutiny as His restored Church. I think if people knew more about Christ's ancient church, they would better understand His restored church. I also don't think they understand the difference between doctrine and policy; doctrine is unchangeable, while policy changes when a change is needed to further Heavenly Father's goal; to bring as many of His children back to him as possible."

Russell sat back and said, "Lee, I've got to get back to work, but before I do, let me urge you to read the Book of Mormon as soon as you can, and as you read, search for the feeling you found while reading the pamphlet, and when that feeling comes, and sometimes it will, you'll know Joseph Smith was a prophet, i.e., this Church is Christ's restored Church."

"Do you have a Book of Mormon I could borrow?"

"I'm sorry. I don't have one in the office, but I'm sure the missionaries will give you one."

"Thank you, Russell. I mean that."

"Thank *you*! And you don't know how much *I* mean that."

Both stood and before Lee headed for the door, Russell hugged him, calling him Brother Richards in the process. Lee's emotions wouldn't let him respond.

CHAPTER TWENTY-SEVEN

"Only three more months," Lee said as he quickly removed the phone from his ear.

Kerry's reply was as expected. "Five months Lee Richards! It's only been two months since I agreed to seven months! We'll get married in five—"

"I bet you count the minutes," Lee interrupted while stifling a laugh.

"That hurt," Kerry giggled. She knew what Lee was doing and was flattered their upcoming marriage was always on his mind. Although she liked the game and always played along, she felt guilty because the memory of her prior marriage wouldn't let her throw caution to the wind and get married right away.

Lee also liked their game, but to him, it was more than that. She needed to be pushed, and he needed reassurance. Anyway, what did he have to lose; there was always a chance she would cave in. "If you know how much I love you, and you still want to wait, does that mean you have reservations about me?"

Kerry had had enough. "I'm not going through this again. I told you, I have reservations about myself. I don't want to jump into another marriage as I did before. Anyway, don't you like dating me?"

Lee knew Kerry didn't want to play anymore, and neither did he. "What are you doing for lunch today?"

"I have an appointment at ten o'clock with Doctor Brown."

"Is something wrong?"

"No. All school nurses have to get a physical every year, and my year's up. I'll call if I get done before noon. Can you get away? We could have lunch."

"Definitely."

Since that first picnic, there had only been one day Lee and Kerry hadn't met for lunch. Even during Lee's trials, both had arranged to have lunch even if it was only a short one.

"I'll let you go, Sweetheart. I'll be at Applebee's. I want to hear your doctor's diagnosis. Maybe he'll prescribe a marriage in two—"

"Lee!"

"Okay, okay. I'll wait for your call."

Lee couldn't help but smile as he hung up. With his hands interlocked behind his head, he leaned back in his chair and thought about his life since meeting Kerry. He couldn't remember a time when he had been happier. He swiveled around and glanced at the clock to determine if he had enough time to squeeze in some work. He didn't know why he was checking; he knew the rest of the day, at least until noon, was a lost cause.

He found himself thinking of the missionary discussions he had had with Elders Johnson and Back. Those two missionaries, teenage kids on a mission for two years, didn't have a clue as to what they were getting into. By the time they came to teach him, he knew more about the Church than they did.

His missionary memories slowly gave way to Kerry. She had given him a reason to be. He hadn't realized how much he had withdrawn from life until he fell in love with her. He smiled when her image appeared in his mind and chuckled when he remembered the calamity of purchasing her wedding ring.

When it came to gifting jewelry, Lee's rule, before meeting Kerry, had been to leave the selection of the gift, to whoever was going to wear the gift. Nevertheless, after visiting practically every jewelry store in Wichita, Lee had considered changing his rule. Fortunately, patience finally prevailed, and Lee arranged to pick up her selection two days later. He also made dinner arrangements at Wichita's most expensive restaurant for the same day. There, he would give her the ring and properly propose; making a memory for both of them to add to the many they had already made.

Nonetheless, on the day Lee was to pick up the ring, the jewelry store called to inform him there would be a one-day delay. Having put more effort into buying Kerry's ring than he had put into getting his law degree, he asked to speak to the manager.

Upon getting the manager, Lee asked him for the number of the store's attorney. When a startled manager asked why, Lee informed him that the failure to deliver Kerry's ring at the agreed time, was a breach of contract. And because the price of the ring exceeded the limit for small claims court, civil court would be the venue, thus requiring legal representation. Lee picked up the ring one hour before his dinner reservation.

"Mr. Richards." Jimmy's voice brought Lee back to the present.

"Yes, Jimmy. What can I do for you?"

"Mr. Richards, you told me to prepare for the Howells' trial as if I was going to be the lead attorney. Well, in doing so, something came to my attention. Could I run it by you?"

"No problem. Close the door, take a seat, and let me help you if I can."

"I need to use your whiteboard and magnets." Without waiting for permission, Jimmy went to the whiteboard, where he attached a map before turning to face Lee.

"As you can see, this is a map of Wichita. Jason told us he was on his way to his mother's church when his accident occurred."

Jimmy then turned and drew a circle located in the top right corner of the map. "This is where Jason lives." Then Jimmy drew a second circle located about a foot below and a foot to the left of the first circle. "This second circle is where his mother's church is located."

Lee wanted to ask a question, but something told him to give Jimmy the floor.

Jimmy then circled an interstate highway, which was in close proximity to the two circles he had already drawn. Jimmy pointed at the new circle and said, "This is I-235."

Both looked at each other until Lee broke the stalemate. "So?"

"Right," Jimmy said, realizing Lee wanted him to continue. "According to Jason's deposition, he had left his house to go to his mother's church on the day of the accident. As you can see, the circle at the top right corner of the map represents Jason's house, and the lower-left circle represents his mother's church. The accident occurred on I-235, which I have circled. You can also see I-235 sort of connects them."

Again, Jimmy looked at Lee as though he was expecting a comment.

"I know you want to make a point, but not as much as I want you to make a point, so make a point," Lee's annoyance was beginning to make its presence known.

"The police report has Jason heading northeast on I-235, at the time of the accident, toward his house. If he were going to church from his house, as he said, he would have been heading southwest, not northeast. In other words, he would have been going from the top right circle to the bottom left circle, not the other way around. That doesn't make sense."

"Good point Jimmy. I don't know how important it is, since we probably…no we definitely won't be putting him on the stand, but good point. Let me think about it, and I'll get back to you in a couple of minutes. By the way, what time was the accident?"

"It was a little after seven in the morning. I'll check and get you the exact time, but I know it was before seven-thirty in the morning," Jimmy said as he started to take the map down.

"Leave the map where it is. I'm going to review my notes on Jason's case."

Lee knew church started at nine in the morning. He also knew Jason had called his mother from the scene of the accident; at least that's what he had told his mother.

If Jason was heading northeast on I-235, at the time of the accident, he certainly wasn't going to his mother's church, and Kerry put Jason's call around nine-thirty, which didn't make sense, since the accident occurred before seven-thirty.

A thought came to Lee's mind. He went to the filing cabinet and retrieved Jason's file. He looked at his deposition but couldn't find what he was looking for.

Then he remembered the notes he took when Jason first came in. However, because he was only concerned about Jason's mother at the time, what information he had about Jason's life was scarce.

Charlie was the only name he could remember from his first lunch with Kerry, but he couldn't remember anything specific. He then checked the few notes he had taken at that lunch. Failing to find him, he picked up the phone and dialed Kerry's number.

"Hi, Love. Sorry to bother you, but I need some information, and I'm in a hurry. I was looking through Jason's file and found

Charlie to be one of his friends, but I don't have a last name. Do you know who I'm talking about, and if you do, do you know his last name?"

"Charlie Zimmer is the only name I can think of."

"That's it. Thanks, Sweetie. Are we still good for lunch?"

"I think so. I'm just waiting to talk to Valynn."

"Valynn?"

"Valynn Brown. Doctor Brown. We're friends."

"Oh, that's right. You're getting a physical. I'll let you go," Lee said, wanting to follow up on his hunch. "I love you Punkin."

"Shouldn't it be Pumpkin?"

"Do you look like a pumpkin?"

"Punkin it is."

The second Lee hung up, he buzzed Jimmy.

Jimmy was only halfway in the door when Lee said, "Find out where a Charlie Zimmer lives."

"Is it important to the Howells' case?"

"Have you found it yet? When you do, or can't find it, then you can ask about its relevance."

"Sorry," Jimmy said as he hurriedly left the room.

It only took Jimmy minutes before he was back. "Here is the address, Mr. Richards."

"Thanks, Jimmy."

When Jimmy left the office, Lee went to the map and circled the location of Charlie Zimmer's address. Having done so, he then stepped back to study the map.

Charlie's circle was even lower, and more to the left than the circle representing Kerry's church. He also noticed that all three circles, Charlie's house, the church, and Jason's house, were all easily accessible to I-235. To get from Charlie's house to Jason's house, Jason would have had to be traveling northeast on I-235, the same direction he was heading at the time of the accident.

"At the time of the accident, you weren't going to church, were you, Jason? You were heading home from Charlie's," Lee said to the map. "Why, I don't know, nor does it make a hill of beans to me. This trial doesn't need you, but I need your mother, so, this is where this little mystery ends."

Lee buzzed Jimmy, "Come get your map, and by the way you're doing great."

CHAPTER TWENTY-EIGHT

Valynn Brown was not only a doctor, but one of Kerry's instructors during her training to become a nurse. They instantly became close friends after graduation, and in fact, Valynn was only one of two people, at Wesley Hospital, who knew about Kerry's life with Sam.

She was as tall as Kerry but very thin; she even looked undernourished. She supported a long, braided ponytail that hung down to the top of her waist. It was a tossup which one captured your attention first, her blue eyes, or a smile that searched for a smile. What held your attention was her confidence, in herself and her profession; she owned any room she entered.

"It's been a long time, Kerry. I hear you got engaged."

"Yes. I'm officially engaged," Kerry said, holding her left hand in front of her nose. "And how are you?"

"If you think we're going to talk about me before we discuss that ring, you don't need a general practitioner, you need a psychiatrist."

Both laughed as they hugged. After both were seated, Kerry began, "I met this wonderful man who happened to have the good sense to offer me this ring. He's a lawyer that—"

"A lawyer!" Valynn's reaction showed Kerry she was impressed.

"My son got into an accident, and Lee, Jason's insurance lawyer, summoned me to his office to see if I would be a possible character witness and—"

"A witness!"

"Say, do you want to know about Lee or not?" Kerry said with a wink.

"Sorry. Go on."

"We went to lunch and have been inseparable ever since. I knew after the second date he was the one, but I think it took him about four dates to realize what a catch he had."

"I'm sure he's great. He would have to be, to measure up to you," Valynn said as she peaked at Kerry's mammogram report.

After an unexpected pause, Valynn began to palpate Kerry's right breast as she asked, "How often do you manually examine your breasts?"

Somewhat alarmed by her doctor's sudden change in demeanor and conversation, Kerry said with concern, "Every month." Valynn's look solicited a more complete answer. "Well, this past year has been a busy one. I know I should examine my breasts more often. Is there anything wrong?"

"Your mammogram reports a category four tumor. A four indicates the need for a biopsy. As you can see, I'm searching for a mass, and when I find it, I'm going to take a fine-needle-aspiration biopsy."

Kerry's weak smile was her only response.

Once the mass was found and the biopsy taken, Valynn gathered her sample, got up, and headed toward the door and the lab. However, at the door, she stopped, looked back, and said, "I know this sounds rehearsed, but I'll say it anyway. Don't worry. There's no definite proof you have cancer, and if you do, as far as

I can tell, it hasn't spread yet, which means we can kill it before it does."

"I know," Kerry's response was barely audible.

"I'm going to take this sample to the lab. I'll be back as soon as I drop it off. Get dressed but don't leave. Kerry, everything is going to be fine."

Everything is going to be fine. During her professional career, Kerry had heard doctors recite those same comments; enough times to know outcomes weren't always fine.

It was only minutes before Valynn came back from the lab, and when she did, she sat next to Kerry and took her hand. "Kerry, as I said, a category four doesn't mean you have cancer. I don't see any physical changes in your breast, which is a good sign. Your mammogram last year showed calcification in your duct glands, but they were benign. If there is cancer, I'm sure it's new and localized; meaning we can take care of it."

Kerry knew the answer to her question before she asked, but she had to ask anyway. "If it is cancer," Kerry hesitated, "am I looking at surgery, radiation, and chemotherapy?"

"Not necessarily. Take a deep breath and listen to what I've already told you. We don't even know if it is cancer. Even if it is, the treatment depends on how fast it's growing and if it's localized."

Kerry started to sob as she bowed her head. "I'm getting *married*, and… and we've never been intimate. Do I marry him before a mastectomy, or after? Or do I marry him at all?"

Valynn felt helpless. "Kerry, you're a nurse. Let's look at this from a nurse's point of view instead of that of a fiancé. *If* it is cancer, and the cancer is localized and new, we can perform a lumpectomy, a partial mastectomy, removing only the mass, a small section of normal breast tissue around the mass, and the lymph nodes in the area. This procedure would be followed with radiation only." Valynn stopped to see if Kerry was listening.

"Go on," was all Kerry could say.

"It's true, that in advanced stages, we recommend a mastectomy, followed with radiation and chemotherapy, but that's in advanced stages. *If* you have cancer, it's probably not in an advanced stage."

Trying to bring some humor to this morbid conversation, Kerry said, "I'm sorry for the scene I'm making. I just didn't want to go into a lopsided marriage, if you know what I mean."

Although Valynn appreciated Kerry's try, she only smiled. "Since we're friends, talk to me about your concerns as a fiancé?"

"To be blunt, if you were Lee, wouldn't you want your bride to be complete on your wedding night; balanced *structurally* as well as mentally?"

"Yes. But would you rather marry him and die after a short time, or be unbalanced and live a long, happy life? If you told him you're going to have a mastectomy, and he didn't want to marry you, what would you think of him?"

Kerry, stared at the floor as she contemplated her friend's questions. Finally, she looked up into Valynn's eyes and said, "I guess I would feel pretty lucky; lucky I found out how important I was before I married him."

"Kerry, I don't know all the details of your last marriage, but we talked enough about Sam for me to know you wouldn't want to go through that kind of marriage again, even if you never remarried."

Valynn hesitated, but only for a second. "Take this the right way. This might be a blessing in disguise. You have a chance to find out who… I'm sorry what's his name?"

"Lee."

"You have a chance to find out who Lee really is before you marry him. And we don't know what the lab results will be anyway."

Tears of gratitude clouded Kerry's vision. As afraid as she was about Lee's reaction, she could see the opportunity this situation had given her. "How long will the lab results take?"

"Three to four hours, but for you, I'll put a rush on it."

"Don't do that. I need some time to find out who I'm marrying."

Kerry's statement caused Valynn to smile.

Kerry asked, "Can I make a call?"

"Sure. I'll give you some privacy. Take all the time you want, but after you leave here, be available by phone. When the results come in, we'll know if there is cause for concern, and if there is, what we should do about it."

As the doctor left the room, Kerry dialed Lee. "Hi Honey," Kerry said trying to choke back emotion. "I know it isn't noon yet, but could we have an early lunch? I have something to run by you."

Lee, remembering Kerry was at the doctor, said with some alarm, "Is everything all right! Do you need me to come to the doctor's office?"

"No. I'm just hungry, and I want to run my test results by you."

"What were the results of your tests?"

"They're not completed yet. I'll tell you what I know when we eat. I'll even go Dutch treat."

"Dutch treat!" Lee said, exaggerating his comment. "You're on. I'll meet you at Applebee's. I'm leaving the office as we speak."

Lee didn't buy what Kerry was selling. He buzzed the front desk and before his receptionist could speak, he informed her he would be gone for the rest of the day.

When Lee got to the door of his office, he stopped as if hearing a voice. He locked the door and went back to the only window in the room. After closing the blinds, he knelt and said, "Father, I'm not too good at this, but please help me think, act, and react to whatever I'm going to hear, in a way that would not only be pleasing to Kerry but Thee as well." He waited for inspiration, but none came.

After getting up, he opened the blinds and headed toward the door. He paused at the door, hoping for some direction. When none came, he unlocked it and left for Applebee's.

CHAPTER TWENTY-NINE

The drive from the doctor's office to Applebee's was surprisingly peaceful for Kerry. When she arrived, she found a parking space and waited for Lee's arrival.

She was no longer worried about Lee's reaction because his reaction would make her decision. At least that was her initial thinking. Then she suddenly remembered Lee's wife had died of cancer. The realization caused her to break down, only taking control of herself when Lee rapped on her car window.

"Hi, Punkin. Are you okay?"

She blew her nose as though a runny nose was the reason; she had a handkerchief in her hand. "I'm fine. I have some concerns, but I'm fine. Let's get a table, order, and I'll tell you all about them."

Lee could tell something was wrong.

After being escorted to a table, and ordering drinks, he could take the suspense no longer. "What happened at your doctor's appointment?"

"My mammogram revealed a mass in my right breast that might be cancerous."

Lee's facial reaction made Kerry emphasize, "It *might* be cancerous. The fact it might be cancerous, tells me that it might not be cancerous, and if it is cancerous, the cancer hasn't advanced. The doctor took a biopsy, and I should know more in about four hours. If the test results are cancerous, the treatment options range from partial surgery and radiation to a mastectomy, radiation, and chemotherapy."

Lee started to comment, but Kerry held up her hand and proceeded. "I know you are an honorable man, but I don't want to marry an honorable man. Well, I do want to marry an honorable man, but I want to marry an honorable man who wants to marry me, knowing I might not be physically complete…and I can understand if you have reservations about that."

Both were silent.

"I would if I were you," Kerry added.

Lee sat up straight. "You would?"

"I know you had a hard time with Gayle's cancer, and I can understand not wanting to repeat that experience. I—"

"I'm sorry," Lee said in a volume that made the waitress carrying their drinks, make an about-face, "Do I have to set you straight before we eat, or after we eat?"

His question embarrassed both of them. "I'm sorry. I didn't mean to be so demeaning. I'll be quiet until you finish."

They both looked at each other as if posing for a portrait. Kerry's eyes were misty. She tried to speak, but every try was met with a lump.

A waiter brought them their drinks and promptly left.

Lee kept looking at Kerry, and Kerry kept looking at Lee. Neither touched their drinks. When the waiter came to take their order, Lee quietly said they needed more time.

After another couple of minutes, Lee said in a soft loving voice, " Kerry, I'm tired of waiting to get married."

Lee waited several seconds for a response that never came.

"We're getting married, Kerry. Do you understand? Regardless of the tests results, we're not waiting for five months, or one month, or for the treatment to begin, we're getting married as soon as possible. Neither of us knows how long we have in this life. We do know we love each other, which is a lot more than ninety percent of the married couples out there. We know the Church is true, and I love you. Hey, that rhymes."

Kerry gripped his hand and raised her eyebrows, indicating she wanted him to cut the cute and continue.

Lee took the hint. "If treatment isn't an emergency, I can see us getting married at the *beginning* of next week, going on a honeymoon to Hawaii, and then coming back for treatment. If that's too soon, then we'll get married at the *end* of next week, go on a honeymoon to Hawaii, and then come back for treatment. Right now, the only important thing in our lives is when we'll get married, and of course what we're going to eat. And before you answer, let me caution you, if you don't want to get married, the dinner is on you."

A small laugh accompanied a single tear sliding down the left side of Kerry's cheek. She didn't know if she had cancer, but she knew she had Lee's love, and Lee's love was more important.

CHAPTER THIRTY

I t was late afternoon when Valynn gave her the test results.
"Kerry, are you ready for some good news?"
Kerry inhaled deeply but didn't say a thing.

"The bad news is you have a *small* mass of cancer cells in your right breast. The good news is, it's localized—it hasn't spread. It's stage one, grade one. Do you remember what those mean?"

"I probably would if they weren't mine."

"Of course. How stupid of me. I'm sure you're rattled right now. Your cancer is not only in the earliest stage of growth, but its growth is at the slowest rate we measure."

Valynn hoped for a response. When she got none, she said, "Kerry, we caught it early."

"Thank god," Kerry whispered.

"That's a good person to thank," responded Valynn.

Valynn hoped for a happier response, but when she didn't get one, she proceeded. "I suggest doing a partial mastectomy or lumpectomy, removing only the cancerous mass and some surrounding tissue, followed by radiation. Of course, along with the lumpectomy, the nearby nodes will be removed for precautionary reasons." Making sure she followed protocol, Valynn added,

"There's always a chance any treatment might miss some cancer cells, but I'm very optimistic."

"When would treatment begin?"

"The best time would be as soon as possible."

"Could it wait a couple of weeks," Kerry said with a proud smile, "so I could get married?"

"I take it a mastectomy wasn't an issue with Lee."

Kerry's failed attempt to respond spoke volumes.

"When are you getting married?"

"As soon as possible, because we want to go on a honeymoon."

Valynn sat down, looked at the biopsy report, and said to herself as much as she did to Kerry, "If the mass had measured a centimeter more, I would say we shouldn't wait. However, the mass is less than two centimeters, and a grade one in stage one, meaning it's slowly growing." Valynn, still studying the report continued, "I think we can put treatment off for a couple of weeks, but not more than that."

Kerry gasped as tears ran down both cheeks.

"Have you got your honeymoon picked out?" Valynn said wanting to bring more sunshine into the conversation."

"Hawaii."

"Hawaii!" Valynn repeated. "On second thought, I think it would be better if your doctor came with you, just a precaution you understand."

"Fine with me as long as you're on another island."

* * * * * *

As soon as Lee heard the results, he set the date of the wedding. Kerry could almost swear he choked up when she told him the test results, but she would never ask.

During her drive home, she couldn't help but notice how numb she was. All her emotions had been spent in the mental transition from a corpse, or even worse, being in a world without Lee, to his soon-to-be companion.

As she entered her house, the turmoil of the day hit her. She plopped down on her sofa and took in her living room, suddenly realizing that within the month, her living room would be their living room. She wanted to stay in familiar circumstances until her treatment was over and had admired Lee for accepting her weird request with no opposition.

"Should I tell Jason I'm getting married?" she said to the room. The question made her sit up. With soberness, she realized it wasn't *whether* she should tell him, but *when* she should tell him. She looked at the clock and was pleased to see it was too late to contact him. *Tomorrow will be soon enough,* she thought as she sought safety on her sofa. However, she didn't have a chance to enjoy the comfort it offered, because she found herself grabbing her phone and dialing Jason's number. She was glad his voice mail was the only thing she heard. She thought about hanging up during its message, but after the beep heard herself say, "Hello Jason. This is your mother. I'm getting married in four days, and I hope you can come. Love you."

As soon as she hung up, she wished she had left a different message. But the more she thought about it, the more she felt empowered for leaving the one she had left. She didn't need his opinion or permission. Those days were suddenly gone. Facing cancer had already changed her, and she wasn't about to return to the old Kerry.

Her pride was replaced with humility as she found herself sliding off the sofa all the way to her knees. Once there, she held that position for a moment as if she didn't know what to do next. When she finally tried to pray, her emotions wouldn't let her.

She got off the floor and went into her bedroom and went to bed; she didn't even disrobe. It didn't take but minutes before sleep pulled a blanket of comfort over an emotionally exhausted body.

CHAPTER THIRTY-ONE

While blotting her lipstick, Kerry analyzed her reflection. Gone was the healthy image of a teenage girl on her wedding day. The person staring back at her had more wear, heartaches, and pain, yet more reasons to be happy and optimistic.

The vibration of her phone startled her, but not as much as when she saw who was calling.

"Jason. Where have you—"

"Tell me you're not getting married!"

Kerry looked at the phone to make sure it was Jason who was calling.

"It's nice to hear from you too," Kerry said with some sarcasm, "and yes I'm getting married. I would have hoped you would be here, or at least be happy for me, but you'll have to agree that was a stupid assumption on my part."

"How can you do this to me, to dad? You don't even know this man," Jason screamed. "You—"

"And neither do you," Kerry screamed back. "And since we're on the subject, how do you know I don't know this man. You never ask about my life anymore. I know Lee! Your father was the man I didn't know, and this phone call is telling me I don't know you either or come to the think of it, maybe I do."

Jason didn't respond for a moment, which allowed Kerry to continue. "I owe you an apology, an apology for choosing to marry your dad. In the past, and I want to emphasize the word *past*, I felt guilty about saddling you with him because your dog is more of a dad than he was or is."

"I don't have a dog!" Jason screamed, "I never had a dog!"

"My point exactly!" Kerry's courage was gaining momentum.

"Jason, because of the mistake I made at eighteen, I've tip-toed around you all my life. But even though I have cancer, I'll bet my future is better than yours."

She thought about giving him a chance to respond, at least about her cancer, but she changed her mind. "Before I hang up, the wedding is in fifteen minutes. Hope you can make it."

Kerry thought she was through, but then realized she wasn't. "I owe you another apology. I should have treated you this way years ago."

Fearing she had said too much, she let another moment of silence follow, hoping Jason would say something. When he remained silent, she added, "I love you, Jason, with all my heart."

Jason's reply was a ring tone.

After hanging up, she looked at the phone and said, "Boy, did both of us need that!"

Her moment of triumph was interrupted by a knock on the door. For some reason, she looked at the phone before replying. "Yes."

The door opened and Jean stepped in. "You haven't changed your mind have you. It's okay if you have since I'm keeping the go-to-a-wedding dress I bought."

"Well, since you're keeping the dress, I guess I'll have to get married. Is Lee still out there?"

"Do you mean in the building or the city?"

"What did I do to deserve you?"

"I don't know, but you should repeat it as many times, and as often as possible."

Their long hug filled them both with emotion.

"Lee is in one of the classrooms with Brother Cruz," Jean said as she stepped back to look at Kerry. "I sure do like him. Do you think Jason will like him?"

"My answer has something to do with flying pigs."

Kerry gave Jean a few seconds to finish laughing before she continued. "Jason just called, and he was "Jason" if you know what I mean. I owe that kid an apology."

"What on earth for?"

"For letting him live this long," Kerry said with a slight hint of a grin.

Jean laughed and said, "Let's change subjects. Are you nervous?"

"You know Jean, I'm not nervous at all, which makes me nervous. I'm doing the right thing, and if I'm not, don't tell me."

"You're doing the right thing. You can feel the spirit when Lee's around, and in the little time I've known him, I've seen him grow spiritually. You certainly can see he thinks the world of you and vice versa."

"Jean, he makes me feel safe. I never felt safe with Sam. Ever! When I married Sam, I was an excited girl that wanted to leave home and become a woman. Hey, I was going to the temple for the first time. I was going to experience intimacy for the first time. I focused on everything but the man I was marrying. That's not happening today. All I can see is a future with someone who loves me; a future with someone who will take care of me; a future with someone who will help me to become a better person. I won't say *concern* hasn't visited me from time to time. However, if I'm making a mistake, and I'm not, I would rather find out by marrying him, than not marrying him. I'm not going to go through life wondering *what if*."

"Good for you. Can you feel the spirit when you talk like this?"

"I can."

"Let me go tell Lee you're ready. Are you ready?"

"I was born ready."

"You go girl," Jean replied as she turned to leave.

Before Jean got to the door, it opened and a head poked in. "Excuse me. I'm looking for Kerry Howells?"

Kerry and Jean looked at each other before looking back at the stranger who had just addressed them.

"I'm Kerry Howells," Kerry said, not sure her answer was correct.

"I'm Laurence Richards. I'm Lee's younger brother."

Kerry and Jean looked at each other again, and then back at Laurence. Kerry slowly reached her hand out, as Laurence walked toward her. "I'm sorry Laurence, I didn't know you were coming. Don't you live in—"

"Hays, Kansas. I live on our father's farm. Well, I guess it's my farm now. When Lee became a lawyer, I became a farmer. Somebody had to run the farm, and I got stuck with it."

Kerry noticed a slight sting in Laurence's comment.

"Laurence, have you seen Lee yet?"

"Not yet. I wanted to meet the woman who could take Gayle's place. Lee thought a lot of Gayle."

"I'm not that woman because I'm not taking Gayle's place," Kerry said somewhat annoyed with Laurence's statement.

"I didn't mean it the way it came out. You can see I'm not the attorney in the family. Let me rephrase what I said. I really thought the world of Gayle, and so did my brother. For him to find someone else, that someone would have to be fantastic. I've come a long way to see if he was right, and I'm beginning to see why my brother thinks you're fantastic."

"That's better," Kerry said with a big smile, followed by a hug.

"I also wanted to meet the person who made him a Mormon."

"I wish I could take credit for that, but I think the spirit gets the credit for that miracle."

"A miracle is an understatement. Please don't be offended, but don't Mormons live in Yoder, drive buggies, and wear bonnets?"

"You're thinking of the Mennonites and Amish," Jean said as she headed his way.

"Oh, I'm sorry. I'm—"

"You're Laurence Richards, Lee's brother. I'm Jean Atlee, Kerry's friend," Jean said as she shook his hand, and then headed toward the door. "I'll see you two in the chapel. It was nice meeting you, Laurence."

After Jean left, Laurence said, "I feel bad about my entrance. I—"

"Don't worry about it. Have you seen Lee yet? Oh, I already asked you that."

"No. We're sort of...you might say...estranged if I'm using that word correctly. You see I'm—"

"Laurence Richards, my brother-in-law to be, who owns a farm, and who is always welcome in my home."

"I like you, Kerry Howells."

"And I'm beginning to like you, Laurence Richards."

"I'll go see my brother now. I just wanted to meet you first. I think I'm going to think the world of you."

Both let their new friendship age for a couple of seconds before Laurence said, "Excuse me for not staying after the ceremony. Hays is a long way from here, and cows only care about getting fed, and milked."

CHAPTER THIRTY-TWO

Russell could tell Lee was nervous. Their conversation had become sporadic, and Lee was on his fifth trip around the room. "Why don't I meet you in the chapel; give you a chance to crawl out the window, and escape to Oklahoma."

Lee didn't respond. He just looked at his watch as he walked to a wall and back.

"Lee, are you okay?"

"What! Oh…oh yes, I'm all right. I'm just remembering." Lee paused trying to remember what he was just remembering. "I'm okay."

"You got me fooled."

"I'm just realizing how big a step this is for me. The Church, Kerry, cancer."

"Cancer!"

"Oh no. You didn't hear that," Lee said, hoping to repair his blunder. "Kerry has cancer, and neither one of us wants anyone to know, at least not right now. It's just little cancer, which will be taken care of when we get back from our honeymoon. You've got to promise not to say a word. Please."

"Don't worry, you never said a thing. Did she get a blessing?"

Lee looked as though he was told *he* had cancer. "No, I didn't even think of a blessing."

"Did you get a blessing?"

"Why do I need a blessing?"

"Oh, I don't know. You're on your second mile in this room. You're getting married in minutes. You just might need some spiritual help to cope with all that. You ought to try one. I hear they work."

Lee was puzzled by Russell's statement until he saw him grin.

A knock on the door, as it was being opened, caused both to turn. When Laurence stepped into the room, Lee immediately went to his brother, too choked to speak. After a brief hug he turned to Russell, and with emotion in his voice, introduced his brother. "Russell, this is my brother Laurence. Laurence, this is Russell Cruz, my best friend."

They both exchanged greetings and handshakes.

"Is this the miracle man that converted my brother?" Laurence asked Lee while looking at Russell.

"Let me clarify something before I leave. The Holy Ghost converted your brother, not me."

"Yes, but you helped," Lee quickly added. "By the way, didn't you say you had a pamphlet for my brother?"

"Are you saying you didn't bring one for your brother," Russell said with amusement.

Lee enjoyed Russell's comment, as he awkwardly looked at his brother and said, "I'm so glad you came. I thought you couldn't leave the farm?"

Russell felt it was time to leave the two brothers to themselves. So, before Laurence could respond he announced, "I'll leave you two alone. By the way Lee, I'd be glad to step down as your best man, so your brother could take my place during the ceremony."

Before Lee could respond Laurence answered the offer, "No. You should stand with my brother. I came to see the bride."

"I can't wait to introduce you," Lee responded. "She's a wonderful person. I know you'll like her."

"I know I will. I just met her."

"You just met her! When?"

"Minutes ago," Laurence said, enjoying his brother's surprise.

"It was nice to meet you, Laurence. I'll let you two catch up," Russell said as he headed toward the door.

After Russell closed the door, and before Lee could respond, Laurence said, "I've been pretty immature about my actions these past years. Dad needed help on the farm when you went to Vietnam, so I put my dreams on hold. I thought you would replace me when you came back, so I could go to Agriculture College at Kansas State, but that didn't happen. Instead of replacing me, staying home, and working the farm, you left for Washburn, to pursue your dreams, never thinking of me. Thus, I didn't get to go to college and resented you for taking my dream. I saw myself as the brother in "It's a Wonderful Life" who gave up his dream so his brother could fulfill his dream. I was very bitter. To be honest, I couldn't stand you until you married Gayle, and when she died, what brotherly relationship we once had, died with her."

Laurence knew what he was saying was hurtful, but he felt it needed to be said. "On the other hand, ever since you've joined this church, you have become a different person. You have shown some interest in something other than yourself. You actually made an effort to keep in touch with me and my family. When I heard you were getting married, I decided it was time for me to become a different person as well."

"Thank you," Lee said. "I think that was an apology." When Laurence stiffened, Lee quickly continued, "Thanks for being here. It means a lot to me."

"See you in the chapel," Laurence said as he opened the door to leave. "You made a good choice in Kerry."

CHAPTER THIRTY-THREE

Lee and Kerry sat in first class as their Boeing 757-330, the largest single-aisle passenger aircraft ever built by Boeing, slipped through light clouds at thirty thousand feet, traveling over five hundred miles an hour. Lee had set out to give Kerry a first-class flight, a first-class honeymoon, and if he could, a first-class life, one that wouldn't be shortened by cancer. So far, he felt he had delivered what he could. Now it was time for God to do his part.

Although Hawaii had been wonderful, both were ready to go home. Having trials to prepare for, a legal trial for Lee and a trial of therapy for Kerry, both thought it wise to take advantage of their long flight and keep to themselves.

It didn't take long for Lee to succumb to sleep. On the other hand, Kerry struggled; her body might have been on the plane, but her mind was in Wichita. After hours of slipping in and out of awareness, she searched the cabin for activity, only to find a few conversations. It seemed the soft monotonous hum of the jet engines, had put most of the other passengers to sleep.

She was grateful Lee was asleep. Up until now, she had evaded any talk about her upcoming treatment, and she certainly didn't want the trip to end with such a discussion. To make sure that didn't happen, she had laid her head against the window and closed her eyes, pretending to be asleep. *Please, God, I've been through so much. Just let this trip end without making my cancer a topic.*

"Would you care for a towel?" The steward's offer startled her.

"Good morning, Punkin," Lee said with a rested smile as he accepted a towel.

"Good morning to you, Mr. Punkin," Kerry said, bringing her tray down while accepting a towel.

Lee brought his tray down as well. "I see you're in a good mood."

Kerry leaned over and kissed him on the cheek. "Why shouldn't I be, after the honeymoon you gave me?"

"Did you get any sleep? Lee's question was sincere.

"Yes and no."

"Are you worried about your upcoming treatment?"

"Have we landed?"

"Of course not."

"Then we're still on our honeymoon, right?"

"Yes," Lee said, knowing where Kerry was going with her question.

"And my rule, which you have honored until now, still applies; we don't talk about anything but our honeymoon until we land. And with that said, in the small amount of time we have before we land, I would like a review of everything we did. Do you remember when we first arrived in Honolulu?"

"I understand. We flew from Wichita to Dallas—"

"Lee! Begin with the lei you gave me when we landed in Honolulu."

"Okay, I gave you a lei after we landed in Honolulu."

"Leeee!"

Lee grabbed her hand as if preventing a slap, grateful for her playful mood. "I gave you a lei after we landed, because everyone who goes to Hawaii should get one the minute, they get off the plane."

Kerry nodded her head in agreement. "Lee, it meant a lot to me to get those flowers. It set a very lovely and memorable tone for the rest of the week. It was the first time I felt the spirit of Hawaii. You told me once when a person goes to Hawaii, a part of that person becomes Hawaiian. That didn't make any sense to me at the time, but it does now. Proceed travel guide," Kerry said as she kissed his shoulder.

Lee resumed with dignity. "From the airport, we took highway sixty-one to the Kailua Valley Lookout on top of the Pali. I wanted you to see what I think is the most beautiful view in all the islands."

"No argument there," Kerry eagerly joined in. "It was breathtaking. I couldn't get over how green the mountains were, or how rugged they looked. It was as if God had clawed deep grooves on the sides of the mountains. And Lee, the wind from the ocean rushed up the side of those mountains about a hundred miles an hour."

"More like seventy but go on."

"And remember the guy making leis and Hawaiian things?"

"Oh yes, those Hawaiian things."

Kerry slugged him, causing Lee to feign pain. "Can I continue?"

Lee raised his arms in a defensive posture. "Yes, but please don't hit me again."

Kerry ignored his gesture. "From the Pali, we went south to the Halona Blowhole. I liked the scenery around the blowhole as much as I liked the blowhole. Then we drove to Hanauma Bay. The water was so clear, and the fish…. We finally went to our hotel, the Aqua Aloha Surf, checked in, and before taking in the nightlife of Waikiki, we took a stroll along the Ala Wai Canal, where large canoes filled with rowers, raced up and down the canal is some sort of competition. You know Lee," Kerry said as she looked into the past, "we could have come home the next day, and it still would have been the best trip of my life. You have to realize, I'm a Kansas girl."

"It doesn't manner where you live, there's only one Hawaii and only one Kerry." Neither said anything as the steward took their towels.

"We don't have much time before we land, and we have a lot more to review. I want to get as much Hawaii in this return flight as I can."

"By all means," Lee said with encouragement. He understood what his wife was doing and couldn't have agreed more.

"The next day we went to the International Market Place, where we had breakfast before going to Kailua's State Park. I think it's my favorite park in Hawaii."

"I agree," Lee said. "I like that beach because not very many people know about it, or should I say *knew* about it. Since our last visit, I wouldn't be surprised if it becomes a tourist attraction."

Kerry raised her arm as though she was going to slug him. "You embarrassed me on that beach."

"I embarrassed you! It wasn't me whose bathing suit was altered by the tide!"

"Yes, and it wasn't me who was standing at attention, saluting my predicament, singing—Oh say can you see." Kerry retorted.

"I think I have a good voice," Lee said as if crushed by Kerry's assessment.

When Kerry giggled, Lee knew he could go on. "Do you remember, on the way back to our hotel, we stopped at the Dole

Plantation Home? And after touring the plantation, we finished the day by eating white pine pineapple, as we sat among the rainbow trees, watching the sunset?"

Kerry's smile answered his questions.

"The next day we went to the North Shore, where we boarded a sailboat, and went to shark's cove for two hours of snorkeling, or at least everyone else snorkeled for two hours," Lee waited for another slug.

"You mean where you tried to kill me!"

"Kerry," Lee said as if her remark was uncalled for.

"You knew I was afraid of deep water," Kerry said as she poked her finger into his side.

"Deepwater to you is anything higher than your waist," Lee said putting his hand about three feet above the aisle.

"Lee, the water was at least thirty feet deep!"

"Was it that deep?"

Kerry's eyes widened as her mouth opened.

Lee quickly spoke, "Listen before you got in the water, you were more buoyant than the boat. If I'm not mistaken, you were wearing an inflated life vest, and carrying two noodles before your foot ever hit the water. And, after getting into the water, you grabbed a life-saving ring that was attached to the boat. Come to think about it, you didn't climb down the ladder, you climbed down my head and back."

"I'm your wife. You're supposed to support me!"

"Financially! Your weight shoved me under the boat, ripping my swim trunks on the boat's barnacles."

The image had Kerry laughing. "I was so afraid."

"So was I, and I'm a good swimmer."

Kerry stopped laughing. "Can you explain how the rope to the life-saving ring, the ring I was clutching, suddenly became separated from the boat?"

"It slipped off."

"It slipped off in your hand! I found myself about a hundred yards from the boat, in thirty feet of water, because it slipped off in *your hand*."

"Kerry," Lee said as if he was hurt by her insinuation. "Aren't you glad I caught it when it slipped off?"

Kerry almost slugged him again.

"On the way back to Honolulu, we stopped at Maui Mikes in Wahiawa, for chicken. Isn't Maui Mikes' chicken the best chicken you've ever eaten?" Lee asked knowing the answer.

"If it wasn't, I wouldn't have gone back two more times."

Lee lowered his voice. "Then the next day we went back to the North Shore and visited the temple grounds. When I get my temple recommend, we'll go back and go through the temple."

"I know we will Lee."

Wanting to stay in the moment, they just held hands.

When the intercom told them their plane was on its final approach to Dallas, they prepared themselves for landing.

As their plane began to drop out of the sky, Kerry was the only one thinking about Wichita and she wanted it that way.

"Kerry."

"Lee, you promised."

"And I've kept my promise, and if you let me speak, you'll see I'm still keeping my promise. But before I say what I'm going to say, and I'm going to say it, I want to remind you this is my honeymoon as well."

Lee's tone told her more than what he said.

When Kerry failed to respond, Lee continued. "In my next journal entry, I'm going to write about this couple who went to Hawaii on their honeymoon. They both knew the wife had been given a cancer diagnosis, but you would have never known it because they were so positive. Can you imagine having cancer in Hawaii, cancer in paradise? After observing them for a week, I thought their approach to their vacation was a metaphoric way to approach life. When I talked to them, I learned they had done everything they could concerning his wife's treatment and trusted the doctors and the Lord to take care of the rest, knowing the rest would be the best in the long run. I bet if I could talk to the husband, he would be so appreciative of his wife's example of showing him how to face adversity; so thankful their honeymoon hadn't been marred by his negative talk. I'm so blessed that you're like his wife. I know you thought about what could be, but I'm glad you steered me to the positives. I hope I can do the same for you from now on."

Kerry's emotions wouldn't let her respond.

As the plane touched down in Dallas, memories of Hawaii touched down as well. Both had a new approach to adversity; one they would need in the future.

CHAPTER THIRTY-FOUR

The night before his arrest, Jason had prayed for help with his addiction. The realization that he was praying scared him more than discovering he was almost out of drugs. He had been up for four days and wanted that lifestyle to end, as well as his relationship with Charlie. However, he needed to secure enough meth to pace his withdrawal.

On the night of his arrest, Jason arrived at Charlie's around seven-thirty in the evening. He was disappointed to find only strangers among those already there. After grabbing his purchase from Charlie, he decided to snort a complimentary pinch of meth before leaving. That's when his world was turned upside down.

The first stun grenade exposed the room with a blinding light of over seven million candelas, giving Jason flash blindness, while the combined intensity of two more grenades, each one producing 170 decibels, disturbed the fluid in both inner ears, causing temporary deafness and loss of balance. Although he had lost his sense of hearing and balance, he only needed the sense of touch to feel the barrel of a pistol being placed behind his left ear as he lay on the ground.

Within seconds after being jerked to his feet, an officer whisked him out of the house to the trunk of a patrol car. There, he was informed he was about to be searched, and if he had any sharp objects, which could injure the officer doing the search, he needed to speak up.

Sarcasm came to Jason's mind but didn't linger. He remembered a warning Charlie had given him—*Since a police officer has the discretion of charging a suspect with as many crimes as he or she has at their disposal, especially if the suspect is going to jail, an abundance of politeness and cooperation should be afforded said officer and/ or officers.*

After assuring the officer he wouldn't be injured during his search, nor would he find a gun or drugs, the officer proceeded. The search was rough, followed by tight handcuffs, Miranda rights, and his placement in the backseat of the patrol car.

As the police officer was closing the car door, Jason looked up and said, "Could I say one thing?"

"Sure, but remember you've been given your Miranda rights!"

Jason wasn't being sardonic when he said, "I want to thank you for arresting me. I think my arrest is an answer to a prayer."

The officer's face registered surprise. He started to respond, but an order from another officer, caused him to shut the door, and head back into Charlie's house.

As Jason sat in the back of the patrol car, he concluded his arrest was indeed an answer to his prayer. However, the longer he sat in the car, the weaker his conviction became, and by the time he arrived at the county jail, it was gone.

Being booked was everything Charlie said it would be—questioning, surrender of personal belongings, and mug shots. After mug shots were taken, he was turned over to a jail cop.

A jail cop is different from a street cop. A street cop asks questions, a jail cop gives orders, at least within the confines of a jailhouse. Even in jail, *Miranda* would have to ask a jail cop for the right to talk.

After check-in, Jason was taken to a room, where the patdown of his person was close to a strip search. From there he was taken to "pit one" a concrete pit containing an enclosed toilet, a free telephone, and benches, all under the surveillance of jail cops from above.

Inside the pit, other jail cops questioned prisoners to see who could post bail. Some charges had a fixed bail, which negated a judge's approval. The owner of serious charges, or a history of repeated offenses, usually got free accommodations for the night.

Although Jason didn't have a record, his charge demanded that he be held for arraignment. When asked if he wanted to call a lawyer, he said no. His dad and Lee were the only two lawyers he knew, and he didn't want to get either one of them involved.

Having refused a lawyer, he was taken to "pit two," a similar but slightly smaller concrete pit. In this pit, he was screened for communicable diseases such as TB and was asked if there were any inmates, gang members or enemies, he didn't want to be associated with. Although Charlie wasn't an enemy, he listed him as one because he just didn't want to be around Charlie for a while.

From pit-two, Jason was escorted to a cellblock comprising two floors, joined by one set of stairs. The cellblock had fifteen cells on each floor, all of which opened onto a common area housing a table, chairs, and a TV. The guardhouse, an enclosed oval structure of glass, high in one corner of the cellblock, housed a guard whose only job was to maintain constant surveillance of the cellblock and its inmates.

When Jason entered his assigned cell, he didn't speak but nodded to his cellmate. Each measured the other, and despite his lack of seniority, both secretly concluded that Jason was the alpha.

The guard who had escorted Jason to his cell ran through a list of introductions with the enthusiasm of a recording—lights went on at four-thirty in the morning, and went off at ten at night; Jason had the freedom to do whatever he wanted from six to ten, the only exception being a mandatory lockdown to clean the common area; whether he wanted to eat or starve, meals would be served in the common area; he wasn't in prison, where *inmates* ran the prison, he was in jail, where *jailors* ran the jail; the stairs could be used for exercise if he fancied exercise.

As the guard walked out of Jason's cell, he turned and pointed to his cellmate, "Any questions, ask him."

Needing time to come down, as soon as the guard left, Jason crashed on his bunk, telling his cellmate he was tired and wanted to be left alone.

* * * * * *

The day after his arrest, he was taken before a judge and arraigned. He pleaded guilty to the possession of drugs and was told that because of his clean record, he would only receive a sentence of one hundred and eighty days. Jason suspected overcrowding had more to do with his light sentence than his clean record.

Back at his cellblock, he decided to contact a lawyer to see if there was anything that could be done about his one-hundred-and-eighty-day sentence. Pride was one thing, one hundred and eighty days was something else.

His dad wasn't even a consideration. However, Richards was not only an attorney, but his representation could also bring discord to a marriage he viewed as a humiliation to both him and his dad.

When he was able to speak to one of the guards he said, "Hey, I want to speak to a lawyer. How do I do that?"

"Well, let's see. You can scream or call one on the phone. I'd call one on the phone if I were you."

Jason laughed to show respect. "Problem is, I don't have his number."

"Kid, they call them phone books."

"I know. I just thought you might know him. He was the former assistant district attorney."

The former assistant district attorney got the guard's attention. "What's his name?"

"Richards is all I can remember, which is embarrassing since he's my new stepdad."

Whether the guard wanted to be the one to humiliate a former assistant district attorney or make points with a former assistant district attorney, Jason didn't know or care. The guard's quick exit told him Richards would soon be at the jail.

CHAPTER THIRTY-FIVE

I*t's nice to be out of that stupid cellblock,* Jason thought as he waited in the interrogation room for Lee's arrival. When Lee came to the door, Jason remained seated. "Richards, you got here fast. How's married life with my mom?"

"First of all, since you're not in our lives, it's great. Second, it's none of your business, and the name's Mr. Richards or I'll walk, and if I do, on my way out, I'll tell the guards you brought me here to sue them because of the way you've been treated. I'll also make it known to your companions that you're my favorite stepson, and that wouldn't be good for you, since some people in here hate my guts. Are we clear, or do you need a demonstration as to how bad I can make your life?"

"Sorry Mr. Richards," Jason said as he looked at the desk in front of him. "Sorry about the personal injury case too. I guess my actions messed up our case."

"Nah. The case was never about you. In fact, your stupidity will probably help me."

Lee's rejection of Jason's peace offering, combined with his personal attack, almost caused Jason to get up and walk out, but one hundred and eighty days is one hundred and eighty days. "Is there anything you or another lawyer could do for me? I know I screwed up, I've learned my lesson, and I want to change."

"And why do you think you've learned your lesson?" How many guys do you think are in here for the second, third, or fourth time, who thought they had learned their lesson? Boy, you have a serious habit, one that isn't easy to overcome, *if* you can overcome it at all. You're in more trouble than being in here."

"That's why I need help. I'll go straight. I just wanted to know if a lawyer could shorten my sentence or get me transferred to a better place."

"It's too late now. If you had called me when you got arrested, I might have been able to do something. Anyway, jail will give you an opportunity to change if you want to change. Believe it or not, the Church is big in this jail, and the Church can help you change."

"What do you mean 'the Church is big in this jail'?"

"What's the worst thing about being in here, beside the people, and your lack of freedom?"

"Boredom?"

"Boredom is right, and the Church of Jesus Christ of Latter-Day Saints can help you with that boredom, along with the real reason you're in here, which is your mindset."

"Wow. You sound like a member."

"I am."

This declaration stunned Jason. After a second or two, he spoke, "I don't want anything to do with the Church. I—"

"Have a good stay, if that's possible," Lee said as he turned to walk.

"Wait!"

"Make it good, this is the only chance I'll give you before I walk out of here."

"Please help me if you can."

"I don't have time to get into your self-absorbed sorrows. Do you want to better your life in here or not?"

"I do," Jason coldly said.

"On Sunday, the Church has a sacrament meeting that lasts one hour. There will be speakers, hymns, and prayers. The only thing missing will be the sacrament. Even if you hate church, it's an hour you can get out of your cell, and more importantly, hear something besides your cellmate, and the guards."

When Jason didn't respond, Lee continued. "On Tuesday, the Church has a class, consisting of a Church Conference Talk on video. After the video, you'll be given a questionnaire pertaining to the video you just watched, a questionnaire to be taken back to your cell and answered. This is not only another hour out of your cell but can give you something to do while you're in your cell. On the following Tuesday, you can bring your filled-out questionnaire back to the missionaries and watch another video, while they grade the questionnaire you just handed them. At the end of the new video, the missionaries will return the graded questionnaire you handed in, along with a new questionnaire pertaining to the video you just watched. There's another hour you can get out of your cell and have something productive to do when you're back in your cell."

Lee had expected an attitude from Jason by now, but it didn't come, which gave him some hope. "Finally, on Friday, the Church has an addiction program, like an AA meeting. This might be the most important hour of your week. Besides, it's another hour out of your cell. I hope you see the advantage of what I've told you. However, what I'm going to tell you now is the most important information I can pass along. You probably don't know anyone who has overcome addiction, because I'm guessing all your friends are addicts. However, I know people just like you, who have overcome their addiction, and I'm telling you, the only way you're going to overcome it is to give your life over to Christ. This has nothing to do with religion: this has everything to do with you qualifying for His help and accepting it when it's given. Nevertheless, the journey begins with you wanting His help."

Both looked at each other with less animosity. Lee could feel the spirit and hoped Jason could as well.

"Can I give you some more advice?"

The question surprised Jason. "Isn't that what you've been doing?"

Lee fought the urge to leave.

"There are sixty inmates in a cellblock; sixty bored butts trying to find thirty seats in a classroom, which means you'll have to get in line at least thirty minutes before the beginning of each class in order to get a seat; that is, until you get some seniority in here, which will allow you to cut in line. Letting your fellow inmates know you're a Mormon, will help you in here. I know you think that's crazy, but most of the time it will help. Remember, the Church is big in this jail, and the fact you are a member will be enough to get you a chair most of the time. Concerning your mother, she's recovering from her cancer treatment."

The startled look on Jason's face told Lee he had forgotten all about his mother's cancer. Lee let his statement sink in before saying, "She's doing okay. Her bouts with nausea, pain, and fatigue are minor, but they're not her biggest problem. You are her biggest problem. She thinks it's her fault you're in jail. We know differently, don't we?"

Lee waited for a response, and when it didn't come, he continued.

"Jason, I want you to like me because if you did, it would help your mother. I'm also trying to convince myself, I don't care about you, but I'm failing."

Lee wanted to say more, but the spirit told him he had said enough, and it was time to leave.

Lee started to turn, but instead said; "I'll tell your mother about your circumstances here."

"Don't do that!"

"Now that I know, I have to. There are no secrets between us, and there never will be. And for what it's worth, I love your mother."

Neither spoke as Lee held out his hand.

Jason was surprised at how quickly he stood and took it.

"If you want to talk, tell the guard. I'll give him my card, but let me warn you, if you give the guards any trouble, they'll lose that card."

Lee thought of one more piece of advice. "If you want to turn your life around, talk to the Lord. He's waiting to hear from you. I'm glad you're in here, and I mean that. I think this is the best thing that could have happened to you…that is if *you* think it's the best thing that could have happened to you."

Jason remained silent as Lee left.

CHAPTER THIRTY-SIX

A week after they got back from Hawaii, Kerry underwent lumpectomy surgery on her right breast, the byproducts being a bruised, swollen breast, and fatigue, fatigue that eventually gave way to strength and energy. Fortunately for Kerry, since her stage one cancer didn't call for chemotherapy, her doctor had given her a two-month hiatus for her body to heal; two months she used to adjust to a new life with Lee.

When she was told her regime of radiation treatment was only going to be eight, Monday-to-Friday sessions, lasting only ten minutes in length, she began her treatment with optimism, optimism that was replaced with skin irritation, swelling, and insidious fatigue, fatigue that made the simplest routine a chore and sleep a constant demand. Although her medical team assured her this *fatigue* would depart within two to three weeks following her last treatment, she was beginning to wonder if it was being replaced by a different fatigue, psychological fatigue that her cancer might outlive her new marriage.

"Today is different," she whispered to a picture of her and Lee in Hawaii. She had gotten a call from Valynn, reporting the results of a recent MRI, which found her to be cancer-free, nul-lifying the need for her future radiation treatments.

After a sobering couple of seconds, she gathered herself with what energy she had, and announced to no one, "It won't be too long before Lee and I are sealed in the temple."

She glanced at the clock on the living room wall, a clock that told her Lee would be home in ten minutes. Kerry gently slid off the couch and went to her bathroom. There she found a mirror, which presented a face in need of work.

"Kerry Hourrigan Claypool Richards, you can look better than this," she said to the mirror as she squeezed her cheeks, checked her eyes and lips, and tried to comb her hair. After a couple of failed attempts to make her hair presentable, she gave up and let it choose its direction as she left the bathroom for the porch swing.

Immediately, after finding the swing, the sun's rays found her, flooding her with optimism as well as warmth. She thanked God for Lee, and for the love Lee gave her. A smile came to her face, as her mind rested upon the new poem she was working on; a smile Jason's image chased away. Although she had phoned Jason several times since the wedding, she felt bad about her hurried disconnections each time she heard his voice mail.

Kerry began to quietly sob, but quickly abandoned that luxury when she saw Lee's car coming down the street. For no reason, she quickly got off the swing, and went inside, heading for the couch, dabbing her eyes in the process. She sat on the couch and picked up a book as Lee walked through the door. Kerry acted as if his arrival had startled her. She laid her book on the couch, stood, and with the expectation of being kissed, stretched out her arms.

Although Lee enveloped her, he didn't kiss her. After an un-comfortable hug, Kerry asked with trepidation, "Lee, is something wrong?"

"I've been trying to decide when and how I'm going to tell you what I'm going to tell you, and there's only one way to tell you."

Lee's remark almost caused Kerry to smile, but she could sense something wasn't right.

"Promise me you'll listen to everything I'm going to say before interrupting me. Please try and hold your questions until I'm done. Please."

Kerry resumed her seat on the couch. "Okay," she softly said in an unsure tone.

"I mean it, Punkin. Just let me talk. Please. Just let me talk."

"Okay."

When that was Kerry's only response, Lee resumed his re-hearsed delivery.

"I talked to Jason today." Kerry leaned forward and started to speak. However, Lee held up his index finger and stared her back to her original position on the couch. When she repositioned herself, he continued, "I saw him at the county jail."

Kerry quickly sat forward again and started to speak, but this time, without prompting, she resumed her original position.

"He's been busted for using meth." He waited for Kerry to react. When she didn't, he spoke with authority, "He's been sentenced to six months."

There was a small gasp from Kerry as she looked down at her lap, eyes filled with tears. "He's a drug addict. I've lost my son."

Even though Lee agreed, he had to give her some hope to hold on to. With strength, he looked at her until their eyes met. "We don't know if he's an addict, we only know he got arrested for having drugs in his possession. It might have been his first time."

"Lee!" Kerry said with irritation.

"Seriously Kerry, we don't know. One thing I do know, whether it's his first time, or he's an addict as you think he is, one thing is for sure, jail is the best place for him right now."

They both just looked at each other before Kerry said, "I'm waiting."

"If Jason got busted on his first try, jail-time will scare him into quitting. If he's an addict, for six months he won't be able to get any meth, he'll have time to dry out."

With a hopeless stare, she looked down at her lap. "That makes some sense. Did he say anything about me?"

"He was sorry he hadn't called. He suggested his drug habit being the reason." Lee wasn't about to say anything different.

"Can I see him?"

Lee had to lie. "He doesn't want you to see him in jail. Also, it's such a short sentence as drug-sentences go. I'm sure you can understand why he wants to get out first. He's not very sociable right now. Kids don't think like we do, especially while in jail. Kerry, he's got some growing up to do, adjust to jail, his inmates, and...."

The look on Kerry's face told him he was saying more than he should.

"Some of this is my fault. I shouldn't have said what I said to him before our wedding," Kerry confessed, as much to herself as she did to Lee.

"Kerry, he had this problem long before the wedding. Anyway, I think he eventually understood your reaction."

"Do you think he's had this problem for a long time?"

"I don't know sweetheart," Lee said as he gave up hope of a meaningful discussion. Then, as if inspired, Lee knew what to say. "He was interested in the programs the Church has to offer."

Lee's remark brought the response he wanted. "What do you mean 'programs the Church has to offer'? He's in jail," she responded as if Lee was stupid for saying what he had said.

Neither said anything for several minutes.

Kerry, still looking at the furniture, broke their silence. "I think I need to see Bishop Knutson. I haven't talked to a bishop in a long time."

Lee was stunned. He wanted to ask why, but her deep thought told him he should wait for a less emotional opportunity.

"I need to talk to the bishop. Could you call his executive secretary, and make an appointment for me in a couple of weeks? I should be feeling much better by then since I no longer need radiation treatments."

Lee was confused and the look on his face confirmed that. "I thought you had a week and a half to go?"

"That would be true if my last MRI didn't say I wasn't cancer-free."

Lee rushed to her and held her tight, burying his face in her hair as he softly cried. When he regained his composure, he kissed her and said, "I don't know what to say?"

"Let's thank the Lord, and then you can make that appointment."

Lee had to ask, "Why do you think you need to talk to the bishop?"

"Lee, ever since I can remember, I've tried to do the right thing. I didn't leave the Church when my husband was making a mockery of me and the Church, nor did I leave the Church when I thought my bishop was taking Sam's side because they were both men and priesthood holders. Time and prayer have shown me I was wrong. Without proof that Sam was lying, there wasn't anything my bishop could have done. Yes, I need to talk to our bishop."

Kerry was silent for a while, and Lee didn't mind.

"I'm tired of being the good girl and getting the bad end of the bargain. I know after the news I got today, I shouldn't feel the way I do, and yet I can't think of a reason why I shouldn't feel the way I do. Could you make that call for me?"

She didn't wait for a reply. She just smiled, got up, and headed toward the bedroom like a robot.

"Yes, I'll make the call, but can I ask you a question first?"

She stopped and slowly turned with great difficulty. "Sure."

"Why can't we view what you've gone through in a positive light?"

"What do you mean? If someone's told you having cancer isn't a bad thing, send them over to me, and I'll straighten them out." Her attempt at sarcasm was without energy.

"You *had* cancer, and I stress *had*, just like a lot of people have had cancer. Cancer will always be around. However, unlike a lot of its victims, you've had the financial means to treat your cancer. You also had a doctor who knew how to treat it, and you've lived in a location where it could be treated. Unlike a great many cancer victims, you weren't alone during your treatment. You lived with someone who loved you and took care of you during your treatment. That's not all. You're not alone when it comes to having a son who *might* be a meth addict, and I emphasize the word might. However, unlike some addicts who live on the streets, your son will go to bed tonight in a warm room, with clean sheets, and a full stomach. And when he wakes, he will put on clean clothes, and have access to the influence of the Church. He has the love of his mother who has married someone with some pull in said jail. He might not take advantage of the Church after he gets out, but he'll take advantage of the Church as long as he's in jail. Being in jail could change his thinking."

"Lee, I can't see jail changing him," Kerry said as if she had given up hope.

"You might be right," Lee said giving up on the possibility of a rational conversation. "But then again you might be wrong. He'll be going to church three times a week while he's in jail, and that's three more times than he was going before jail. Don't search for ways to change your son, search for ways to connect with Heavenly Father. Have faith. Believe in God enough to throw your common sense out the window and do what he wants you to do."

He thought about shutting up, but lawyers don't do that. "Kerry, you're married to the best thing that has ever happened to you. Only my modesty prevents me from elaborating."

"Lee, what I love about your modesty, is how modest you are about your modesty," Kerry said as she joined Lee in a smile.

They hugged for a moment before Kerry looked at Lee and said, "You're right. I finally have a husband to handle these things, and I think I'll let him handle these things."

Lee smiled.

"Do you mind? I'm tired. I'm going to lie down if you don't mind?"

"Sure, Punkin." Watching Kerry's listless attempt to go to their bedroom, wore Lee out. He was glad no more was said about Jason.

CHAPTER THIRTY-SEVEN

Bishop Knutson stood six-five and weighed 340 pounds. He had huge feet, broad shoulders, and broader hips. His wide smile took your eyes away from his enormous waist, a moving billboard advertising his love for food.

After a handshake, the former farmer who had turned barber, motioned with arms that could pick up a cow let alone scissors, for Kerry to be seated.

"Sister Richards, it's nice to finally have a one-on-one with you. I'm sorry this didn't happen when you moved into our ward. How do you like your new ward?"

"I love this ward. Everyone has been so nice to me."

"Was it hard moving out of your old home?"

"Yes and no. I loved my old home, but it turned out to be easier for Lee to take care of me in his house. Plus, it's closer to his workplace, giving us more time together."

"We're glad to have you. I've wanted to formally meet you before now, but I also wanted you to finish your therapy first. It's finished, isn't it?"

"Yes. I'm beginning to get my strength back. I'm here to see if you can help me get my testimony back."

Kerry's statement took the bishop by surprise. "Are you losing your testimony?"

"I guess not, or I wouldn't be here."

Kerry waited for the bishop to reply, and when he didn't, she continued with some emotion in her voice, "Bishop, my testimony has taken a bit of a hit lately."

The spirit told the bishop to keep quiet, and he obeyed.

Both were uncomfortable as they waited for the other to speak. When no one did, Kerry began to rise out of her seat. "I shouldn't have come."

"Don't leave," said the bishop in a whisper.

Kerry, dabbing her eyes, slowly sat back down.

The bishop gave her tissues and waited.

It took a couple of minutes for Kerry to compose herself, and when she did, she spoke with some bitterness in her voice. "I was born into this Church, and I've always done what I was supposed to do. I was morally clean when I went to the temple. Throughout my horrible marriage, I was a faithful wife to my husband, a good mother to my child, and a faithful member of this church."

Tears and more tissues demanded a pause.

"For my efforts, I was served divorce papers on Mother's Day."

She stopped and took a breath.

"Months later, my ex-husband was caught having an affair, and if that wasn't humiliating enough, only when he was caught having *another* adulterous relationship, was he excommunicated."

The bishop wanted to explain that a bishop can only judge what he knows but instead waited to see if Kerry would continue with her ex-husband's excommunication. When she didn't, he said, "I'm sorry. Going through that must have been hard. A bishop, like any judge, can only make judgments on what he knows. I don't know what your bishop knew at the time, so I won't comment if you don't mind."

Kerry accepted the bishop's reluctance. "How the ward reacted throughout this entire circus, was the hardest thing for me. Honestly, I felt shunned by the ward."

"Do you feel like you've been shunned by this ward?"

"Not at all and believe me when I say I'm thankful for that."

Kerry clasped her hands and laid them in her lap. "Could I ask a favor?"

"Sure."

"Coming here to talk with you has been harder than I thought. Could you please refrain from interrupting?"

"Sorry. Go ahead."

Kerry, resting her weight on her crossed leg, ever so slightly leaned forward and said, "When my son moved out to go to college, whatever relationship he and I had, moved out with him. If we have one today, I'm not aware of it, and it certainly isn't the mother-son relationship I want. For example, you know he didn't come to my wedding when I married Lee. However, did you know minutes before our wedding, he called me, not to wish me luck, but to chew me out for betraying him and his father?"

Kerry sat back with a resigned look. "Add all that up and throw in cancer and having a kid in jail for drugs and tell me God is letting this happen to me for my own good. Is divorce, humiliation, cancer, and my son's addiction and incarceration what I need? And don't come back with 'some people have it worse' because that just makes my argument. If I didn't have Lee, I don't know what I'd do."

This wasn't the first time the bishop had heard such confessions and reasoning. His past experiences had taught him any response coming from him would have little chance of being heard, let alone understood. However, he still had to try.

"I'm certainly not going to tell you I know how you feel. No one can completely know how you feel, or what it's like to be in your shoes. However, because of my calling, I've listened to a lot of people, and their stories have given me a unique perspective about life. Would you like to hear my perspective?"

"No."

Her answer surprised him. He had never had that answer to that question before. He didn't know what to say, which was fortunate since Kerry wasn't done.

"But I probably should hear what you have to say, so go ahead," Kerry said with resignation.

"I've had members, with hardly any problems, wonder if God really cares, and I've had members, whose lives are worse than what you've described, testify that he does care. Kerry, we see the world through glasses of perception. We interpret what we see as reality. Only when we look at the past through the lens of hindsight, do we get a more accurate picture of the present. With hindsight, I've looked back at some of my trials and realized I wasn't ready for the help or answer Heavenly Father would eventually give me. In fact, what I wanted wouldn't have been the best, or even a good solution for me or someone I loved at the time of my request. Hindsight has made me realize my biggest obstacle during a crisis, isn't the crisis, but my inability to see the future."

The bishop realized Kerry was listening, so he continued. "Although hindsight clarifies the past, our inability to see the future skews our perception of the present. That's why it's important to have faith in a God who has seen the future."

"Thank you," Kerry said with sincerity. "In other words, what you're saying is our present always makes more sense when viewed in the future. Yet, because the present isn't in the future, it can't be viewed with hindsight."

"Well said. If you could see what was going to happen in the future, you would know how to better live in the present. Are you beginning to see why we should go to our Heavenly Father when asking for advice about the present, or the future? Remember, forgiving yourself doesn't fix the past as much as it enlarges the future."

"Yes, but since He knows the future, why isn't He answering my prayers about the present?"

"Maybe He is. I don't know. Maybe an answer would impede the reason for your trial. Maybe you're not ready for the answer. Maybe strengthening your faith is more important than solving your problem. I believe how you react to your circumstances, is more important than your circumstances."

When Kerry didn't respond right away, the bishop decided to take their conversation in another direction.

"Let me give you some questions to think about. Stipulating there is no God, if one man believed in God, and another didn't, which one would have more comfort in his trials?"

He didn't give her a chance to respond. "Now let's stipulate there is a God. Which one would find more comfort in his trials? The answer is the same for both questions. The man or woman who believes in a god will always have more comfort in facing his or her trials, and the good news is, there is a God. When it's time for you to have your answer, God will give it to you, and the answer will have been worth waiting for."

"I'm tired of waiting," Kerry retorted. "He needs to give me a break."

"Maybe God's already given you a break, and you haven't rec-ognized it. Do you think you would have ever met Lee, if...what was your ex-husband's name?"

"Sam."

"Do you think you would have ever met Lee if Sam hadn't divorced you?"

Kerry shook her head.

"The husband you didn't want is out of your life, and the hus-band you've always wanted is in your life, to help you with cancer you would have gotten, regardless of your church affiliation or marital history. Lee didn't make your son an addict or a convict, but he'll be there to help both of you deal with it. Your son is off the streets, drying out in a jail where he will be given the opportunity to affiliate with the church. Did you know about the Church's connection with our jail?"

"Yes. Lee told me," Kerry said with more trust.

"Do you think he would have anything to do with the Church if he wasn't in jail?"

"No." Kerry's response had some hope.

"Are these blessings a coincidence?" the bishop asked himself as much as he did Kerry. "I don't know. I do know God is watch-ing you, and he cares for you. I think he's been in your life a lot more than you think."

Tears of hope and appreciation demanded more tissue.

"Kerry, there have been times when I felt I'm in the fourth watch of a personal struggle, and God is just watching me strug-gle. Sometimes I think He's not answering my prayers because I'm unworthy of His time. Then there are times I think He's teaching me a lesson, which only makes me mad. It's only when I remember He knows the future and that He's on my side, do I forget myself and move forward. Kerry, if you don't give up, you'll be all right, in fact, everything will be to your good. That is if you don't give up."

After a comfortable silence, the bishop asked, "Have I helped?"

"More than I thought you would."

Kerry's statement caused the bishop to smile. It also gave him the confidence to continue.

"Kerry, your experiences can prepare you to live with those around you as well as help you live with God. Your cancer has given Lee the opportunity to show his love. Your son's incarceration will bless both you and your son if you have patience, and your son will bless many for generations to come."

Kerry leaned forward. "What do you mean 'your son will bless many for generations to come'?"

"I don't know. I didn't intend on saying that, but I'll tell you this, your faith in your Savior will eventually reveal why you're going through all of this."

"I'm beginning to understand Bishop. I know I'm blessed to have this church, Lee, and my son. I also have Jean, a good friend to talk to, and that's more than a lot of people have."

The Spirit told him the meeting should end. "Thank you for coming in."

"Thanks, Bishop."

"Remember He's always watching you," the bishop said while shaking Kerry's hand, "and He knows what we're going through because He's already gone through it."

As they walked toward the door the bishop said, "I guess it won't be too long before I see you and Lee for Lee's temple interview."

"You're right. It's coming up fast. I guess we'll see you then."

As Kerry left the bishop's office, she had more hope, and her future had more meaning.

CHAPTER THIRTY-EIGHT

Kerry, waiting in the foyer for the bishop to finish interviewing her husband for his temple recommend, couldn't believe all that had taken place since their marriage a year ago; cancer, marriage, a honeymoon, surgery, radiation, and a primary calling to teach five-year-old's. She left her past when Bishop Knutson opened his door and invited her to enter his office and take a seat beside her husband. As the Bishop walked around his desk, he noticed Kerry's stare and offered an apology, "Forgive me for my attire. I square dance on Friday nights and should have changed."

The bishop wore a deep-purple cowboy shirt, adorned with white ivory buttons. His Western Bolo tie, pointed to a decorated belt made of alligator skin, joined by a buckle that looked like a license plate. However, there was nothing special about his blue jeans that dived into a pair of white cowboy boots carrying a silver tip on the point of each boot.

Kerry forced herself to look at his face. "Looks like fun to me. Can anyone join?"

"I don't need the power of discernment to know you're making fun of me," the bishop said with a huge smile.

The bishop looked at Lee, and then at Kerry, "I'm glad both of you took the temple preparation classes even though I know it was your second time Kerry. I think every married couple in the church should take those classes. The principles they teach are eternal, offering direction for a happy marriage and a happy life."

The bishop waited for comment and when none came, he continued. "I'm sure it's no surprise to you, Kerry, that I've just found your husband to be worthy to go to the temple and get his endowment. I know you're familiar with the temple, but with your permission, I've saved my "temple talk" for both of you."

Both Lee and Kerry squeezed hands and looked at each other as if they were earth's only inhabitants.

This time when you go to the temple, focus on the *feeling* of being in the temple more than what is going on in the temple. Sometimes people going to the temple for the first time are so overwhelmed with the endowment, they forget to enjoy the spirit."

"I appreciate that," Kerry said. "It's been a long time since I've been to the temple, but I can remember my first and only time was intimidating."

The bishop set up and smiled. "Well, now that I've finished my "temple talk" let me see if I know what's going to happen this Saturday."

Somewhat surprised, yet pleased the interview was over, Lee and Kerry looked at each other as if they had won something.

The bishop enjoyed their reaction. "I understand everyone is meeting at the church parking lot tomorrow at nine o'clock in the morning and going from there to the Oklahoma City Temple."

He looked for verbal confirmation and when it didn't come, he asked. "Right?"

"Right," both said in unison, followed by laughter.

"Lee who is your escort?"

"My escort is Russell Cruz."

"He's a good man. I take it he will be your witness at the sealing?"

"Yes, he will."

"And Kerry, who will be your witness at the sealing?"

"Jean Atlee will be my witness."

"Do I know Jean Atlee," the bishop asked.

"She's a dear friend from my old ward."

"Since it's been a while since your first time through the temple, you might want her beside you as an escort."

"I've already thought of that."

"And the sealing will be at eleven-thirty?"

"That's correct."

"Well, that sounds great. I can't wait. As a cowboy at heart, may I say, I'm glad when the good guys win."

Although there were tears all around, emotions were checked as the bishop asked," Is there anything else you want to ask or talk about?"

Lee and Kerry looked at each other, shook their heads, looked back at the bishop, and simultaneously said, "See you Saturday."

"See you Saturday," the bishop replied.

After hugs, Lee and Kerry went to their car. When Lee opened the car door for Kerry to get in, through tears she said, "I'm so glad we're doing this."

"So am I," Lee said as he kissed her on the cheek. "Saturday will be a good day."

When she broke down and cried, Lee hugged her and waited for her to stop. When she finally regained her composure he asked, "What's wrong?"

"I wish I knew how Jason was doing. He's been out of jail for a week and no contact. I wish he would just call me, and tell me where he is, how he's doing, whether he's hungry or cold. I know he doesn't have a place to live."

"Kerry, I have a good feeling about the future. I think something is going to happen that will be a blessing for all concerned. If we trust in the Lord, He'll tell us what to do and say, when it's time to say and do. I just know the future is going to be better than we can imagine. You'll see. Saturday will be the beginning of a new life for all of us."

CHAPTER THIRTY-NINE

"Knock again, I don't think he heard you," Kerry said after Lee's second attempt at knocking on Russell's door. "No, he heard me," said Lee. "I hear him coming."

Russell was surprised to find Lee and Kerry standing at his front door. "What are you two doing here? I'm just getting ready to leave for the church parking lot where a group of people will convoy down to the Oklahoma City Temple to witness the sealing of Lee and Kerry Richards."

Suddenly, his facial expression went from humor to concern. "You're still going to the temple, aren't you? You haven't—"

"No!" Lee interrupted with a chuckle. "Before going to the church parking lot, we wanted to stop by and talk to you privately. Can we come in?"

Embarrassed that he hadn't already invited them in, Russell holding the door, quickly stepped back and said, "By all means."

Once everyone was seated, Russell asked, "I haven't done anything wrong have I?"

Both Lee and Kerry were grinning as she said, "I don't think you could do anything wrong."

Russell's face was expressionless. "You'd be surprised."

"Well let's just say, you haven't done anything wrong as far as we're concerned."

"And I'm thankful for that," Russell replied. "But, since we don't have much time before we have to be at the church parking lot, what can I do for you?"

Lee and Kerry looked at each other and then back at Russell. "We just wanted to personally thank you for making it possible for us to be together, and the Spirit told us to tell you that before we got together with everyone at the church."

"That says a lot about you guys," Russell replied. "The spirit can suggest a lot of things, but individuals have to be worthy enough to notice, and have enough faith to act. Thank you for your kindness."

He turned to Lee. "I know the experience that came from reading the pamphlet gave you a testimony. And I bet you think that experience is the reason you're going to the temple today, but it isn't. Yes, it *helped* you get to where you are, but it isn't the reason you have a temple recommend."

"You're wrong Russell. Listen, I know that experience is the only reason I'm going to the temple today."

"No, it isn't. It's why you joined the church. You're here today because you've used that experience to grow. If you hadn't taken that experience and tried to live the gospel, your initial testimony would have eventually left you, and you would have coasted into complacency. I know what I'm talking about. But I'm sure you've been given enough advice concerning the temple. So let me ask you who your escort is going to be?"

"If they'll allow two lawyers in a temple at the same time, would you be mine?"

"I can't think of anyone I'd rather escort than you. I'd be honored."

"Will you witness my sealing as well?"

"Again, it would be my honor."

Russell gathered himself. "Would you two forgive me if I offered you a tiny, tiny bit of advice about the temple?"

Both Lee and Kerry laughed as they nodded their heads.

"Don't forget how you feel when you're in the temple, and try to find that temple feeling when you're out of the temple. I'm warning you; you can take the Holy Ghost for granted, and without his help, your testimonies, this church, this religion, and especially his access, can be replaced by an evil influence without you knowing it. I took my testimony for granted. I grew up in the Church, attended Primary, Young Men, and Seminary like I was supposed to. I had no trouble bearing my testimony on Fast Sunday. At nineteen, I went on a mission, even baptized some people, came home, got married in the temple, and had a family. As the years went by, I even became a bishop."

"A bishop!" Lee said. "I didn't know that."

"The fact I was bishop when I was excommunicated, is what's important."

Silence filled the room.

"I'm not going to give details, and I hope I can rely upon your discretion to keep my excommunication between us. Let's just say I took my testimony for granted, and I don't want either of you to follow in my footsteps. My world was the church, not my testimony of the gospel. I preached the importance of working on one's testimony; I just forgot to work on mine."

Russell could tell he had a captive audience. He gave them just a moment to gather themselves before continuing. "What does my short-sightedness have to do with you two going to the temple? I was married in the temple, but afterward, I didn't attend *regularly*. Please attend *regularly*. Going to the temple *regularly* will help you view your testimony in a unique way. I'm not saying going to the temple regularly will replace spiritual actions outside the temple, but I am saying, going to the temple *regularly* will help you to accomplish what you're here to accomplish. Notice how many times I used the word regularly. If you don't have time to go to the temple, make time. If you're unworthy, do something about it immediately."

Russell stood and then quickly sat back down. "When I was excommunicated, I thought I would notice a big difference, but I didn't at first. However, as the weeks and months went by, I could tell the spirit was slipping away, and when it was gone, it was obvious it was gone. I didn't fall to zero, I fell below zero. It was as if I was in *Satan's* world, not a world with Satan in it, and believe me there's a difference."

Russell could tell he was in jeopardy of overstating his point. So, he waited for inspiration as to what to say if anything. He didn't have to wait long. "If you're not prepared to receive what the temple has to offer, the temple is nothing more than a big, beautiful, white building. On the other hand, if you bring the right attitude to the temple, you can have a spiritual experience like no other. If going to the temple has been your goal in life, you're in danger of losing all you've gained. The temple shouldn't be the goal of this life, but a tool in which to obtain the goal of this life, which is to get back to your Heavenly Father."

He could tell it was time to stop. "We need to go," Russell said as he stood. "If you wait a minute, I'll get my coat and follow you in my car to the church parking lot."

"No problem. If we weren't staying in Oklahoma City tonight, you could ride with us," Kerry said.

"I appreciate that, but we can talk after the sealing. Anyway, you need to be alone and share your feelings, and I want to stress the word *feelings*. This is going to be a great day for you both."

* * * * * *

Back in the car, Kerry and Lee waited for Russell to pull his car behind Lee's, and when that was accomplished, Lee headed down the narrow streets of the housing complex, with Russell a couple of car lengths behind.

"Wasn't that something about Russell?" Kerry said in reflection. "I think he has a point. I've taken my testimony for granted many times."

"I think you're right. Kerry, let's do the simple things. Let's try and notice when we're taking our testimony and blessings for granted. Let's—"

Lee never finished his sentence because he was dead.

Due to the parked cars along the street, Lee never saw the car that T-boned his car as he entered the intersection, a speeding car driven by two teenagers going for a joy ride in their parent's sports car. Nor did he experience the force of impact that pushed his car sideways into a telephone pole, trapping Kerry in the process.

CHAPTER FORTY

Russell couldn't believe what he had just witnessed. What startled him even more than the accident, were the boys' attempt to flee the scene. However, when they realized there was a witness, they both slumped down in their seats and waited for their fate.

Once out of his car, Russell attempted to open Lee's door. When he couldn't, he tried the door behind him with the same results. Failing to gain entrance, he went over to the other side of the car to attend to Kerry. Although her door was blocked by the telephone pole, the door behind her was accessible. After finally getting into the car through the right rear door, he found her unconscious but still breathing. He then moved to Lee and checked for a pulse, and when none was found, he dialed 911.

As he was calling, he noticed a crowd beginning to form. After giving vital information to the dispatcher, he again checked Kerry to see if there was anything he could do. When he realized there wasn't, he said a quiet prayer over the distant sound of sirens.

* * * * * *

After stabilizing Kerry and confirming Lee's death, paramedics, police officers, and men from the tow truck pushed Lee's car away from the telephone pole. Once Kerry's door was free, firemen pried it open, allowing the paramedics to remove Kerry to an awaiting ambulance.

While this was happening, the two boys were interrogated, handcuffed, and transported downtown to be booked.

Russell was torn between following the ambulance and going to the church parking lot to inform everyone what had happened. Rationalizing there was nothing he could do for Kerry, he decided to go to the parking lot.

When Russell arrived at the parking lot, he found Jean, the bishop, and several couples waiting for the arrival of Lee and Kerry. His alarming demeanor drew their attention as well as silence. After informing the group as to what had just happened, the bishop said a prayer and then asked if anyone knew how to get in touch with Jason. When no one could answer, Jean suggested soup kitchens and parks. The Elder's Quorum President made assignments to search those areas, and those assigned dispersed with urgency. Jean, Russell, and the bishop decided to go to the hospital in separate cars in case individual errands would be required at a later time.

When they met at the Emergency Waiting Room, Jean asked Russell if he knew how to get in touch with Laurence.

"Laurence. I forgot about Laurence. You're talking about Lee's brother in Hays?" Russell said, deep in thought.

"I think it's Hays," Jean replied. "If I'm right, he lives on a farm outside of Hays, Kansas. Someone needs to call him. I think it would be better to hear about his brother's death from a man, rather than an emotional old lady."

Russell started to say something, but decided to put his arm around her, and let her cry instead. When she composed herself, he excused himself to call Laurence.

* * * * * * *

It was three and a half hours before Kerry was brought out of surgery. During that time, many came to find out the latest and express their concern. None stayed more than twenty minutes, most leaving sooner, all leaving their concerns for Kerry's condition, and their pledges to help.

A doctor wearing blue surgical attire, drew everyone's attention as she entered the waiting room. "Mrs. Richards is out of surgery. Is her son here?"

"We're still trying to locate him," said Jean. "How is Kerry?"

"As you know, she has been through a traumatic experience, but she's out of danger, and that's all I can say for now. If her son arrives before she regains consciousness, notify a nurse."

As the doctor left, Russell and Jean looked at each other. "I'm no lawyer, but I didn't like it when she said, 'that's all I can say.'"

"I'm with you, and I am a lawyer."

"Do you know if Jason is in or out of jail? Jean asked with some judgment.

"He's out of jail, but the day's still young. I've heard he's living in a park. This isn't going to sound nice, but I hope I can have a talk with him before he sees his mother. I would like to help him have the best attitude he can have before seeing her if you know what I mean."

"I know what you mean, and I agree," Jean replied.

Russell was going to say something else but stopped when Bishop Knutson and Jason, walked into the waiting room.

"Excuse me, Jean, I need to talk to Jason."

"Go ahead. I don't want to talk to him."

"Please, don't tell any of the nurses Jason is here until I talk to him."

"Jason who?" Jean said as she turned to take a seat.

It was obvious Jason didn't like being at the hospital, and he didn't care who knew it.

"Bishop, could Jason and I have a word alone?"

"No Russell. We both need to have a word with Jason."

The bishop's remark caused Jason's conceit to wane.

"What if I don't want to talk to either of you?" Jason said as if the thought had just occurred to him.

Jason, at the moment, you're a visitor in the hospital. Give us any trouble, and you could be a patient, was the only thought that flashed across Russell's mind. "Jason, we're concerned about you and your mother. Please give our concern some concern. What do you have to lose?"

The bishop and Russell escorted Jason to a vacant room. Once inside, Russell turned to the bishop and asked, "Could I do this?"

"Be my guest. I'll guard the door."

"Jason, if you just listen for a moment, and I mean listen, not hear what I'm going to say, but listen to what I'm going to say, this won't take long. This won't be a lecture, because I'm not here to judge you. I'm here to see that your self-importance, or whatever is wrong with you, doesn't hurt your mother. None of us know how bad your mother has been hurt. What we do know, is when you see your mother, unless she says otherwise, all of us will be with you. Do you understand?"

Russell didn't give Jason a chance to answer. "It isn't a decision for you to make, but more of an investment in your future. If you don't upset your mother, I'll give you some money for the street. You can use it for food, shelter, drugs, I don't care. Think about what I'm saying. As long as you help your mother, you will find help. Now let's go wait for your mother to wake up."

The bishop started to remind Russell that Jason could find out the condition of his mother but decided against it.

Jason's demeanor told Russell and the Bishop their attempt to reach Jason had failed.

Once in the waiting room, Jason sat down and opened up a magazine. Sensing everyone's dislike, he pretended to read.

It seemed like an eternity; before a nurse came and told everyone that Kerry was awake, and wanted to see Russell, Jean, and Jason. As they walked toward Kerry's room, the bishop told Russell, he would be glad to help them with a blessing if Kerry requested one.

When Kerry learned her bishop was in the waiting room, she told Russell to invite him in as well.

Everyone was surprised to see how injured Kerry was. Her right leg was in a cast, and the right side of her face was covered with one large bandage. However, she welcomed them all with a small portion of a smile that managed to escape the bandage.

Jean and Russell cautiously went to separate sides of her bed, while Jason and the bishop stood at the foot of the bed.

When the bishop attempted to speak, Kerry painfully raised her left hand, which stopped him before a word was uttered. "Come close so I don't have to speak very loud," her voice was clear but weak.

When all were in their place, she began, "When I'm done talking, I want a blessing, and then I want some sleep. I don't have the energy to answer questions right now, but I do have something you all need to hear. Russell, do you have a recording device to capture what I'm going to say?"

Without a word, Russell took out his phone and turned it on.

When Kerry saw that he was ready, she spoke. "I think I've had a vision. But it doesn't matter whether it was a vision or a dream. I've just been communicating with Heavenly Father and his Son, and all of you were mentioned during that communication. I also want to tell you, Lee is happy."

She paused to let what she had said sink in. You could tell Kerry was pleased with the expressions of shock and concern for her sanity.

"Thank you for remaining silent. While on the operating table, I saw Christ. I knew it was Christ because Heavenly Father told me it was his son. We talked and Christ asked me if I wanted to be with Lee or go back for a short time to help my son straighten his life out. As you can see, I chose to help my son."

Jason could feel everyone's eyes, as he stared at his mother with contempt.

"As you can see, the broken window next to me in the car has scarred my face, and the impact of the telephone pole has broken my right leg. What you can't see is a missing spleen, which was taken during surgery, and the return of my cancer."

Her statement sucked the air out of the room. No one spoke. No one knew what to say.

"Again, thank you for not commenting. Concerning the return of my cancer, it happens; the odds were against it, but it happens. The Lord told me about my cancer before giving me the choice to come back. When I asked to come back so I could help my son, he gave me a plan to help us, help Jason, and he wanted all of you to be witnesses concerning that plan."

Kerry, along with everyone in the room, looked at Jason to see his reaction. Seeing only disgust, they looked once more to Kerry for instruction.

"Jason, they say I have about six months to live, which means you have about six months to change or continue to live on the streets or in some jail." Kerry's statement had power and finality.

"This is what I mean by that statement. You can get off the streets, at least until my death, and if you complete the assignment, I'm about to give you, you will receive my entire estate. If you don't, you won't receive a dime, and you'll be put back on the streets knowing that going back was of your making."

Kerry could tell Jason's pride was starting to surface, so she quickly continued. "Meantime, the house Lee and I were living in, is available to you so long as you abide by the following conditions: There will be no drugs in the house, which includes any drugs inside you when you're in the house. The house, as well as you, will be spot-checked by anyone Russell chooses, at any time Russell chooses, if that's alright with you Russell?"

"No problem," Russell said, as he looked at Jason.

"Thank you, Russell. Heavenly Father said you would agree."

Kerry's statement caused Russell to humbly look at the floor.

"Russell, you'll be paid from the estate." When Russell tried to object, Kerry closed her mouth and eyes until he stopped. When he gave up, Kerry continued, "Jason, you will also have an allowance and our other car. Your only job will be to write a manuscript centered around Lee, me, and yourself. Of course, you can include those in this room, our friends and acquaintances, anyone you deem necessary. However, everyone's name, and I repeat everyone's name in the manuscript will be changed to protect his or her anonymity. It's also not for dissemination unless Russell agrees. Gather any appropriate information you need. For example, go through my journal, my dad's, and Lee's journal. Yes, I got Lee to begin one when he joined the Church. Interview me and my friends, and Lee's friends, even Lee's family if you desire. Do anything you can think of in order to write your manuscript. You did well in journalism before you got dumb and threw your college away. Use that training to write your way off the streets, and into something we can be proud of. Be forewarned. They say I have six months to live, but they could be wrong, and who knows if I will be able to be interviewed in three months. I might not be able to talk. You really don't know how much time you have, so get writing."

Kerry turned to everyone else. "If he comes to you, I would appreciate you helping him." Everyone smiled and nodded their heads in compliance.

She turned back to Jason, "When I die, and your manuscript isn't completed, but you have made a good-faith effort, I'm sure Russell will give you a reasonable time to finish it. He will be the judge of whether you inherit my estate or inherit the street. Is that okay with you Russell?"

Before Russell could answer, a nurse entered the room. "Kerry, you need your rest."

"This is one of the nurses I worked with years ago," Kerry said with pride and love. Her comment brought emotion to the face of the nurse, which pleased Kerry. "Could you give us just a moment?"

"Make it a short one," the nurse said as she turned to leave.

When the nurse was no longer in the room, Russell agreed to Kerry's prior request, which brought relief to Kerry. After a couple of deep breathes, Kerry continued, "I would like to see each one of you in the future. It's going to get lonely in here, and I don't think I have six months."

She regretted saying her last sentence. She sensed she was feeling sorry for herself, and that certainly wasn't something she wanted them to take from the room.

"I would like to have a blessing from the bishop now."

Before anyone could say anything, Jason blurted out, "When can I get the keys to the house and the car, and some money so I can eat?"

Jason's statement shocked everyone. With tight lips, Russell said, "I'll get you those things when I'm appointed power of attorney. Is that alright with you Kerry?"

Kerry nodded, truly embarrassed and disappointed at what had just happened. After a moment of awkward silence, she said without emotion, "Bishop, after my blessing, take Jason back to wherever you found him."

She then turned to Jason. "Jason it's your obligation to get Russell's phone number, so he can give you the things I'm offering, when and only when he decides you should get them." '

Still looking at Jason she said, "And Russell, there's no hurry about transcribing this conversation, or getting a power of attorney if you know what I mean."

"I'll transcribe your wishes as soon as I get back to my office."

"Take your time," Kerry replied as she kept her gaze on her son.

The silence in the room was palpable; a silence that was broken by Russell. "Jason, get smart and at least act like you care about your mother, and if you can't do that..." Russell gathered himself. "Remember, you're the one who can keep you off the streets, and I'm the one who can put you back on the street, and for your own good, I'll do it."

Kerry's smile showed her approval. "Grow up Jason. I love you. I think you love me too, and if you don't, I don't want to hear it."

Kerry's next statement surprised all of them. "Jason, would you leave the room so the spirit can be here during my blessing."

Jason left, and after the blessing, the bishop squeezed Kerry's arm and went into the waiting room where Jason sat in a pout.

After a short minute, Russell left as well, and upon entering the waiting room, went over to Jason. Both stared at each other for a moment before Russell reached in his pocket and pulled out a twenty-dollar bill. "Because I think the world of your mother, I'm giving you this money. When I get power of attorney, I'll pick you up, give you the car and house keys, along with a month's allowance minus twenty dollars, and drive you to the house. Word of advice. I'd make it easy for me to find you when I'm ready to find you. I'd hang around soup kitchens, libraries, or Riverside Park. Believe me, when I tell you, I won't waste much time looking for you."

When Jason took the twenty, Russell turned and left, followed by the bishop and Jason.

Jean had wanted to leave with Russell, but she couldn't. With everyone gone, she went to Kerry and kissed her softly on her good cheek. With tears washing her face, she whispered in Kerry's left ear, "In the future, I expect a poem for the writing club."

Only smiles and tears were exchanged as Jean winked and left the room.

CHAPTER FORTY-ONE

As Jean drove toward Serenity, a three-story nursing home in the newer part of West Wichita, she was thankful the snowfall the night before had been light. If it had been any heavier, she would have canceled her trip to visit Kerry.

While maneuvering through the slow traffic that follows any snowfall in Wichita, she marveled at Lee's foresight to double his insurance policy after his marriage to Kerry. Whether a premonition or fate, his insurance investment, coupled with the settlement from the accident, was more than enough to financially secure Kerry's future.

Finally, Jean turned into a long street, flanked by tall, barren trees, trees, which would outlive every resident in the facility she was driving toward. Since it had been over five months since Kerry's surgery, she doubted Kerry would live long enough to see these trees bud.

As Jean parked her car, she checked her watch to make sure it was lunchtime. She preferred this time of day because she could enter without being too obvious. It was a time when a large number of the ninety-six occupants, occupants driven by the hunger for companionship as much as food, would congregate into the dining area. These residents, like their counterparts all over the world, just wanted to be wanted, and this *want* created a necessity for them to slipstream behind anyone, trolling for attention, a necessity created by their selfish children who only visited their families on birthdays, Thanksgiving, and Christmas.

Entering Serenity always brought wonderment. The dining hall, an area resembling a small courtyard in a French village, was immediately on the other side of the front door. It gave visitors and residents alike, a euphoric impression of gaiety and control, a facade often destroyed by the arrival of an ambulance.

After Jean entered the building, she quickly took the elevator to the second floor. After exiting the elevator, she walked down a long lighted hallway to Kerry's apartment. Instead of knocking, she opened the door and called out before going in. She always felt awkward about doing this, but that was the way Kerry wanted it.

Kerry, seated in a recliner, greeted Jean with as much energy as her health would allow her, "Hi, my best friend."

Ignoring what she saw, Jean replied, "You're looking good."

"Thank you, you old liar."

Jean smiled and gave her a gentle hug. Then she took her recording device out of her handbag and switched it on before taking her seat.

"Thanks, Jean, for recording our conversations. Jason needs them for his manuscript."

"How's he doing on his manuscript?"

"I don't know. He must be doing something right, or he'd be out on the street." Both laughed as they thought of Russell.

"One thing I do know, he records all his interviews so he has a record of any findings or conversations he might want to put in his manuscript."

"What do you mean by putting conversations in his manuscript?"

"This conversation might be in a chapter."

"You mean this conversation is going to be in his manuscript?"

"Maybe. Don't worry. If it is, our names will be different. For example, Jason has given your character the name of Jean. So, when your character speaks in the novel, it will be read as Jean speaking. When my son's character speaks in the novel, it will be read as Jason speaking. Does that make sense?"

"So, my character's first name is Jean."

"That's right."

"So, what's my character's last name?"

"I think your character's last name is Atlee. But get this, my son, or should I say, Jason, has given my character the name— Kerry Hourrigan Claypool Howells."

"What!"

"The names Hourrigan and Claypool are middle names he picked from my ancestry; Kerry is a name he made up, and he picked Howells because of my Welsh roots, and who in the Church doesn't have Welsh roots," Kerry said with some humor.

"I think I understand," Jean said. "A recording of our talk today might be in his manuscript in some form or another, and if it is, and if he picks something I've said, the novel will record Jean as saying it instead of my real name. If you say something he chooses, the manuscript will record Kerry's character as saying it. What is—"

"Lee…Lee Richards. The character's name of my beloved is Lee Richards."

Kerry was silent for a moment as if honoring her late husband.

"Remember my anonymity requirement. I think what he's doing is smart. I can't wait to read about the conversations I had with my dad."

"How can that happen? He can't record your dad. Your dad's dead."

"That's true, but he has access to my dad's journal, as well as mine and Lee's. He has our writings to glean from, and I'll tell you what Jean, I can certainly see God's hand in my dad's fanaticism concerning journal keeping, why he passed it on to me, and why I passed it on to Lee."

"To be honest, I didn't think your plan would work."

"First of all, it isn't my plan. The Lord gave me the plan during my surgery. That's the only reason I had any faith in its success."

"Is Jason in compliance with the plan?"

"I think so. I guess Jason wasn't doing much at first, so Russell made him produce a one-page plot summary of what the manuscript was going to be about. It seems to have worked."

"Good for Russell. I'd like to see that summary."

"You can. I got it right here. I'll read it to you."

Kerry searched through a couple of things before finding the summary. "Listen to this. The manuscript begins at the deathbed of Gayle Richards, a woman who had suffered from Multi Myeloma for two years, a woman who had searched the disciplines of medicine and religion for a cure; a search that made her husband Lee, mistrust those disciplines; disciplines represented by Kerry, the attending nurse; a Latter-Day Saint who had been served divorce papers that very day; divorce papers dissolving a temple marriage, causing her to question her own faith, as well as worry about her young son Jason; a boy who, years later as a young man, would reunite them when Lee represented him in a personal injury lawsuit."

"That sounds like what really happened between you, Lee, and Jason."

"See his genius. Instead of trying to create a fictional story in six months or less, he decided to write a fictional history instead."

"You're right. That's smart. Go on reading."

"Their reunion generates a mutual attraction strong enough for both to continue seeing each other. During their courtship, Lee attempts to show Kerry the fallacy of Christian religions, and in doing so, is maneuvered into reading a pamphlet from her church, an exercise that results in his own conversion. They get married and set a date for their temple marriage. However, their anticipated temple marriage is challenged with one setback after another; Kerry's breast cancer, Jason's incarceration for drugs, making him homeless after his release from jail, and a car accident on the way to the temple, leaving Lee dead, and Kerry injured. During the surgery to repair her injuries, the Lord gives her a plan directing Jason to write a manuscript around the time frame of Kerry, Lee, and Jason's relationships. Since her cancer has returned, he has to write the novel in Kerry's lifetime, which is expected to be six months or less. If he fails, he becomes homeless once again."

"Does Jason's character finish the novel before you die?"

"He won't tell me."

"What's the theme of the novel?"

"He won't tell me."

"What happens to Jason in the novel?"

"He won't tell me."

"Doesn't that bother you?"

"I don't think what Jason writes in his manuscript is as important as Jason writing a manuscript. I've already seen a change in him. He even gave me a kiss on the forehead last time he was here."

"That's an improvement!"

"Do birds fly? Who knows, maybe he'll tell me he loves me before I die."

"Let's change subjects. How are *you* doing Kerry?"

"How do I look?"

"You look great, considering."

Kerry laughed. "Considering I have cancer or considering I'm dying from cancer."

Jean laughed, mainly to support Kerry.

Kerry reached for and held Jean's hand. "I'm sorry. I didn't mean for my question to put you on the spot. I know I've lost more weight since your last visit, but I'm okay."

When Kerry didn't continue, Jean took advantage of the lull, "Enough! I came here to get cheered up, not necessarily to cheer you up. Let's talk about something positive. Have you positively decided where you're going to be buried?"

Both laughed; Kerry because she loved Jean's humor, and Jean because she couldn't believe what she had just said.

"At first, I decided to be buried in Stafford, in the vicinity of Lee and Gayle's grave. But then I changed my mind. My friends are here, and who knows, Jason might want to come and see my grave. And then I changed my mind again. If he wants to see me, he can make the drive."

"Do you think you'll change your mind again?"

"Probably."

"Have you had many visitors?"

"Mainly you and the regulars; Russell, the bishop, Jason."

"So, Jason has become a regular?"

"He has. When the Lord gave me the idea about the manu-script, he told me Jason would come around. Even Jason told me he feels different."

Kerry stopped talking as she tried to change positions. When Jean tried to help, Kerry smiled, and with a quick shake of her head, waved her off.

"Jean, I feel I am very close to the veil. I'm excited to see Lee and my parents again. I'm even excited to meet Gayle. If Jason shapes up, I hope he asks for Laurence's permission to do Lee and Gayle's temple work, as well as ours. If he doesn't, I guess I'll have to wait."

"How does Russell think Jason's doing?"

"Russell and I are somewhat skeptical. We don't know whether he's changing because of his predicament, or whether his change is genuine. Frankly, we couldn't care what the reason is."

"Does the bishop still come as often as he did?"

"Not as often, but he still comes, and when he does, we talk some church. Mainly he lets me know he's just there for me. However, it doesn't matter whether it's Russell, the bishop, or you; we all end up talking about Jason."

"Do any of the people in your old ward come to see you?"

"Not one."

"How about your new ward?"

"A few. However, to be fair, I don't really know many people in my new ward. I think those who come, do it out of respect for Lee. He was only in the church a year; nonetheless, he made a lot of friends. But guess what!"

"What?" Jean said, joining in Kerry's excitement.

"I enjoy you more than anyone." Kerry tried to continue but stopped and closed her eyes. Her expression was one of discomfort. When she opened them, she gave Jean a weak smile and said, "I don't think I have much time."

Kerry's comment took Jean by surprise. She was going to respond, but the spirit told her this was Kerry's time to talk.

"You know when we're born, we have no idea of what time is, and don't for decades after our birth. Laying in this nursing home has given me time to think about *time*. I remember my dad's mantra, which addressed a bad habit of visiting regrets for what he had or hadn't done. That's all I seem to do when I'm not sleeping. Yes, I think about Lee, which is the brightest part of my day, but other than that, all I think about are my past mistakes."

Jean had no clue what to say.

"And there's no rhyme or reason in my thinking. I might flashback to being mean to a girl when I was in elementary school and then speed forward to losing my temper at work. I don't worry about the future; the future's been taken care of. I just ping pong between the past and the present. I don't know why I focus on my mistakes more than my successes, but I do. I hope after I die, I can see my life through rose-colored glasses. I hope Heavenly Father wears rose-colored glasses."

"I guess you're right. None of us think much about our time down here, especially when we're young. Why should we? We have all the time in the world, a lifetime of time. In our later years, we don't realize our bodies have been dying since our mid-fifties, or before. Only when dying comes to our attention, do we begin to analyze our life as well as our death. I think you're more afraid of leaving Jason, than dying."

"Jean, Jason is going to be okay. I'm sure he'll get his manuscript done, and face life like all of us do. If he gets his act together, he'll have the church, and you guys to help him, and I think he's getting his life together."

Realizing she should leave, Jean said, "I have to go honey."

"Maybe you should. I can hardly keep my eyes open. But before you go, I have a poem for you. I know you'll say it's good because that's what you do, but the poem is my attempt to make the reader understand life from the perspective of a person who sees it slipping away. Although time is common to everyone who comes to earth, it is a personal companion until it becomes the possession of another spirit at birth. Don't give the poem to Jason until I'm gone."

Kerry failed to control her emotions as she handed the poem to Jean.

"I love you Kerry, a bunch of names I can't remember, Richards."

Jean's name attempt caused both to laugh.

After giving Kerry a hug, she turned off her recorder, put it in her handbag, and left the room.

While leaving the building, a nurse shouted, "Jean, could I have a minute?"

Jean sensed a grave concern in the approaching nurse.

"If anyone wants to visit Kerry, they should do so sooner than later, and the family should be available at a moment's notice during the next couple of months."

"Is her death that close?"

"I hope she has a month or two, but I doubt it."

"But she seems so—"

"Alive," the nurse completed Jean's sentence.

"Yes."

"Isn't that a godsend?" the nurse said before reacting to a summons from another resident.

As Serenity became smaller in the rearview mirror, Jean was glad she had the bishop and Russell on speed dial.

CHAPTER FORTY-TWO

J ason could feel the large crowd staring at him as he waited for his mother's funeral to begin. He wondered how many in attendance were honoring their friend, and how many were there to see the wayward son, the troublemaker that had brought shame and disgrace to his mother.

Russell, Jean, and some others he didn't know, sat in the middle of the second pew. None of them had asked him to join them, which was fine with him since he wouldn't have accepted anyway. Not because he had anything against them, he just didn't want to be pitied, if that was even possible. He wanted to be alone, and that's why he sat at the end of the first pew, far from the closed coffin that held his mother.

Thanks to Bishop Knutson, he had had some alone time with his mother's body earlier that morning in a viewing room. When he saw his mother's body, he had an emotional breakdown, which surprised him. He didn't understand what the basis for his breakdown was, whether it was seeing his mother's body for the last time, or whether it was the realization that after the funeral, he could lose the house, car, and stipend he was receiving. He knew he had accomplished almost two-thirds of his manuscript, but he didn't know if that was enough to keep him off the streets. He did know he was changing. He just didn't know why.

The room focused on Bishop Knutson, as he approached the podium to outline the morning's program. When he finished, he sat down, and the congregation sang one of his mother's favorite hymns, followed by a prayer by Russell. After the prayer, Jean walked to the podium and gave her talk. After her talk, his mother's doctor gave a eulogy that only mention Jason once. A closing song and a prayer from someone unfamiliar to Jason closed the service. The bishop immediately stood and announced there would be a graveside service in Stafford, Kansas. Jason didn't know whether to leave immediately for Stafford or follow the hearse. He decided to follow the hearse.

He had never made the hour and a half drive to the Stafford Cemetery. He knew it was where Lee was buried, but that was all he knew about the area. He had mixed feelings about his mother's choice of cemeteries; Stafford was a long way to visit, but visiting would buy him points with Russell, as well as get him away from Russell's supervision.

The few who made the drive acknowledged his presence with a handshake and condolence, but nothing more. Other than that, everyone treated him the same as they did at the church, and he reciprocated by distancing himself from the group.

The service began with a prayer from Jean. The bishop then quoted scripture, gave a very short talk, and dedicated the grave. Russell ended the service with a closing prayer, and shortly thereafter people began to leave. As they did, the bishop personally thanked each one of them for their attendance. Jason surprised himself, as well as everyone else, when he did the same.

After everyone had left, the bishop came up to Jason and said, "Jason, I'm going to head back now. Are you okay?"

"Yes, Bishop. Thanks for asking."

"How's the manuscript coming?"

"Writing it has been harder than I thought. I underestimated the amount of information I needed in order to accomplish what my mother wanted. I hope everyone understands I'm trying."

"Did you record today?"

"No. I didn't feel right about it. Plus, I was personally here. However, I must confess, I did make some notes."

"Has Russell looked at your work?"

"Yes."

"Are you still living in your mother's house?"

"Yes."

"I think the fact you're still living in your mother's house, says it all."

Both smiled.

"Jason, you'll find everyone is on your side if you're side is the right side."

Both fell silent until Jason put his hand on the bishop's shoulder, and said with emotion in his voice, "Bishop, I'm trying my best. If it's all right with you, I would like to stay in mom's house until I finish my assignment. "

"Jason, that's up to Russell. The fact that you're still living in the house, speaks volumes."

Their hug was meaningful.

"I'm leaving now. You should be alone with your mother. I'll see you from time to time, and if I can help, give me a call."

As the bishop headed toward his car, he said over his shoulder, "Keep writing. Your mother's watching."

Jason was too moved, to respond.

CHAPTER FORTY-THREE

In the months following the funeral, Jason's drive from
Wichita to the Stafford Cemetery had always been lonely,
that is, if you didn't count the passengers named guilt,
shame, and fear. However, because this trip would provide the
needed material for the last chapter of his manuscript, an accomplishment that would meet his legal obligation to Russell, and
his moral obligation to his mother, peace was his only passenger.

When he arrived at his mother's gravesite, he parked his car,
said a quick prayer, and grabbed his recorder before heading toward her grave. Although there was no one to record, recording
helped him capture the feelings that always accompanied his visits to his mother's grave, spiritual feelings resulting from months
of repentance, feelings that had crept into the manuscript he was
writing.

When he arrived at his mother's headstone, he cleared away
some leaves, dried dirt, and bird droppings. He was amazed at
what had accumulated since his last visit ten days ago. "If I lived
in Stafford, your headstone would be cleared every day."

Jason stared at his mother's headstone for several minutes before closing his eyes to pray. His prayer was longer than usual,
and when he finished, he turned his recorder on, placing it in

his shirt pocket so the microphone would be close to his mouth, ready to capture the conversation he was about to have.

"Hi, Mom. I love you. You probably know everything I'm going to say, which isn't fair, but I'm going to bring you up to date anyway. Russell, Jean, and the bishop have approved what I've written so far, and even though I have the final chapter to write, Russell has turned your estate over to me. Thanks, Mom."

Emotion made Jason turn his recorder off, close his eyes, and attempt to control the moment. After another quick prayer, he turned his recorder back on and spoke to his mother once more.

"Mom, when you first offered me a way to get off the streets, I only took your offer to do just that, get off the streets. As you already know, since then I've gotten off meth, my high horse, and my pity party." He smiled as he heard what he had just said.

"My necessary investigation into the lives of the characters in this manuscript has changed me. By looking at life through their eyes, I see my world differently. I certainly understand what the Lord was doing when he told you to make this manuscript my carrot. If it wasn't for your vision, or inspiration, or whatever happened to you in the hospital, I don't think I would be alive today, let alone getting ready to go on a mission in four months. Did I—"

The realization of going on a mission drove him away from his mother's grave. It took him longer than usual to come back, but when he did, he continued, "Did I hear you turning over in your grave?" Emotion quickly swallowed the humor in his question.

"Mom, becoming like Christ is the sole purpose of my life. It begins with a decision to repent, followed by a commitment to repent, a commitment whose noncompliance is unacceptable, and ends with my life. While the Lord makes repenting possible, holding to the rod makes it probable, and bearing my testimony makes it easier. This is my testimony of Christ. To me, Jesus Christ means more than an example, repentance, and atonement. He organized the world I'm standing on, and the atmosphere I breathe. His example and teachings are so important to my well-being, a god made sure they were captured in scripture, preached by prophets, and brought to my attention by the Holy Ghost. His sacrifice is the only sacrifice that could satisfy justice, let me return to my Heavenly Father, and belong to His eternal family. What touches me the most is the fact that His love for His father and me are the only reasons for His actions. He is a god and the Savior of the World. He is also my brother and my friend, and I testify of this in His name, even Jesus Christ."

Jason paused to reflect on what he had just said. "Looking at our history, yours and mine, it's no wonder we had bad programs. Did you notice I spoke in the past tense? Momma, concerning my bad programming, Dad was the bad programmer, not you. And I'm proud to say, I've gotten out of the way, and let the Lord reprogram me. I'm sorry it took your cancer and my homelessness to do that. I just want you to know I've done it, or at least I'm on my way to doing it, changing that is. I also want to ask Lee's forgiveness for the way I treated him when he visited me in jail. If he isn't listening to this conversation, would you tell him?"

Jason couldn't believe how powerful the spirit was. He had to turn off his recorder, walk away, and wait for control to join him. When he thought he could record again, he came back to his mother's grave and proceeded with his catharsis.

"I also realized Heavenly Father will answer my prayers when my thoughts, decisions, and actions allow Him to do so, when my requests are in harmony with his will. Thus, when I pray, to show respect, I wait for an audience, and when I get one, I try to remember to plead for courage, strength, and forgiveness in following his direction. And I'm here to tell you it works."

The wind picked up slightly, making Jason question whether the cause was the spirit, a sign from his mother, or just the wind. After a couple of minutes of silence, he determined it was just the wind.

He sat on the gravestone opposite his mother's. "I couldn't wait to get this manuscript done, so I could get on with my life. However, after getting into a routine of thinking about chapters and the storyline, I found myself building my whole day around writing. Writing this novel has become my life, and right now, I'm enjoying my life. So, when I get back from my mission, I'm going to go back into journalism. With my felony, I don't think WSU will accept me, but BYU might since I'll be a returned missionary. Don't worry, that isn't why I'm going on a mission. I'm going on a mission because the Lord wants me to, just as finishing this manuscript is what the Lord's wants me to do."

He took a piece of paper out of his shirt pocket and upon reading it, smiled and looked at his mother's headstone. "Mom. I've written a mantra of my own. It helps me handle my addiction. Don't worry, even though I'm tempted once in a while, and not just about drugs, I'm doing alright. It helps to know that all temptations require an awareness that demands a decision concerning that awareness. Now when I'm tempted about anything, I focus on a decision instead of the temptation. That focus could be changing what I'm doing, my surroundings, or reminding myself you're watching me. No matter what the temptation is, I always try to focus on a decision instead of the temptation, and this mantra helps me do that."

After a short pause, he looked at his mantra, and read it to the world. "Since the present never stays, the future never arrives, and the past is always here, I make my past enjoyable by remembering *awareness* always demands a decision that changes everything; a decision I focus on if necessary."

He scooted off the headstone, and sat down on the grass in front of his mother's headstone. "I'm going to leave in a couple of minutes, but before I do, I want to read the poem you gave Jean. She finally gave me a copy, and I've read it again and again. The *wouldn't it be* poem was great. I wished I had read it when you first gave it to me, and the *want* poem was creative and witty, but this *time* poem—"

He suddenly looked at the grass in front of him. His emotions wouldn't let him continue. However, after several seconds he persevered. "Your poem about *time*, the one Jean gave me, is the most thought-provoking poem you have written. Not because it was the last one you wrote…well, I guess that might have something to do with it, but the circumstances…."

He choked up again. He kept staring at the poem hoping to find control. When control joined him, he carried on. "As I read your poem, I want you to know, I now look at time with a perspective only this poem could have given me."

Because he knew his emotions were beginning to take the moment again, he quickly retrieved her poem and began to read:

It's All About Time
By Kerry Richards

TIME caught me as I fell into mortality.
It took me years before I recognized her,
And even then, I virtually ignored her

I can't remember our formal introduction,
Whether we were friends or enemies,
Rivals or companions, I just can't remember.

Now I see her as life's chameleon,
Changing from a word to a biography,
A passport to a prison, forever to now

Written with the pencil of experience,
Corrected with the eraser of repentance,
She is the paper that collects my life.

While revising my final manuscript,
She becomes a biased editor.
Camouflaging success, magnifying failure.

I can't blame her for the plot.
I only hope rose-colored glasses,
Read the story I should have written

As we walk to my mortal departure,
I don't want to let go of her hand.
For, unlike our first meeting, I know she's there.

But I relent so she can wave goodbye,
Only to watch her catch another,
Seeing my fear through eyes of indifference.

After he finished his reading, he didn't say anything for a long time. Then he suddenly broke down and cried longer than usual, longer than he wanted. When there were no more tears, he looked at his mother's gravestone. "Each day, I thank the Lord for giving both of us more than six months; for you to live, and for me to change." He paused to gather himself, and in a shaky voice said, "I want you to know, I've changed."

Only when a sprinkle of rain touched his face, did he decide to leave. He got halfway to his car, turned back to the gravestone, and spoke. "Mom...Momma, keep watching. I know Heavenly Father is."

As the wind picked up and drops of rain became more frequent, he turned and went back to his car. It took him some time before starting it, but when he did, he headed toward Wichita, to write the last chapter of *Months to Live, Months to Change: A Novel About Addiction, Atheism, Apostasy.*

ACKNOWLEDGMENTS

Marie, I want to thank you for your many rereads, revisions, and encouragement. I needed your faith in this book as well as me.

A special thanks to Dr. Rymer for the promotion you've given this book. Your comment on how the book had given you a laugh, a tear, and an unexpected ending, gave me the courage to proceed with its publication.

Dorothy, I want to thank you for a keen observation and necessary edit, as well as your encouragement.

Lynn, your excitement was needed, timely, and welcomed.

Stan, you will never know how much reading both revisions touched me.

To my daughter Lacey and granddaughter Sophia. Thank you for wanting to listen to me read this book over the phone. It allowed me the platform for improvement.

ABOUT THE AUTHOR

With the exception of drug addiction, Richard has walked in the shoes of all the characters in this novel. He has vicariously explored addiction and incarceration while on an inner-city service mission for his church. He has observed cancer and been its victim. Although he has experienced apostacy and atheism, an unexplainable spiritual experience has left him a strong proponent of his faith. He is a Vietnam veteran, and a retired consultant concerning the pathophysiological response to soft tissue damage resulting from a whiplash accident.

He has published several booklets and articles, one article winning Today's Chiropractic Magazine Association of Georgia's gold GAMMA award for Best Service Journalism in the Business-to-Business category. He has published an instructional booklet that resides in a prestigious Chiropractic College, and been a guest lecturer at three colleges. For fourteen years he presented 12- and 16-hour seminars to doctors and attorneys in the United States, and Canada. He and his wife Marie, are retired and living in Salt Lake, Utah. They enjoy visiting family in this country and Marie's birth country of Wales.